Husk

Husk

To Chris + Sarah
Thanks for your Love.
Rick Chitwood

Rick Chitwood

Library of Congress Control Number:		2010914142
ISBN:	Hardcover	978-1-4535-8145-2
	Softcover	978-1-4535-8144-5
	Ebook	978-1-4535-8146-9

This book was printed in the United States of America.

To order additional copies of this book, contact:
Xlibris Corporation
1-888-795-4274
www.Xlibris.com
Orders@Xlibris.com
85447

PROLOGUE

They were dead already. Their bones crushed as the Moon dragged the lunar craft into her belly before turning her glare back toward Earth. In the foggy quiet, the luminescent Moon studied her reflection in the waters of Hong Kong, water that lapped hard against the trawling boats, the shrimpers, the old, the worn, the wooden yachts, and the buoys' clanging bells to warn of danger. And the water, empowered by the Moon, stormed up the sand on its belly, gaining ground with every push forward. Wave after wave, it took the shore like the troops at Normandy, heaving forward to the very edge of town.

Yet to the east, in Wellington, New Zealand, stranded fisherman gulped coffee and surveyed the remnants of a sodden battlefield. Silhouetted against the rising sun, an orgy of gulls shrieked and dove amid a hundred dark hulls keeled over in the muck. Flopping fish, hapless crabs, every bit of ocean life had been left naked by the receded sea. Gorging themselves on the carnage, the gulls discharged themselves on the unfortunate souls arriving at the docks for duty. Waiting for the tide to return, the sea goers missed the glint of the seething Moon on their western horizon.

And even further east, on a launch pad, 39-A, Kennedy Space Center, a lone white steed stood at attention. Muscles taut, quivering with the heat of anticipation, he scanned for the Moon's approach. His white armor, outfitted with two Aries X solid rocket boosters, shone in the slanting sunlight, obscuring from view the letters U-S-A-H-O-P-E on his side. On his back rode the hope of humanity, the hope of new conquest: lunar habitation. The great stallion stamped, kicking up dust and sending the gators deep into their ponds, but the mobile launch platform held tight. He waited. A soaring bald eagle circled and came to rest on his reinforced carbon-carbon nose. The foreboding orbiter grunted and groaned. As the snow-headed creature took flight, talons ready for a fight, he glanced down into the window of the crew module and saw two very human, very fragile eyes staring back at him.

Mission commander Colonel Kimberly Anderson watched the eagle soar the skies around the command module. If she had believed in omens, she might have thought to analyze this one, but she didn't. Instead she considered an early conversation with NASA's head administrator. "Unusual seismic readings," Jack had mentioned. "Stay vigilant."

"Colonel? . . . Colonel Anderson?"

The colonel blinked hard, cleared her throat, and returned her mind to the upper deck of the crew module, where apparently only four of the five crew members were preparing for takeoff.

"Huh?"

Sitting next to the colonel in the pilot's seat (if you can call reclining on your back with your knees pointing up "sitting"), Major Sam Lathem tried again to get her attention.

"Colonel? You okay?"

She wasn't sure whether it was the Pentagon's pressure or the loss of the lunar craft *Pinta* on Survey II, but something was not right. The rush to return to the lunar surface choked her confidence in the leadership.

"Colonel?"

"Yea . . . ah . . . I'm okay."

"You were humming."

"Was I?" The colonel's eyes drifted back toward her port window.

Lathem leaned forward and caught a glimpse of the feathered wing racing toward the inlet. "Quite loudly, actually."

Anderson's gaze drifted to the instrument panel directly in front of her. Lost in anxious thought, she observed nothing.

"You okay, Colonel?"

"Let's just get this bird in the sky, Major." Anderson arched her back with a groan and then ran down the launch sequence checklist for the third time. "Propulsions?"

"Check."

"Avionics?"

"Check."

"Life support?"

"Check."

She paused to buckle herself into the seat harness. Anderson called over her shoulder to the seat directly beneath her, "Captain Davenport, this being your first trip to the Moon, and on behalf of NASA, I have been cleared to brief you on a well-kept government secret: we've never really been to the Moon . . . We circle the globe and then land in area 51. The set is magnificent."

The colonel was not given to much levity, and this attempt at humor, like most of her other attempts, fell a little flat. However, it did accomplish her goal. Captain Edward Davenport, medical officer, released the breath that he had been holding.

"Just get this thing off the ground in one piece?" Davenport asked. Sweat beaded his pale upper lip.

"That's the plan," the colonel replied.

She called back to Martinez, "Mr. Martinez, cargo secure?"

"Locked and loaded. Let's go be heroes."

"Heroes, Mr. Martinez?"

"Sure, why not? We're the front edge. We're Ponce de Leon, Lewis and Clark, Glenn and Armstrong. We're laying life and limb on the line for humanity. We *are* hope, my compadres."

Colonel Anderson turned and stared deep into the eyes of the young, energetic explorer. She wished she had half of Martinez's enthusiasm. "Point taken, Mr. Martinez. I imagine the world will never be the same again."

Anderson shifted her attention. "Mr. Rogers? How's your neighborhood?"

"Ready, ma'am."

"Major Lathem?"

"All systems are go."

Colonel Anderson nodded and returned her attention to the console in front of her. Quad-redundant was in agreement. "Let's light the fires, gentlemen." Closing her eyes for the briefest of seconds, she shot a prayer to the heavens and then depressed the two buttons marked Mission Control.

"All systems are go for launch."

CHAPTER ONE

The sky blue 1965 ragtop Mustang pulled off the Bennett Causeway just before crossing the Indian River. Major Robert Haistings flipped the radio to 740 AM and grabbed his binoculars from the glove box. The WWNZ commentary droned through the heavy summer air.

"Near the tarmac at Cape Canaveral, members of the press corps have taken their positions and dignitaries fill the stands. A quiet hush has come over the crowd now that the sun has begun its march to bed, throwing pink and orange ribbons behind the brilliant white spacecraft . . ."

Bobby glassed the cape. Even in the August heat, a crowd of onlookers packed both beaches and bridges. Twilight launches always pulled large numbers as they promised a spectacular light show. This one would not disappoint.

"Colonel Kim Anderson commands today's mission. She and the crew of the Hope *are scheduled to complete phase one for the planned lunar outpost."*

Normally Bobby experienced launch from inside the orbiter. However, after the Survey II disaster, his wife, Carol, had asked him to keep both feet firmly planted on terra firma. They had argued, she had cried, and he had taken a long walk. It's hard to live on the edge with a wife, a child, and two mortgages. He had put in his paperwork, pulled out of Survey IV, and promised Carol there would be no more space missions—but he was still fully committed to space exploration. He was not leaving NASA, he told himself. He was just changing jobs. He would be ground support—loyal to a fault—to the brave men and women who explored the unknown.

The astronaut inside him, however, was still fascinated by the sight, the smell, and the unmitigated power of liftoff. No, Bobby couldn't miss the launch. He would watch the space transport *Hope* embark on its journey with adventure in his eyes, a smile on his face, and satisfaction in his heart. At least that's what he wanted to believe.

As the radio announcer talked more about the mission, Bobby longed for space travel. Leaving the binoculars on the front seat, he got out of the car, slammed the door, and paced the length of the Mustang three, six, nine times. He snatched up some of the gravel crunching underfoot and hurled it at the Indian River. "Not this trip."

Nothing could relieve the pounding in his chest, the itch in his hand to hold the throttle, or the reality that he would always from this point on see the earth from a myopic perspective—the ground would always be right in front of his face. He leaned back against the door. "You're still a pilot, buddy." It was good self-talk.

"It's seven thirty-seven here in Central Florida. The launch sequence for space shuttle transport Hope *is just seconds away . . ."*

Bobby reached back into the car for the binoculars and climbed onto the back of the passenger seat to improve his vantage point. He leaned down and turned up the radio.

"The transport is headed for Space Station Delta where the five crew members will transfer to their lunar module and proceed to the Moon. Scientists around the world expect the five-trillion-dollar research laboratory being built on the lunar surface to yield numerous medical breakthroughs, and with the outpost in place, the possibilities for manned space travel are endless."

A gust of wind brushed its cold fingers across the back of Bobby's neck and down his spine. He shivered from the chill but kept his focus on launch pad 39-A. There the great metallic white stallion stamped impatiently. He flared his nostrils and snorted, whinnying as the Moon crested into view. Eyes flashed red. His entire body quaked.

"People around the world anxiously await the answers Hope *will bring back . . . in ten . . . nine . . . eight . . . seven . . ."*

"We are go for main engine start."

"Five . . . four . . . three . . . two . . . one . . . , and there they go."

"Houston, we have liftoff!"

"Roger, Commander. Go with throttle up!"

"Roger, Mission Control. Going with throttle up!"

Hearts raced; knuckles turned white; *Hope* shook.

Like a needle slipping through viscid fabric, the rockets propelled the space transport *Hope* through the atmospheric canopy. They penetrated the earth's safety net in seconds. And the battle began.

Chapter Two

"Primary rockets away . . . tanks have separated . . . Prepare to cease burn on my mark: three . . . two . . . one . . . mark." Major Lathem followed the colonel's orders, and an eerie quiet permeated the cockpit.

Anderson sighed before she spoke. "Mission control, this is Survey III aboard the *Hope*. Propulsion systems disengaged."

"Copy that, Hope. Please open cargo bay doors." Outfitted with solar panels, opening the cargo bay doors provided cooling for the hydraulic system and power for the orbiter.

"Roger, Houston. We are transitioning to a rotating rest period." The team had been up since 0400 hours, not that any of them had slept well. Anderson figured that Davenport hadn't slept in a week, and he wouldn't now either. Davenport had the first watch with Major Lathem.

The colonel detached her harness, floated out of the command seat, and began removing her bulky liftoff suit. Chief Engineer Sergio Martinez and NASA's expert geologist Andrew Rogers also unbuckled, disrobed, and air-swam toward what passed as "crew quarters" in the new generational orbiter. They secured themselves into the rectangular niches intended to allow sleep during their zero-gravity flight. As usual, Rogers had trouble fitting his six-foot-five-inch frame in comfortably.

"The wife had us redo our wills last year," he said as he settled in. "I specified an extra-long casket for my burial. Gave measurements and everything. Didn't want the government to cram my body into an average-size box for all eternity. Six hours of commanded rest in one of these vaults is enough for anybody."

"You shrink when you die, you know," Martinez commented.

"Good. Then I'll have plenty of room to kick around."

"I personally don't plan on staying connected to this old shell, *mi amigo*. Cremation's the way to go. I'll be long gone."

"But where to?" the colonel asked.

Rogers snickered. "He'll already be used to the flames before they send his body through the crematorium."

Martinez turned off the light. "You surprise me, my friend. I didn't think you would want to contaminate Earth's precious soil with your remains. But hey, if you want to be worm manure, more power to you."

"Organic fertilizer, my man, of the most premium quality."

"Six hours' sleep, gentlemen."

Martinez and Rogers quieted down, and within minutes, rhythmic snoring came from Martinez's berth. The weightlessness of outer space negated the effects of weight on his nasal passages, but apparently, Martinez had other issues. Nonetheless, the colonel found the noise distracting. She tried to clear her mind and allow rest to wash over her, but nervous anxiety continued to stir her thinking.

After a few more minutes of mental gymnastics, the colonel abruptly released herself from the sleeping berth and headed for the cockpit. She'd made nine previous trips into space, including two to the lunar surface, had aborted one mission just after takeoff and cut one mission short after losing her life support's primary backup, and had always come through the fire proven. But with retirement only as far away as *Hope*'s return to Earth, her jaded confidence suffocated any anticipation. Then the alarm sounded.

CHAPTER THREE

Even on a Tuesday evening, Club Chameleon in Houston was hopping. A promise to bring old Chicago tunes out of the closet had lured the faithful and the young . . . and those who actually remembered the band. People and music pushed outward on every wall, spilling out onto the street through the open door.

The dance floor heaved rhythmically under the glow of ever-changing lights, and the wait staff threaded their way through walls of smiles and winks to set libations onto small round tables surrounded by the seated customers.

At the bar, a strong tanned hand reached for a scotch. Five well-groomed fingers lifted the glass from counter to lip, and just above the rim, hazel green eyes continued their relentless gaze at an eighteen-year-old brunette three tables away. Eyebrow and glass rose ever so slightly in salute. The girl's boyfriend scowled and moved his chair to break the man's line of vision. The man's face curled into a grin.

His French silk shirt almost as expensive as the gold chain around his neck and the cologne on his face, the man stood up and scanned the room. A dark-haired beauty with rich tanned skin in a shimmery low-cut sheath that changed color with the dance floor looked his way and then returned her bored attention to the giggling couple at her table. A fourth chair was empty.

He sent a chardonnay to her table and slipped into the waiting seat as she looked around for her benefactor. He offered his hand. "I'm Frank."

She smiled and grasped the wine stem instead. "What, no line with the wine?"

"Did you need one?"

"Not particularly."

Setting the glass down, she returned the handshake. "Margo."

He embraced her slender fingers, lifting them to a kiss in one moment, eyes grazing the deep plunge of her dress in the next.

Margo waited a beat then gently pulled her hand back. "So, Frank, what do you do?"

"I'm the OIC of the planned lunar outpost."

"That's not just a pickup line, is it?"

"No, I'm the OIC."

Margo's friend, a curvy, mahogany-skinned woman in a form-fitting red dress, interrupted her own rapture with her new gentleman friend to comment. "Did I just hear you say you've been to the Moon?"

Frank leaned back and smiled. "Not only have I been to the Moon, I'm the officer in charge of the current operations. Colonel Frank Thompson."

The woman flashed a grin at Margo. "So, Colonel, just what does the OIC of the planned lunar outpost do?"

"I lay out the work schedule, put the teams together, and then make it all happen."

"Un-hun, my girl, Margo, here is in training."

"LaDee, shhh," Margo reprimanded.

"Really?" Frank signaled the server for another scotch. "What's your specialty?"

"I have a PhD in geophysics."

"I'm bringing a geophysicist with me on the next launch."

"I know. We work for the same company."

"You work for Tectonics?"

"Yes. In fact, NASA is currently evaluating my hypothesis."

"Tell me about it."

LaDee got up from the table. "Whoa, girl. Hold on." She pushed her chair in. "C'mon, Matthew, let's see those size tens on the dance floor. There's about to be a lot of mumbo jumbo at this table." She grinned at Margo. "See ya, girl."

Margo folded the corner of her cocktail napkin and then looked up at Thompson. "As I assume you are aware, previously the Earth's rotation slowed by about fifteen microseconds each year, basically due to the transfer of rotational energy to the Moon and the frictional drag of tidal movement. At the same time, the transfer of angular momentum and rotational energy to the Moon increased its forward direction, causing it to orbit farther away from the Earth, increasing the Earth-to-Moon distance by about thirty-eight millimeters annually. In short, days should be getting longer and the Moon should be slowly moving farther away."

Margo leaned back and crossed her legs. "However, over the last five to ten years, the average spin rate of the Earth has increased rather than decreased. We can explain this shift as occurring because of an apparent decrease in the Earth's mass distribution, most likely due to postglacial rebound—are you tracking with me so far?"

Thompson motioned for her to continue. "The sparkle in my eyes should tell you the lights are on upstairs."

"Right." Margo grabbed a handful of peanuts and distributed them as visual aids on the table. "So without the weight of the immense glacier ice pushing down on most of the continents, the Earth's crust has slowly decompressed, much like a depression in your carpet eventually releases after furniture is moved. The crust's movement away from the Earth's center, because it lacks symmetry, has caused the Earth's rotation to accelerate. Unlike the figure skater, who pulls body parts closer to center to spin faster and moves the extremities farther from the center to slow down, the decompressing crust, with its thicker continents and thinner ocean basins, moves outward unevenly. Therefore, the shifting mass acts like a shot put or discus as an athlete heaves it around and around faster and faster before launching it. The centrifugal force causes the spinning body—in this case, the Earth—to increase its rotational momentum. It speeds up.

"The puzzle comes because if the Earth's rotational speed is increasing, a higher amount of energy should be transferring to the Moon, causing the Moon to increase its distance from the Earth even more. However, lunar laser ranging experiments in the last four years indicate that the Moon has all but halted its movement away from the Earth. In fact, the statistics show that if you take the average distance throughout the elliptical orbit, the distance from Moon to Earth has decreased. The Moon has begun to descend into a lower orbit."

"Your point?"

"I think that the Moon's core has grown more dense due in part to its overall increase in proximity to the sun caused by its previous higher orbit. The exposure to higher temperatures would then liquefy the nonrigid mantle surrounding the core, releasing gas from underground cavities. Recent basaltic flow had to come from somewhere. I think we may be seeing the 'waking up' of the Moon. Spectrograms have actually observed increasing levels of carbon vapor—more carbon than previously believed even existed."

Thompson's eyes began to gloss over. Knifing his fingers through his hair, he stole a peek at another short skirt.

Margo's voice pitched louder. "I know this is mostly speculative, but I fully believe that we are witnessing the very early beginnings of life on the Moon. The carbon is there. We've discovered the frozen ice we expected in the lunar poles and the shadowed regions. I believe that the composition of the Moon is morphing, making room for the combining of the first molecules of life."

"Interesting."

A long-legged blonde brought Thompson another scotch. He neatly swirled his glass, jiggling the "rocks" out of stacked formation. Margo looked from the glass to Thompson's face.

"Am I boring you?"

"I've heard all this before."

"But you don't buy it."

"I think it's worth looking into. That's one reason we're bringing your man with us on Survey IV."

"When is that?"

"I'm forty-one days out right now."

"I would give anything to go up with you."

Thompson raised an eyebrow. "Anything?"

Margo didn't answer.

Frank's grin spread Cheshire style. He stood up and offered a hand. "Shall we join your friends?"

Margo allowed him to help her up, and the pair stepped onto the dance floor to the beat of *Saturday in the Park*. Taking her by one hand, Frank slipped a hand around her waist and spun her around. He was light on his feet and moved with grace. When the tempo slowed and the lights dimmed, Frank moved in close for an easy two-step. His lips brushed her ear.

"I could get you on a mission sooner than you think." He slid his hand down to the small of her back. "After dinner, we could check the schedule. See if I can work something out for you."

"Or I could earn the spot on my own."

"You could, yes. I bet you could. But my way would be faster"—Frank spun Margo around and lowered her into a dip—"and guaranteed." Helping her regain her balance, he shrugged. "It's up to you."

They returned to their table to find LaDee on the way out with her latest catch.

Frank helped Margo with her chair and then slipped down into his. He reached across the table and gently laid his left hand on hers. "Shall I order dinner, or would you like to get out of here?"

Margo stared at his hand. She stroked the narrow band of light skin wrapping around his tanned ring finger. "You're married?"

Frank shrugged again. "Does it matter?"

"Yes, it does."

An amused smile spread across his face. "Then, no, I'm not married."

"Care to explain?"

"If you need me to be single, then I'll be single. Just think of me as a single guy."

Margo pulled her hand back from under his. "What kind of crap is that?"

Like a clawed, velvety paw snatching its prey, Thompson caught Margo's wrist between his thumb and forefinger and, with a swift twist, raised her fingers to his lips, kissing them one by one.

"Listen, beautiful, life is about choices. Each choice you make leads you down a particular path. When the opportunity comes, you have to make the right choice. Most people miss out on life because they are afraid to make the hard choices. Opportunities slip through their fingers. This is your opportunity to take the path that leads to the lunar surface. Make the right choice, and you'll be standing in moondust before the end of the year."

"And if I choose to call your wife?"

Thompson's eyes narrowed slightly, but his smile remained smug. "Then you are choosing to never step foot in an orbiter."

Margo leaned in. "Do the words 'sexual harassment' mean anything to you?"

Shaking his head in amusement, Frank replied, "Choices, choices, sweetheart. It's all about choices."

He stood up, retrieving a solid-gold card case from his right pants pocket. "I see you need a short while to think about it." He tossed a card on the table. "Give me a call when you change your mind." He dabbed at the corners of his mouth with a napkin then excused himself and returned to the hunt. Margo watched Thompson brush up against a buxom blonde on the dance floor. Within moments, the two were caterwauling along with the band, and Margo gathered her purse and headed out.

*   *   *

Fumbling for her set of keys in the dark entryway, Margo heard the phone inside her two-bedroom condo ring.

"Come on, Margo, open the stupid door."

Margo stuffed the mail in between her teeth and scrambled through the door, dropping her work clothes into a bin labeled "Dry Cleaners" and continuing on to the living room toward the phone, which had stopped ringing. Nothing except the light had changed since she had left the gated community that morning at six thirty. When she had gone to work, the August sun had reached through the crystal-clear glass window to fill the room. Now the moon chose which parts of the room to touch with her cool, blue glow: a rectangle of the bamboo floor, clean, fresh and environmentally friendly; an alphabetically arranged spice rack on the kitchen counter just beyond, ready to be employed for dinner;

and the dust-free entertainment unit with a picture of Margo's mom and dad at center stage. Ten miles away and they still had not seen her new place.

The message light begged to be checked.

"Socs, I'll bet you fresh fish that was Mom and Dad calling."

Margo turned on the light and shuffled through the mail: "All junk." Placing two more bills on an ever-increasing stack of notices, she called out, "Should I listen to the message?"

Socrates didn't respond.

"I'm going to get me a dog."

With an extra-large diet soda in hand, Margo made herself comfortable on the couch, being careful not to disturb the sleeping keeper of the condo. Staring up at a beautiful sunset landscape of Roswell, New Mexico, Margo dreamed of simpler days. The large two-by-four-foot black metal-framed photograph was the only color print that graced her eggshell white walls. She hit Play.

"*Hi, Margo. Sorry we missed you. Hope you're not asleep already. I know your social life has been a bit, um, plain lately. Have you heard from NASA yet?*"

Margo hit the Cancel button. "More junk." She laid Thompson's card by the phone.

Her cell rang. She answered. "I'm in."

CHAPTER FOUR

"Godspeed, Kim. Hurry home."

Bobby watched *Hope* fly until it became less than a speck through his high-powered lenses.

He slid back down into the driver's seat and put the key in the ignition. A low rumble sounded over the constant roar of cars on the causeway. The wind swirled and scattered the morning's newspaper across the backseat. Looking northwest, Bobby spotted the edge of a cold front racing to meet the rising moon. It was clashing with the stifling August air, creating miles of dark towers. He swung open the door to raise and batten down the top of his passionate hobby. He gave her a pat on the rump and returned to the driver's side.

Bobby was only halfway home when the fury of the heavens caught up with him. The southbound lanes before him filled up with bright taillights. Bobby switched lanes left and then right and then left again, only to find his path completely blocked. He saw the emergency lights in his side-view mirror before he heard the siren over the pounding rain. Three ambulances and a fire response vehicle flew by on the left shoulder, barely avoiding his door handle.

Bobby looked at the dashboard clock and cringed. Carol was going to be irritated. He punched Home on his cell. No signal.

Bobby tapped the steering wheel a few times with his fingers and then checked the signal again. No go. Already in neutral, he punched in the clutch and methodically rotated the stick through the gears. He fiddled with the ancient radio to pass the time.

"Police officials continue to caution all women to avoid walking to their cars alone at night until the A1A rapist has been apprehended. Twenty-three vic—"

"Unhappily married? Looking for love? Register at . . ."

"In other news, continued global warming and resulting rising seas are being blamed for coastal flooding in Hong Kong. Scientists warn that an unabated increase in fossil fuel production and consumption will only . . ."

"The Pacific Ring of Fire is lit up tonight, registering three earthquakes—4.5, 5.1, and 6.0, respectively."

"Give me a break," Bobby muttered. "Is there any good news?" Bobby hit the brakes hard as lightning lit the sky.

Time seemed to slow as an eighteen wheeler in the northbound lanes swerved into a jackknife. The tanker swung laterally, running over a Mini Cooper, and then collected several other small vehicles into its petroleum-encased web, dragging them off the road. Their drivers bailed out almost before the cars came to a stop. The truck cab turned, twisted, and flipped, sending bits of gravel, grass, and glass flying, finally coming down on its grill in a deep, water-filled ditch. Bobby could see the bloodied face of the truck driver, whose eyes pleaded for help.

"Oh God, help him!" With eyes searching up and down the roadway, Bobby opened his door. Preferring to acquiesce to type A heroes, Bobby hesitated and looked for one. Seeing no one, he stepped up. Two other men ran up behind Bobby just as the tanker exploded into flames.

The shockwave knocked Bobby to the ground. He staggered to his feet and shielded his face from the heat with his hand. He inched forward. The trucker yelled for help.

The two young Samaritans looked at Bobby for direction. "Get the door open."

Shielded by his cab, the trucker worked his seatbelt loose just as the would-be rescuers forced open his door. "Can you move?" Bobby asked.

"Help me to my feet and I can run."

Face red with rain-washed blood, the driver took two steps and collapsed. Bobby pulled the driver's right arm over his shoulder and grabbed the driver's belt in the center of his back. "Let's go, let's go!"

The larger of the other two Samaritans followed Bobby's lead on the left side. They were up and moving fast from the flames.

By the time they were laying the driver on the asphalt shoulder, the paramedic from the previous traffic accident was checking the driver's vitals.

As Bobby moved back toward the tanker, a hysterical woman appeared through the smoke. "My baby, my baby!" she screamed as she pulled on the back door. The Mini Cooper's roof collapsed to the roll bar, jamming the door. Flames shot out of a crack in the tanker just eighteen inches above the crushed roof.

The other two Samaritans pulled the woman back from the flames. Bobby took two steps toward the car only to be pulled back by a firefighter who had arrived by foot. "The truck is coming. Wait for the truck."

The tanker's aft compartment exploded, engulfing the car in flames.

The firefighter took off his helmet, listened, and peered hard into the blaze. He leaned into Bobby and whispered, "She's gone."

Then another tire blew, the flames receded, and the smoke cleared just enough for the firefighter to catch a glimpse of the little girl's waving hand.

Two more tires blew as the fire truck pulled up. Without any hesitation, the firefighter replaced his mask and helmet and rushed into the unknown flames. His buddies pointed their hoses just above his head. Half the water vaporized in the heat, and the other half cascaded down upon the firefighter and the Mini Cooper. Bobby marveled at his courage and laughed out loud two minutes later when the firefighter came running from the flames, carrying the little girl in his arms. And he wondered. Would he be so brave?

CHAPTER FIVE

Returning to his Ford Mustang, Bobby started to inch his way home amid thoughts of his own little girl—strong willed and determined, just like her mother. He checked his cell again; still no signal. His wife, Carol, would not be happy.

Carol was a five-foot-three-inch dynamo who had a tongue and a mind to match the fire in her hair. She was enough to turn anyone's head, including Bobby's, which she could spin with a smile. Even after fifteen years of marriage, she still took his breath away. They had met in his third year of college. Carol O'Conner was a grader for Professor Moseman in the English department. She was not impressed with Bobby's writing prowess. Carol had bled all over his final paper. Moseman's only comment was "Talk to the grader." Bobby made an appointment for the following Monday at two o'clock in the afternoon. Over the weekend, he did a little research on Carol.

She was cute, small in stature, and one year younger but one year ahead of him in school. He considered intimidation, but that wasn't his style. He would simply come in strong and confident and give logical reasons why the grade should be advanced. The content itself, like the degree of difficulty in gymnastics, should pump the grade one letter all by itself. "Be gentle, Bobby," he told himself. "You don't want to be a jerk—you just want to raise your grade."

At one forty-five, Bobby made his way to the Hurley Building. Denim shirt, stone-washed jeans, and leather sandals softened his presence. He would keep his sunglasses on and take them off for effect upon meeting her. He would be in complete control.

Carol was filing grades. She turned away from the four-drawer file cabinet as Bobby walked in. The glasses came off, and he was stunned. He tried not to check her out. He tried to keep his eyes on her eyes. He had never seen eyes as blue as hers, set against flawless skin and the most perfect nose—she was gorgeous. He was speechless. He just stood there frozen in time, unable to move. Then she did it. She smiled. His knees almost buckled.

Fifteen years—and forty-five minutes—later, Bobby whipped into the driveway of his flat, four-bedroom, Spanish-style home in Satellite Beach. The deluge had tapered down just before the lightning struck. The thirty-foot royal palm in the front yard burst into electric fire. Bobby slammed the Mustang into reverse and flew out into the street, creating separation from the burning tree. Electric fire fairies floated down onto the driveway only to drown on the rain-soaked concrete. The light rain continued to soak the smoldering palms, extinguishing the flames.

Distant lightning filled the air as Bobby pulled back into his drive. A paranoid affect overtook the unflappable pilot as he walked through the front door, dripping water over the mosaic-tiled entryway.

In a pink nightgown, five-year-old Stacy Haistings scrambled out of her mother's arms and dashed over to greet her daddy. "Did you hear that?"

"I did." Bobby looked toward Carol. "It struck the palm by the drive."

"You okay?"

"Just a little wet." Bobby shook his head and sprayed Stacy with droplets. She squealed.

"Bobby," Carol scolded, drying her hands with a dishtowel, "stop that. You're as bad as a dog."

Bobby noticed that she was still wearing her lace camisole and skirt. He pulled her in for a kiss. She let him then pushed him away.

"Ugh." She playfully snapped the dishtowel on his hindquarters before tossing it to him. "You're late, and you're wet, Major

Haistings. Dry off and eat your dinner before your daughter court-martials you."

Stacy giggled. "I sentence you to one bedtime story, Daddy."

Bobby set Stacy down and told her to go pick out her story. Following Carol back into the kitchen, he apologized for being so late.

"The sky broke loose, and there was a half-hour delay on US 1 due to an overturned eighteen wheeler."

"You stop and help?"

"Yeah. I helped two other guys pull the driver out. But I also watched a firefighter run through a blaze to rescue a little girl. What is it in a man or woman that would motivate them to run into the flames of an overturned tanker truck that could vaporize the block at any moment?"

"I'm not sure."

"I wish . . ."

"You would if it was your family." She bumped him with her hip playfully.

"I hope I never have to find out." Surely, love would bolster his courage.

"Why don't you go tuck your daughter in, and we'll talk later, after you get a chance to eat."

Bobby found Stacy sitting on her bed, flipping through the book she had chosen. After two trips through the same book, Bobby tucked Stacy in and kissed her good night.

Carol was setting Bobby's reheated dinner bowl on the table when he arrived in the kitchen. He sat down, and Carol wrapped her arms around his broad shoulders and rested her cheek on the top of his damp head. "You went to the launch, didn't you?"

"I'm hopeless." Bobby took a bite of the steaming black bean soup and then returned her gaze. "I couldn't stay away."

"I don't want you to regret your promise and then blame me."

"It was my choice, Carol. You asked and argued your case. I made the decision." He took another bite. "Don't get me wrong—I never said it would be easy. You know me, I love the adventure."

"I know."

"Some days will be harder than others. Today, it's not that hard."

"What do you mean?" Carol finished wiping down the counter.

Bobby put down his spoon. "Two reasons. First, there are way too many global peculiarities."

Carol sat down next to Bobby. "Such as?"

"We've had more than twenty named storms this year, seven major hurricanes, and it's only the first of August. In the last six months, we've had more measurable earthquakes than we had in the previous decade. Who could have even dreamed that a tsunami would hit Boston Harbor? Who knew there was a fault line off Greenland?" Bobby took a couple bites. "There's flooding up and down the northeastern seaboard and weird tidal shifts, not to mention meteor showers like never before. And many people are pointing their finger at the moon. Something's not right."

"And second?"

"This whole Survey III mission is moving way too fast. I don't like it. Satterfield's memorial service was only two weeks ago. I was in flight school with that guy. He had three kids—all teenagers. I'll tell you something. You couldn't pay me enough money to be on that mission right now."

"That's fine by me. I like you home." Carol handed Bobby his napkin.

"I'll bet you even money Kim Anderson wishes she was on solid earth right now."

"I wish she was too." Carol stood to refill her coffee cup. "She'll be okay, won't she?" Bobby didn't answer. "Jack's in the loop," she called over her shoulder. "He won't let the mission get away from NASA again, will he?"

After a short tour in the air force, Jack became a NASA test pilot and then took two trips into space before settling comfortably behind the chief's desk. With a superior attention to detail and a genuine love for his teams, Jack was well respected at NASA. So no one thought twice when he got preoccupied with his brother's sudden death shortly after the lunar craft *Pinta* entered lunar orbit. General Buchholz stepped in during Jack's absence. No one blamed Jack for the crash except Jack.

"Bobby?" Their eyes met as she returned to her seat. "I've known Kim my entire adult life." A long-time family friend, Carol looked up to Kim as a mentor.

"I know. I remember." Bobby finished his soup.

Carol pushed her cup away from her and leaned in close. "Bobby, Kim will be okay . . . won't she?"

"She'll be fine." Bobby smiled, took Carol's hand, and pulled her out onto the back deck to show her the harvest moon as it fought with the clouds to be noticed. As he did nearly every night, Bobby searched the skies. Carol relaxed back against his chest, and he wrapped his arms around her. A steady wind fluttered her skirt around his legs and cooled the humid air.

Two shooting stars brought a smile to her face. "Nights like this, even I can see why you're so drawn to space."

On Mercury Road in Satellite Beach, Florida, Bobby Haistings kissed the soft curve of his wife's neck. Two hundred miles above them, finally free of its encumbrances, the mighty stallion galloped mach speed through the darkness toward its pit stop on Delta. In California and across the mid-west through Texas and up into Boston, Massachusetts, again it began to rain.

CHAPTER SIX

At Mission Control in Houston, Texas, red, yellow, and green console lights added their own rhythm to the buzz of the room and the flickering computer screens. Personnel bobbed up and down from their stations like prairie dogs, sticking their heads up to sniff and then disappearing at the first sign of shadows skimming over the grass.

Glassed into his own office box behind the rows of engineers, scientists, and military personnel, Dr. Jack Sooner, chief of operations for the National Aeronautics and Space Administration, plowed through the latest flight details transmitted from *Hope* and compared it with information previously gathered during the tragic Survey II mission.

Sooner rubbed his eyes behind his glasses and closed the report. Stale coffee saturated his once-sharp mind. His tie removed, sleeves rolled up, and remnants of last night's Danish just above his belt, Jack grabbed the remote and unmuted the LCD screen built into the office wall. CNN was showing Hurricane Otis's landfall at Puerto Vallarta, Mexico. With swirling ferocity, the wind whipped broken palm fronds and roof boards onto the boiling, frothy beach. Angry water pounded the shore, slamming into piers, sand, and rocks and then exploded, spraying foam and saline high into the sky. The wind howled as the salt spray rained down on the incoming surge, a million plinks hitting ground zero like the rapid volley of machine gun fire.

Jack turned up the voice-over.

"World in crisis. Behind Otis, on the Pacific Mexican coast, Tropical Storms Pilar and Ramon are lining up for their turns at wreaking havoc. While our Pacific coast is being hit with more water than it can handle, in Wellington, New Zealand, yesterday's record low tides have remained. Hundreds of boats are still bogged down in the mud, and even the evening's high tide failed to bring the water back up to the docks.

"Dr. Ramesh Gupta of the International Oceanography Institute reports of tectonic plate movement in the Pacific Ring of Fire."

Jack muted the television and grabbed two antacids from the large bottle in his desk drawer. Chewing the chalky tablets, he pressed the well-worn button on the speakerphone and dialed the extension for the on-duty astrogeologist.

"I need the latest data on lunar seismic activity."

"We've lost two of the geophones left behind by Survey I, sir, but . . ."

A fresh stomach geyser blasted the antacids. "What do you mean 'you lost them'?"

"Sorry, sir. Communication from geophones Alpha 3 and Delta 1 ceased at 0218 Zulu, coinciding with another meteor shower in that region. But we still have three left accounting for two different sectors, sir."

"What do you see?"

"Not much. Most of it is minor, and it is restricted to sector D214."

"Send it to me ASAP."

"Yes, sir."

Within seconds, Sooner's printer began spewing out pages filled with the zigzag heartbeat of the Moon. Standing and leaning over the papers spread out before him, Sooner scanned the seismic report and then flipped through a dozen of the latest eight-by-ten glossies of the Moon. The printer's beep interrupted his concentration. He picked up a final document from the tray. A moon landscape stared back at him from the paper. At the bottom, a caption read "Moonface as seen from EPSOLONON Observatory at 0830 Zulu."

Jack sank into his chair. *Not on my watch! Not again.* Sooner ran his fingers through his thinning hair. Taking a deep breath, he picked up the phone but hesitated before dialing. He tapped the number keys on the dial pad, without pushing them. His right middle fingernail clicked over and over again on number nine. Jack picked up the moonscape again and studied it. *I won't just hope for the best.* He dialed the Pentagon.

"Get me General Buchholz!"

"One moment, please."

"It's Sooner. We need to scrub."

"What's the problem?" Buchholz was calm and assertive.

"I think lunar seismic activity has created an unstable LZ and may have caused a change in the Moon's rotation. Any change at all and our navigational calculations would be off. They could miss the landing zone by hundreds of miles. It's too risky to land."

"Are you sure? What does Thompson say?"

Sooner gripped his pen hard. "Haven't talked to him."

"Good grief, Jack. I know he's paint on a pump handle, but I want him in on this from the get go. Brief Thompson on your findings, and then I want to see both of you in your office in twenty."

"Minutes?"

"Yes, I'm in Houston. I take it you didn't catch my press conference this morning."

"I was busy. We do have a team in space."

"Just keeping the public informed, Jack. Why I came to Houston in August is beyond me. It's hot, it's wet, and it smells—kinda like my left armpit. You boys ought to get hazard pay."

Jack grunted. *You're the hazard.*

"Call Frank. He flew in yesterday. I'll see you both in twenty."

Nineteen minutes later, Jack found himself standing between the two empty chairs on the visitor's side of his own desk. Reclining in Jack's chair, in a surprisingly crisp uniform with a barrel-chest full of medals, including a bronze star with clusters for bravery under fire, General Lee Buchholz rested his high-glossed, black cowboy boots on the desk and filled the office with smoke from his smoldering cigar. His effort to extinguish the flame was less than adequate.

The bronze star on Buchholz's chest glared at Jack. Twenty years ago, the old cowboy from Nebraska had risked his life for his men. It was a story Jack had heard countless times.

Colonel Frank Thompson, impeccably dressed in an expensive dark suit and red silk tie, stood at the desk's corner and flipped through the report Jack had left on the desk. Jack ignored him and eyed the boots. The general returned the strong bead.

"My apologies, Jack." He shifted his boots to a small space of unused desk real estate. "Thompson, what's your take?"

"I know Dr. Sooner has the team's best interest at heart, General, but I think a scrub is certainly premature." Thompson paused to flash his winning smile: artificially whitened teeth, thin lips, and a slight cleft in the chin. "The chief tends to be a bit of a mother hen with his teams, you know. These men know the risks. They're up there to gather data and lay a foundation for the research lab. I've said it before. The increased seismic activity may be a wrinkle in the overall plan, but it's just as well it's happening now, so they can analyze it now. After all, we're planning to stay on the Moon quite a long time." He studied the moonscape in silence for a moment and then added, "We'll be much more prepared for the future, don't you agree, Jack?"

"No, I don't agree." He snatched the report off the desk where Thompson had placed it. Peeling the pages back quickly, he shoved the picture in Buchholz's face. "Look at the picture, General!"

"I'm looking. What in Sam Hill do you expect me to see?"

Sooner held up the picture next to a framed photograph of the Moon that decorated his wall. He pointed to a ridge crest on the right side, just beyond Mare Fecunditatis. "There! That ridge should not be there. Even if we assume tectonics theory, it shouldn't be happening this fast. The lunar surface is dangerously unstable."

Picking lint from his left sleeve, Thompson asserted, "You don't know that, Jack. That ridge could just as easily be the edge of a new impact crater. Nothing out of the ordinary."

Sooner, red faced with veins popping out of his forehead, glared into Thompson's arrogant eyes from six inches away. Jack had never understood how such a narcissist could rise to the rank of colonel. Thompson's minty fresh breath soured in Jack's stomach. "I'm telling you, something is happening! We don't have to risk lives to gather data. We could send probes."

The general rolled the cigar in his mouth and stared at the black and whites as if he might see something move. "I'm not convinced, Jack. We've known about moonquakes since Apollo. Never been an issue. If they're coming faster and harder, it probably has more to do with superior instrument detection than actual movement. Regardless, if there is a problem, we will handle it."

"There is no handling an unstable surface," Jack insisted. "We don't even have the full report on why the lunar craft *Pinta* crashed." Jack put his hands on the desk and moved closer to the general's face. General Buchholz still reclined in the chair. "General, you may not have known Len Satterfield, but pilot error would be the last conclusion I would come to with him at the helm."

"Jack, Jack, I know he was a friend, but there's no need . . ."

Jack leaned in and lowered his voice to a deep growl. "Lee, I don't know how you got it done, but you have circumvented NASA's entire safety protocol. In all the history of the National Aeronautics and Space Administration, we have never, I mean, never, sent another mission up following a complete loss of ship and crew without a full investigation. Forget full—we've hardly even begun to investigate. It reeks of political excrement."

The general met Jack's stare without blinking.

Thompson shrugged and spoke up. "The world changes, Jack. Volcanoes erupt. Dinosaurs die out. Glaciers descend and retreat. More is at stake here than a few casualties. If we don't stay on top, someone or something else will."

Jack felt the acid rising but kept his lock on the general. "Is that how you stomach it?" He felt a diatribe erupting from his gut about the state of the American military, but he forced it back down. "We're talking lives—men and women with families." He shifted his gaze to the ribbons on Buchholz's chest. "Where is your sense of humanity, Lee?"

"Enough!" The general pulled the plug from his mouth. Sooner gritted his teeth as General Buchholz stood up.

"Jack, I'm going to go with Colonel Thompson on this one. This activity or change in the terrain, whatever it is, isn't anywhere near the quadrant where our team will be landing. You're asking me to worry about a California earthquake while sunning myself on Miami Beach. Didn't get this far by running scared." He looked around for a makeshift ashtray and settled on a dirty coffee cup on the walnut credenza. Snuffing out the smolder, he headed for the door. "It's a go. And Jack, if you can't handle the pressure, I'll find someone who can."

Stiffening his jaw, Jack ground his molars and swallowed a million inappropriate comments. "Just so we are clear, General, I'm officially filing a protest of warning."

"You do whatever makes you feel better."

Thompson, smile still gluing his cheeks to his ears, reached out to shake Jack's hand.

"You're doing good work, Jack. Try not to get your underwear in a knot."

Jack kept his hand by his side. "I don't see you putting your life on the line."

"Actually, Jack, I'm going to ride in the command seat of Survey IV."

Caught with his fly down, Sooner noticed that Buchholz also looked surprised. Jack could tell that Thompson was enjoying the leg up.

"With Major Haistings's withdrawal from the active astronaut program, I'm next up on my list."

The general turned and abruptly cantered out of the room. "Ride with me, Colonel." Thompson followed in hot pursuit.

Jack waited until Thompson had shut the door behind him. He grabbed a notebook from his desk that read "NASA/United States Armed Forces Joint Project" and flung it across the room.

Sooner's phone beeped with an incoming call. Jack left the folder and its contents where they had fallen.

"Sooner here."

"Jack, it's George Miller." He was a reporter for the *Washington Post* who boasted of a friendship with Jack.

"George, I don't have time for twenty questions right now."

"You following the news, Jack?"

"What do you think?"

"Right. What do you know that we don't?"

"The government's not always keeping secrets, George. We're scientists here, not politicians." Jack glanced at the paperwork all over the corner of his office floor and could not help but grumble internally.

"Whatever you say, Jack. Now, off the record, Tectonics is saying that the irregularities on the Moon are causing the weather disturbances on earth? What's NASA's take?"

Through the glass wall, Jack stared blankly at a meeting of the minds taking place right in front of him—engineers and scientists apparently still attempting to determine the cause of a stray alarm in *Hope*'s auxiliary navigational system. Heads bent together over computer data, messages relayed into space, the men and the women of NASA Mission Control responded to the latest challenge of their mastery of all things technical and scientific. Jack pushed a button and closed the automatic blinds.

"C'mon, Jack, give me something."

"George, you tell your readers that weather patterns on this planet fluctuate as a natural course of action. We have been in an *El Ninõ* pattern for three years now, and there is no sign of it stopping. El Niño has been known to cause damage to the reefs, which in turn affects wave action, shore erosion, and tidal basins. We live in a cause-and-effect world. Everything has a consequence."

"So there is no lunar connection?"

"We are experiencing natural phenomena well within the normal range of cyclical fluctuations. The stars are just lining up right now. That's all. Thanks for calling."

"Wait! I have information for you."

"Have a nice day, George."

"Your mission is in jeopardy."

"Good-bye, George."

"There are covert players." Jack hung up the phone, took off his glasses, and massaged his closed eyes in a counterclockwise motion. His back ached as the disc between L4 and L5 disintegrated a little bit more. Another painkiller would play havoc with his nervous stomach. Was the mission in jeopardy? What did George mean by "covert players"?

CHAPTER SEVEN

Colonel Thompson followed the general as he exited the building, walked down the six concrete steps, and climbed back into the large black SUV that sat outside the administration building, waiting to return the general to the airport. Buchholz reigned in his tongue until both doors were closed. Thompson let the silence ride until the general broke it.

"Any way we can get Haistings back?"

"I doubt it. He seems pretty happy in the training division. I hear he's a good teacher. But more importantly, his wife is happy."

"Frank, do you know what you're doing?"

"Yes, sir, I do. I've stayed current. I want to go."

Thompson watched the scowl on the general's face ease up. Buchholz took a long draw on his cigar and scanned the passing traffic. The furrowed brow remained.

"Can we push the Survey IV mission up a couple weeks?"

Thompson quickly pulled his smartphone from his pocket and began reviewing the calendar with one eye on his phone and one on the general.

"Why?"

"Could we do it? . . . Is it possible?"

"I'm not sure we can get a transporter ready any earlier. They are still having trouble with the Yeager's heat shield. Besides, the next Aries X rocket is at least thirty days from ready. Word is we will be pressed to launch in forty days."

"What about the Russians?"

"After the whole Iran thing, they are not renting to us anymore. You know that."

"What about the X-102 space transport? I hear Captain Graham has been in the saddle all week."

"The X-102? I've got two problems with that. The X-102 is experimental. We don't even know if it can dock with the Delta space lab. And Bonham is a wealthy egocentric jerk. I don't like him. I don't trust him. I don't want to owe him anything."

"The X-102 is the future, Frank." The general's eyes rested heavily on Thompson. "Question is, can we move up the future?" Buchholz handed Thompson a one-third cut file folder with "X-102 Confidential" handwritten across the top. "It's not just experimental, and it was built to dock at Delta."

Thompson flipped quickly through the file. "Begging your pardon, General, what's the hurry?"

"Frank, something's happening up there. The Moon is as jumpy as a mare in heat."

"Not in our sector."

"True enough. But I don't know how long I can hold the NASA boys off. Jack has friends, and he can be very persuasive. You heard him—he wants to send unmanned probes to the lunar surface. If Anderson and her team don't bring us some favorable intel, they'll pull the plug."

Thompson coughed hard and said, "We can't afford that."

"No, we can't. We need to take a good look at the X-102. Just bring Graham in and appropriate that transport any way you have to." Buchholz glanced at the driver and cleared his throat. "Legally, of course. Just get me the X-102, Frank."

Thompson raised an eyebrow. The mischievous smile returned. "Yes, sir."

CHAPTER EIGHT

Jack Sooner sat in his car sipping home-brewed coffee from an old "Forty but Sporty" coffee mug. An occasional nibble on a plain bagel and cream cheese did little to calm the butterflies fluttering in his gut. *Why am I here?*

He viewed his team on a very thin line. Camping out at Mission Control is what he should have been doing. *Why am I sitting in my car trying to rendezvous with a* Washington Post *reporter?*

With both eyes trained on the front door of the Moondust Café, he waited. "Why am I meeting this guy? I don't have time for this." But he waited. Miller's last text message had said NASA was being used by an outside agency. That outside players would prevent Jack from scrubbing the mission. He no longer had control. *Not on my watch!*

Jack observed three sorority girls enter and one bearded professor exit the trendy coffee shop. Through the glass walls, he could see young professionals reading newspapers and two different groups of college kids sharing the latest news about who knows what. There was too much laughter for serious study.

The sound of screeching tires directed his attention to his rearview mirror. A half block back, an old gray four-door sedan, with a dented front left fender and no license plate, came to a stop with the right front tire up on the curb. The scruffy driver with disheveled hair, wrinkled suit, and heavy shadow stumbled out of the car and staggered over to the newspaper bin. "Drunk. It's not even ten in the morning, buddy. What an idiot."

The man kept his head down. "Embarrassed are you? Hey, buddy, if it bothers you that much, try not drinking before noon."

A pretty blonde in a short green skirt caught Jack's eye as she exited the café. She hadn't walked ten feet before a five-foot-ten-inch Norwegian fireplug with a chiseled chin caught up with her. "It figures." The couple turned around and headed in Jack's direction. Her colors and curves captured his imagination. Swedish ancestry, he guessed. When they reached the front end of his car, Jack turned red. The fireplug caught him checking out his girlfriend. The chin just smiled.

"Great, I'm not even a threat!" Jack sucked in his ever-expanding gut and flexed his right bicep—not that anyone could see. Ten years of desk work and no exercise routine had taken its toll. "My wife still loves me."

With a lap full of crumbs and a stomach full of bagel, his left thumb scratched the steering wheel and his eyes bounced around the block like a nervous thief. "Mr. Miller, you are thirty minutes late." He retrieved two antacids from a small blue pillbox on his dash, popped them in his mouth, and chased them with the last bit of coffee. "Mr. Miller, I'm going to give you five more minutes."

He reached over and turned on the radio and actually found a station on low-band AM. The DJ segued into an interview with some quack who talked about the end of the world, Judgment Day, and Armageddon. "I don't need that." Jack turned off the radio, placed the key in the ignition, and started his car. He gave one last quick look around and slipped the transmission into drive. Just before he turned his wheel away from the curb, he spotted Mr. Miller across the street, wearing blue jeans and a black T-shirt. He slinked out on foot between two buildings. "Where's your car, George?"

George nodded toward the café and then turned back as if window-shopping on the other side of the street. "Are we supposed to sit back to back and pretend that we aren't talking? I hate this cloak-and-dagger trash."

Jack put his car in park and turned off the ignition. Grabbing a little handheld recorder from his glove box, he exited the vehicle nonchalantly. Not wanting to blow his cover, Jack strolled into the Moondust Café without looking back or around. Two steps in and the place erupted in chatter and emptied onto the sidewalk like a fire drill.

"Call 911!"

"Did you see that?"

"Is he dead?"

"He was drunk!"

"Call 911!"

"I called 911. The police are on their way!"

Jack followed the crowd outside, only to find a covey of people standing around the figure of a man in the middle of the street. He looked for George. The commotion must have scared him off.

"A guy in a gray four-door sedan hit him. Never braked! Hit him front and center, dragged him fifty feet, and then sped off." The fireplug spit the words out. His deep voice surprised Jack.

"Did you get a license plate?" Jack asked.

"Didn't have one! I think it was the same car that was parked down the street with one tire up on the sidewalk. My girlfriend and I both saw it."

"Did you see the driver's face?" Jack continued to search for George in the crowd.

"No, it was buried in a newspaper. Did you see him?

"I think he had been drinking," offered the sweet voice of his girlfriend.

Sirens blared and lights flashed, pushing the crowd back enough for Jack to get a glimpse of blue jeans and a black T-shirt. "Oh no!" Jack ran toward George but got clotheslined by a policeman.

"You'll have to stand back, sir."

"But I know him."

"Were you with him?"

"No, I was meeting him."

"Did you see who hit him?"

"No, but that fireplug over there saw the whole thing." Jack nodded toward the curb.

The police officer motioned for the fireplug to approach and Jack Sooner slipped away through the crowd. He knew what he had to do.

CHAPTER NINE

Racing back to Mission Control, Jack slammed his car into park and walked briskly to the steps, which he took two and three at a time. *This is not good, not good at all.* Ten feet from the front door, he had his pass card out and was yelling, "Open up! Open the door!"

Jack ran the hallways and used the stairs—the elevators were too slow. Passing a variety of people, Jack acknowledged no one. Breathing heavily, he burst into his office, ignoring his secretary's greeting, and closed the door behind him.

After four landline calls, three favors, and a promised bottle of fine wine, Jack Sooner found General Buchholz in Washington. He wasn't surprised when the voice on the other end said, "National Security Agency."

"He's dead, Lee. He's dead. Someone murdered George Miller."

"Slow down, Jack. Tell me what happened."

"I'm pulling the plug, Lee. I'm bringing them all home, now."

"Take a breath, Jack, and listen."

"Listen to what? George Miller is dead. Did your people kill George?"

"My people? My people are your people. We're on the same team, Jack. I don't know what happened to George. You can give me the details later. But please try to understand: the death of a *Washington Post* reporter has nothing to do with NASA or the Survey III mission.

"George said we are being used. I don't know what you are trying to accomplish, but NASA is about exploration, not subjugation. NASA is not supposed to be involved in military action. This is my team, and I'm bringing them home."

"That is your choice, Jack."

"It is my choice."

"That's right, it is your call. But choices have consequences, Jack. I chair the committee that oversees your position. You can be replaced . . . you can be replaced before you make that call."

Jack slammed the phone down and pushed back from his desk. *George was right. They won't let me scrub.*

The phone rang. "Jack, I need you to simmer down." It was Buchholz. "I don't know what I need to do to convince you, but this is the honest truth. I don't know anything about the death of George Miller. We had a picture perfect launch, and the *Hope* is on schedule. I see no reason to abort. Stay the course, Chief. Let's stay the course."

NASA's chief wiped his nose, twisted in his seat, cracked his neck, and then sat up straight and said, "I'll stay the course under two conditions."

"Which are?"

"First real sign of trouble, we bring them home."

"And?"

"You find out what happened to George Miller."

"I'm in Washington, Jack."

"And George was killed here in Houston. What's your point?"

"What do you want me to do from here? Aren't the local police investigating?"

"Use your connections, General. Find out what happened to George. He was no Joe Blow USA. He was a high-profile reporter. I'm sure NSA has a file on George. They probably know what he had for dinner last night. They certainly know what he was working on. You find out what he was working on and give me a plausible explanation of his death and we'll keep moving forward."

"That will take some time."

"Take the time, but keep me in the loop. Or I swear, General, I'll go to the press."

"Don't do anything foolish, Jack."

"I'm serious, Lee. I'll pull the plug on the evening news. Before you can make a single phone call yourself."

"You're in the loop, Jack. Just give me some time."

"I'm waiting."

CHAPTER TEN

Hope continued to gallop through the black darkness toward the man-made change station between earth and the near frontier. A fully operational space station, Delta remained in constant orbit 276 miles over the earth and housed seven to ten research and military personnel. Tours of duty lasted fifteen months; the seven-member crew was in the middle of their second tour. Visitors were a welcome sight. Spotting the *Hope* electrified the space station.

"This is Delta to Survey III aboard space orbiter *Hope*, do you copy?" Anderson glanced at her chronograph. The last hour had slipped away as Anderson and her team disconnected the fourth backup navigational system. It was the only way to silence the alarm. Delta's transmission came in right on schedule.

"Roger, Delta. We copy."

"We have you on screen. Please adjust your heading ten degrees starboard on your vertical axis."

Anderson flipped the covers off two switches. Lathem counted down for the burn. Anderson fired the right thrusters and then shut them down two and a half seconds later.

"Congratulations, Hope, you are on target."

Thirty-five minutes later, Delta stretched out an arm, and as the space transport eased into its doughnut ring hand, the space station tweaked *Hope*'s nose and hugged her close. Then Delta maneuvered a short tube, her umbilical cord, from the platform to match up with the round door on top of the shuttle. After interlocking, the hydraulic doors hissed open, revealing electrical, hydraulic, and life-support connections. Five thousand points of contact lined up perfectly.

"You are clear to board."

Davenport and Rogers entered the space station through the bulkhead door, a thick two-by-three-foot rectangle on one large hinge. Commander Morgan greeted them and then gave them a quick tour of the space station. Anderson, Lathem, and Martinez stayed behind to deploy the lunar module *Santa Maria* from the cargo bay, a task they completed without incident, and then the trio joined the others aboard Delta.

They ate; they slept; they enjoyed a bag of coffee with the crew. Then at 0600 hours Zulu, the military designation for Greenwich Mean Time, they boarded the *Santa Maria* and disembarked for their final destination. With the help of the Earth's rotational whip and two long blasts of their main rocket, the crew settled into their trans-space glide.

Mission commander Colonel Kimberly Anderson tried to shake off the morbid sense of doom still clutching her heart. If anxiety is the fear of the unknown, Kim wallowed in the unfamiliar. She surveyed the crew module. Next to the galley, Martinez monitored the lunar craft's instruments. Looking more like an anxious groom than a seasoned astronaut, Martinez repeatedly set and reset circuit breakers, and checked and rechecked instrument lights. *I've made everyone nervous.* Rogers chewed on his fingernails while he inspected the communication console for condensation; Lathem studied the survey maps. Known as a bit of a maverick, Lathem was too freewheeling for the colonel under normal circumstances. Then again, the colonel had never met a man so eaten up over space travel. First and last at the gym, the once-married bachelor had passionately trained for the mission. Even Lathem's hands looked muscular.

A broad smile rippled the colonel's cheeks as she remembered Major Lathem bounding off of Searcher after Survey I's return. "Can I go again?" Like a twelve-year-old after his first roller coaster ride, the major ran to the back of the line. He hadn't been on anyone's short list to go again so quickly, but he was a good thinker who worked well under pressure. The colonel was glad Major Lathem had finagled his way on board.

Minutes later, Davenport joined the others in the command section of the *Santa Maria*. Bumping hard into Anderson, Davenport awkwardly maneuvered through the passageway. Anderson stretched her left arm out and slowly rotated her shoulder forward.

"Sorry. Shoulder bothering you, ma'am?"

"Anxious to play doc, are you?"

"Just doing my job, Colonel." Davenport took hold of Kim's arm and tested the joint.

Colonel Anderson winced, "The body's not what it used to be."

"It's a good thing NASA's standards aren't as stringent anymore. Thirty years ago, neither one of us would have qualified for this flight. I have a full range of drugs that I can give you—can't have the command lunar pilot seizing up before we reach the Moon."

"The colonel don't need no stinking drugs." Martinez put on an unusually thick Spanish accent. "No way, man. The colonel, sheez a woman of steel."

Chuckles filled the cabin. The colonel shrugged off the offer of meds and winked at Martinez, who returned to checking instrument lights with the end of his pen. The colonel had handpicked Martinez, who had modeled the training manual during the months of prep. He was wound tight, but was by the book, with attention to detail. Anderson liked that.

Glancing down at the flight plan, Major Lathem said, "Colonel, Chief Sooner is expecting contact."

"Then Mr. Rogers will have to evacuate my seat."

Newest to Anderson's team, Rogers floated out of the command seat. "Just keeping it warm."

Their eyes locked. "Thanks." The colonel positioned her earpiece. "What's that noise?"

She turned to see Martinez clicking his black government pen over and over. "Mr. Martinez, you want to stow that pen?" The clicking continued.

"I'm anxious to get started." Martinez tapped the oxygen meter.

"Well, try to relax, Mr. Martinez. Just keep doing your job and we'll be fine."

The colonel waited for hookup with Sooner and watched Martinez pick his pen back up and click it one time before Lathem reached over and snatched it out of his hand. "Marty, how's that little boy of yours?"

"Man, he is growing so fast! We got him in St. Mary's this year. He starts in a couple weeks. I'm bummed. I'm going to miss his first day of church school."

The colonel began jotting down figures on the console pad, manually double-checking the flight control instrument readings. "I didn't know you were a churchgoing man, Mr. Martinez." The linkup had not yet been established.

"Sort of."

"What do you mean 'sort of'? You are or you're not," Anderson questioned.

"Well, I believe in God. I've been a Catholic all my life. My cousin is a priest."

"What about you?"

"The wife takes my boy to mass every week. She never misses." His chest heaved with pride.

"Do you go with her?" asked Anderson.

"When I can."

Rogers jumped into the conversation. "Give me a break, Marty. You've never missed a Sunday softball game in your life, unless you were on a mission."

A big toothy grin overtook Marty's face. "I go on Saturday night."

"When? When was the last time you were in church on a Saturday?"

Marty paused sheepishly. "I was in church three weeks ago." He sat up straight. "Now what do you have to say? Uh ha! I go to church!"

"Yeah, I was there too. It was your sister's wedding."

The big toothy smile was back. "Forget you, man. I go to church when I can."

"For what?" Davenport asked.

"I told you, I believe in God." Martinez clasped his hands together and rolled his eyes to the avionic panels that roofed the cockpit. "Lord, have mercy. I'm flying in a titanium can with a bunch of heathens."

"Quiet!" Anderson adjusted her earpiece and pressed the comlink again. "I'm sorry, Dr. Sooner. Go ahead."

"Be careful, Kim. Though not in your quadrant, lunar seismic activity is increasing. Lay the footer and gather as much information as you can. But be wary."

"Copy that. My nerves are on alert."

"No one here seems to think the events pose a credible threat. Maybe I'm just turning into an addled old grandpa."

Colonel Anderson smiled but did not laugh. Memories of Batman sheets and Wonder Woman pajamas washed over her soul. A picture of her own four-year-old grandson in nothing but Sponge Bob underwear, red galoshes, and a terry cloth cape leaping into her arms from the back of the couch warmed her heart. "Yeah. Hey, Jack. Keep an eye on us."

"Will do."

"Thanks." Anderson ended the transmission with the turn of a dial.

Rogers went back to egging Martinez. "So you believe all the stories in the Bible are true?"

Martinez glared at Rogers through the corner of his eye. "We've had this conversation before."

"I know we have. But I've never gotten a straight answer out of you. I just don't understand how a man can come out of Cal Tech and still believe in the children's story found in the Bible."

"You're going straight to hell, man."

"Maybe so, if there is a hell. It's kinda hard to be afraid of going to a place that you don't believe exists."

The colonel reached up, pulled, and then reset the group of three right thruster circuit breakers. "You don't believe in God, Rogers? Even after an up-close look at the stars?"

"No, Colonel, I don't. A man has got to deal with the hard facts of reality and quit hoping in the make-believe. Humanity is going to follow the dinosaurs into extinction if we don't give up our fairy tales and start coming up with real solutions. No disrespect intended, Colonel, but the biggest fairy tales are the ones in the Bible: the crutch of humanity. If humanity is going to be saved, we gotta save ourselves. That's why I'm in the space program."

Anderson glanced out her view window just as a shooting star streaked across right to left. "I was hoping for a little more."

CHAPTER ELEVEN

Bobby, sweat beading his forehead, lay next to his sleeping wife and watched as the morning sun tiptoed across her pillow, highlighting her magnificence. Not wanting to wake her or fall back into disturbing sleep, he carefully unwound himself from the damp sheet and slipped out of bed. Shuffling into the bathroom, he saw the same face in the mirror that he had seen in his recurring dream: green eyes, sandy hair, and profound guilt. It was his face. But it wasn't his fault—he tried to stop him. Five years of counseling couldn't be wrong, could it? Bobby washed his face and tried to forget it. He pulled on a T-shirt and found his way to the kitchen, rubbing his eyes and scratching various parts of his body.

Bobby tossed fresh grounds into the coffeemaker and opened the front door to grab the *Orlando Sentinel* from the doorstep. It was old school, but Bobby liked holding the paper in his hand. A second paper was found with a yellow slip of paper stuffed inside the plastic wrapper. It was marked Complimentary Copy. Bobby picked up both papers, grabbed his laptop from his office, and headed out onto the back deck.

He dragged a lounge chair to just within the morning rays stretching under the portico then sat down and unfolded the Orlando paper.

The Buccaneers wanted a new stadium. The FDA planned to approve Pfizer's new carcinoma vaccine within the year. Two earthquakes rocked Indochina during the night.

Bobby turned the page and scanned for anything newsworthy. RECORD RAINFALL ACROSS NATION. Bobby glanced up at the robin's egg sky. MORE METEORS, SETI WEIGHS IN. *And the search for extraterrestrial intelligence goes on.*

A small breeze set the fan blades above him into a slow, lazy spin. Bobby unrolled the complimentary paper—yesterday's edition of the *Washington Post.* The front page showed flooding along the Potomac. Jefferson's circular colonnaded structure along the Tidal Basin, rather than the host for a stream of curious tourists, had become an island for one. The story proclaimed that long-predicted effects of global warming were taking hold. Soon the Jefferson monument might become less of a memorial and more of a memory.

Following the continued article, Bobby turned the page and noticed a yellow note stuck to a column on page three. "What do you know?" it asked. Bobby pulled the note off the newsprint and crumpled it. Underneath was a picture of government watchdog reporter George Miller. His weekly column followed.

"Whatcha doin'?"

Bobby jumped then smiled at the round face surrounded by tussled hair, peeking through the patio door. "Waiting for you."

Stacy shuffled outside in her kitty-cat slippers, hugging a well-loved bunny. "Are you finished yet?"

"No."

"Well, let's get to it. We gotta know what's goin' on."

Bobby lifted the papers from his lap to make room for her. "Yes, ma'am." Bobby pulled the metro section from the stack and unfolded it to reveal the nearly half-page picture spread across the front page. Front and center was a magnificent picture of three fat lightning bolts striking three tall downtown Miami buildings simultaneously.

"Oooh . . . ," Stacy said, "that can't be good."

"What's not good?" Carol asked, setting Bobby's coffee on the table. Her satin robe revealed just the right amount of thigh.

"Thank you." Bobby turned the paper so she could see the front page. "The paper says there have been over one million lightning strikes in the state of Florida over the last two weeks. One thousand people have been hit."

"That's not good."

"That's what I said, Mommy." Stacy fanned herself with one of the papers on the table next to Bobby. "It's hot already. Can we go swimming?"

"Right now? You haven't even had breakfast," explained Carol.

"I'm not hungry. I'm hot."

Carol leaned out from under the covered porch and peered up at the clear blue. "I guess breakfast can wait."

"Yes."

"Go in and change, Stacy. We'll meet you back out here." Stacy skipped into the house. Bobby followed Carol back to their bedroom. She tossed him his blue flowered trunks and disappeared into the closet while Bobby sat down on the bed, lost in thought. A moment later, he started getting dressed. When he looked up, Carol had returned and was giving him a puzzled look.

He looked down at his shorts "What, did I put them on backward?"

Carol smiled. "No, just wondering which moon you were visiting. I asked you three times if the paper said why we've had so many lightning strikes."

"God's taking aim."

"I'm serious."

Bobby shrugged. "Most everyone is citing global warming and rising ocean levels." Bobby retied the waistband cord on his trunks.

"How does global warming increase lightning?"

"Something about higher water temperatures and levels causing a change in ocean currents . . . and surface air moving with the water. Apparently, cool water and air are moving down the Atlantic seaboard, colliding with the warm-air flow following the Gulf Stream."

Bobby opened the bedroom door for his wife, and they headed toward the deck. "Of course, George Miller has another idea."

"That DC reporter who did the story on you?"

"Yeah. He sent me his column in the *Post*, but it's just a regurgitation of what's been on the Web for a month now. He's suggesting that NASA is quietly investigating a theory concocted by a company called Tectonics, where a change in the Moon's orbit is affecting the tides and redistributing the earth's water. The redistribution of the earth's water supply will supposedly put new pressure on the tectonic plates and cause increased earthquake activity."

"Is that possible?"

Bobby didn't answer.

"Bobby, is that possible?"

"I don't know, Carol. Cosmic events like they are talking usually happen over eons, not weeks."

They stepped outside. Dressed in her favorite pink and white polka dot bathing suit, six-inch ruffled skirt, hot pink plastic sunglasses, and a white cotton sailor's hat, Stacy sat on a thick aqua blue beach towel, chasing toe jam.

"What took you so long? It's time for swimming!"

"Today's the day, pumpkin," Bobby said, with a gentle smile.

"Tomorrow."

"That's what you said last Saturday, and the day before that and the day before that . . ."

"Tomorrow, Daddy. Tomorrow. I want to do it tomorrow." Stacy bit her lip.

"You're ready for the next step."

"Tomorrow, Daddy. Tomorrow I'll take the next step."

Carol leaned in and whispered in Bobby's ear, "Don't push her."

Bobby offered Stacy his hand. "Ready?" Stacy grabbed hold, and they walked across the cool stamped deck and both stepped down into the water at the same time. Stacy stopped at the first step. Bobby pushed out and squatted in the shallow end submerging his torso up to his armpits.

Turning toward Stacy with his palms turned upward, he urged, "Jump!"

Without hesitation, Stacy jumped. "Good girl. Let's try that again." Stacy took her place on the top step and Bobby inched backward. Again and again she jumped.

"This time I want you to get all the way out of the pool and jump from the side." They moved away from the steps, and once again Stacy flung herself into Bobby's arms.

"Have I ever missed you?"

"Nope. My daddy's the best." She laid a big wet kiss on Bobby's cheek. A gust of wind blew the newspaper off the table and into the pool. Carol paddled after it.

"Do you trust me?" asked Bobby.

"Yep."

"Have I ever missed you?"

"Nope."

"Have I ever dropped you?"

"Nope."

"So you trust me?"

"Yep."

"Then it's time to go to the diving board."

"Nope."

"But you said you trusted me."

"Yep."

"Then today is the day to jump from the board."

In his strong arms, Stacy looked deep into Bobby's eyes. "You promise?"

"I promise. Feel that muscle." Bobby flexed his right bicep into a rock-hard boulder developed in the gym three days a week and shifted his eyes to see if Carol was watching. Her body shook from suppressed laughter.

Stacy poked his muscle and then giggled.

Bobby made his face serious, "That one there scares me sometimes."

Stacy wrinkled her nose and squinted one eye as she looked up into his face. "You'll catch me?"

"I promise."

Stacy scurried over to the diving board, stopping short of climbing up. She stared for a moment at the whiteboard. "You can do it, pumpkin."

She climbed up on her knees and stood to her feet slowly, just as she had done the last three times. From inside the pool, Bobby grabbed the end of the board and pulled his head up. "Stacy, I'm here."

Stacy took two small steps toward her daddy and then froze, "I'm scared, Daddy."

"It's okay to be scared. Being scared helps you to be smart."

"I must be really smart."

"That's okay. Courage is not the absence of fear. Courage is the overcoming of fear."

"I know, I know."

Bobby gently let go of the board and began treading water. "Trust me, Stacy. Don't jump on my head. Jump to my hands." With those final words of instruction, Stacy launched herself into Bobby's hands. After a splash and some frantic kicking, she was latched on to his neck. Carol clapped. Bobby cheered.

Stacy was all smiles. "Let's do it again, Daddy."

Bobby caught her again, ten—then twenty times. Clouds began to fill the sky, but Bobby didn't notice.

"Move back, Daddy, move back."

"Swim, swim, swim!" Completely focused on Stacy, Bobby now let her hit the water on her own and then swim the meter and a half to him.

"It's fun, Mommy. Come and jump with me."

Kaboom!

The first clap of thunder emptied the pool. The second sent Carol and Stacy indoors to make a late breakfast. With hairs standing up on the back of his neck, Bobby wrapped himself in a towel and sat back down to his newspapers. *George Miller dead at forty-seven.* "What is this?" His eyes scanned the article. *Still looking for hit-and-run driver.* Thick black clouds stormed through the stratosphere, stacking up like a giant Teton haltering the sun, shielding its light. Sun released his grip; night returned to Satellite Beach.

Then, with a blinding flash of lightning and a deafening boom, the lights went out. Bobby stepped out from underneath the protection of the portico and looked for lights in the neighborhood. He saw none. He marveled at the darkness. Not even the screen on the back side of his porch would reveal itself. He turned toward the house to see two small lights moving—the girls had candles. A thick drop of rain hit him in the face. He ducked back under the portico and started carefully toward the door.

But another flash of lightning revealed someone standing on the far side of the pool. Bobby turned quickly, squaring his shoulders to where he had seen the man. He yelled out to the blackness, "Can I help you?"

No answer. Eyes wide, blood coursing through his veins, Bobby took shallow breaths and searched. The pool area was completely screened in by a twelve-foot screen wall and topper. The only access was from the house and a locked screen door. Bobby searched for a tear in the screen—maybe his unknown guest cut his own door. No opening was found.

Bobby maneuvered next to the house, protecting any approach from behind, and searched for his guest through the darkness. Bobby hunched over and looked hard. No one. He could see no figure of any sort. Another quick flash of lightning revealed the man still perched on the diving board. Bobby moved slowly over to his pool equipment and grabbed the pole with a skimming net. He removed the net and moved slowly to the edge of the pool. "What do you want?"

The lightning danced in the sky, creating a strobe effect. In the wind, the visitor seemed to move in syncopation now on the far side of the pool. Garbled by the relentless rain, the visitor spoke. "For such a time as this, Bobby Haistings."

Bobby shifted his weight from one foot to the other. "Who are you?" His pulse raced out of control. A crack of thunder pushed Bobby back from the pool. Rain crashed down hard. He searched for his visitor through the wet curtain without success. He was gone.

Bobby sat for a long time under the porch roof, watching, waiting, and listening for any sounds beyond the wind and the rain. The deck light came back on. The clouds began to ease and break up to the northwest. Bobby toweled his hair dry before standing to his feet. He walked the perimeter of his backyard, inspecting every square inch of screen. No holes or rips were found. Everything was as it should be. Stopping in front of the latched screen door—the only possible entry point—Bobby pushed his hair back with the palm of his hand. It was locked, tight and secure. It didn't add up. He turned toward the house and went inside, locking the sliding door behind him, unaware of the strange guest sitting on his deck.

Chapter Twelve

It began as a slight shimmy that ran down the entire fuselage, but it never developed into the violent shaking as it had on previous trips. The column vibrated fast but minutely, almost a hum in Rocket's hands as he reentered the earth's atmosphere in the privately developed X-102. Rocket leveled off in the now steady craft and began his slow descent to the TopAir International test field in New Mexico.

Having temporarily traded in his orange NASA flight suit to moonlight as a TopAir jockey, Captain Steve Graham, a.k.a. Rocket, had flown the same craft into space and back five times in ten days. The X-102 could not only dock with Space Station Delta, it could carry nine passengers and three crew members on each round-trip, and most remarkably, with a runway takeoff and landing, it could be turned around in twenty-four hours to fly the loop again.

Rocket accelerated and banked right over the White Sands Desert. Two balls of light, one white and the other a bronze sparkler, tracked just above and in front of the leading edge on either side. Rocket watched them, mesmerized.

"X-102, we have you in sight. We'll be under your belly in five."

"Roger that. Catch me if you can." The strange lights stayed on his wing until the two chase planes pulled up just under his horizontal stabilizer, then they melted into the setting sun. Rocket checked his instruments.

"X-102, all shields are in place." The T-38 chase planes gave their report.

"Excellent! I'm headed for the hard deck."

Like fresh cream from a clay pot, the X-102 poured out of the sky onto TopAir's lone runway; the chase planes shot past to prepare for their own approach. Rocket bounded out of the cockpit into the presence of Andrew Bonham, TopAir's owner and CEO.

"Did we get that yaw problem fixed?"

Rocket quickly released the strap on his black helmet and lifted it off, revealing his bright red hair, freckles, and Opie ears. "Yaw control was good. That is one sweet ride."

"So"—Bonham's lips spread into a thin smile—"what do you think? Are we ready for Delta?"

A wild grin spread across Rocket's face. "Shoot fire. She's good to go."

"That's what I wanted to hear." Bonham clapped Rocket on the back. "I just got off the phone with Frank Thompson. He's approved the Delta docking protocol and wants the NASA boys to take a look at my ship." Bonham dismissed the chase plane jockeys with a wave. "Let me take you back to your hotel so you can shower and change. We'll talk over dinner. You can write your report later."

"Sounds real good, sir." Rocket took a quick glance back at the X-102's wings, then, carrying his helmet in his right hand, he followed Bonham to the coal black custom bus displaying an eight-foot-high depiction of the X-102 on its side.

"Rocket, I'll be in the back if you need me. Otherwise, just ask Liz." He winked at the young woman holding the door for them. "That's what I pay her for." Bonham headed toward his office in the rear of the bus.

"Hi, Rocket. Good to see you again." Liz had that twangy Arkansas accent. A little thing, barely five feet tall, and not much more than ninety pounds, she revealed every ounce in her spandex exercise outfit. She smiled big with ruby painted lips. Of Middle Eastern descent, her dark olive skin set against her dyed blond hair gave her a unique beauty. Rocket's face tinged red. He nodded a hello. Liz took his helmet and hung it next to the door. "How was your flight?"

Rocket let out a low whistle. "Smooth as whole milk."

"Are you hungry for a snack?"

"You got some Texas toast?"

"I sure do, honey. Sweet milk too." She grabbed him by the hand and walked him the four steps to the table and booth. "You just sit your tired body down right here, and I'll fix you the best sweet toast you have ever tasted."

Liz turned around to the kitchenette and tossed two pieces of Texas toast into a small toaster oven. Rocket sat down and started unlacing his boots.

"Here, darlin', let me get those boots for you." The bus started rolling as she knelt at Rocket's feet.

"That's okay." Rocket brought his knee into his chest, pulling his boot out of her grasp, but Liz took hold and pulled it back down. She looked up at him with an amused smile. "It works better with your foot down here, honey." She untied the right boot.

The toaster oven dinged, sending Liz back to the kitchenette. Rocket started breathing again and quickly untied the left boot and then removed both. Liz pulled the toast from the oven, placed it on a saucer, and then poured the thick, sweet milk on the bread.

"Can I get you something to drink?"

"Water's just fine, thanks."

Liz set the snack in front of Rocket and slid in next to him. Rocket nudged over to his left. She filled the space.

"Rocket, how come you've never asked me out?"

He continued chewing. "This is real good."

"You didn't answer my question." She wrapped both hands around his right bicep. Rocket dropped his toast into his lap—milk side down.

Liz reached in to get the toast. "Here, let me get that for you." Rocket jerked his leg up, smacking the table and spilling his water but successfully shielding his toast.

"I got it." He scooted to his left again.

Liz grabbed a damp cloth from the sink and followed him around the table. "Let me clean this up."

"It's okay . . . really." His smile squared off. "I'm just going to change anyhow."

"Rocket, are you gay?"

"No, ma'am."

Her bright white teeth shone between her perfectly shaped lips. "Then I do believe you're shy!" She laid hold of his right arm again. "Well, I'm free tonight after dinner, and around here, you don't have to ask twice."

"We don't really know each other that well."

"How are we supposed to get to know each other if we don't hang out?" She snuggled up to his arm, pressing her body into his.

"We could talk."

"What would you like to talk about?"

The bus driver hit the brakes hard after being cut off, shoving Rocket into Liz. Rocket's ears burned even more crimson. "Pardon me, Elizabeth. I didn't mean to lean into you."

Her eyes twinkled. "You can lean into me anytime."

Rocket regained his balance. "Well, um . . . Elizabeth, do you believe humans are alone in the universe?"

"What?" Her nose wrinkled.

"What about God?"

"God?" She laughed. "Are you pulling *my* leg now?"

"No. Do you think he's real?"

Liz let go of Rocket's arm. "I'm not sure about the whole god thing, but I'm very spiritual."

Rocket leaned toward Liz. "Once you've been out there"—Rocket peered out the window and then turned back toward Elizabeth—"it makes you think maybe there is a God."

She slid to the end of the booth. "I'm not interested in religion."

Rocket filled the space again. "I'm not talking about religion."

Liz stood up with a disappointed smirk and said, "Pity." She waltzed to the back of the bus and joined Bonham.

Rocket finished eating his sweet toast just as the bus pulled up to his hotel. Sock footed, Rocket debarked.

"Rocket!" It was Bonham from the back window. "I'll pick you up again in two hours."

"Yes, sir."

Rocket hurried to his room and took a long cold shower. With wide shoulders, a well-developed chest, and a solid six-pack, Rocket wrapped a towel around his thirty-inch waist and answered the room phone on the seventh ring.

"How was the test flight?" Colonel Thompson asked.

"Sweet. The X-102 is incredible, Colonel. For the very wealthy, it will be the ride of a lifetime."

"Good to hear. How fast is your turnaround?"

"We can turn it around in twenty-four hours. Less for a lower-atmosphere flight."

"Good. I'm cutting your leave short. Need you back tomorrow."

"Tomorrow? I don't know if I can get a flight back tomorrow."

"You won't need a flight. You will be flying the X-102."

"Does Bonham know it?"

"Not yet, but he will. We want to get a good look at the X-102 to insure Delta interface. We're looking at using it on Survey IV."

"I'm not sure Bonham will be ready to let it go yet."

"You leave that to me. Plan on another twenty-four-hour turnaround, and I'll see you tomorrow night."

Rocket hung up wondering how Colonel Thompson would convince Bonham to turn over his billion-dollar investment to the US government.

CHAPTER THIRTEEN

The *Santa Maria* began its lunar orbit right on schedule. Sailing over the crater Ptomeaeous, Colonel Kim Anderson looked left for Plato, Aristoteles, or Hercules, three of the larger craters to the designated north. But having begun their descent, all three were hidden behind the Alps. So the colonel set her gaze for Mare Tranquilitatis, whose perimeter rim had grown higher and thicker with new basaltic outcroppings. Anderson sensed a difference she didn't like. She wiped her face with a handkerchief. "Major, I need the coordinates now!"

"Almost complete, ma'am." Lathem looked back and forth from the view screen to a chart indicating navigational landmarks. The next trip would prove simpler once they established the coordinates for the new lunar positioning unit.

"Major?"

"I got it. I got it. Adjust seven degrees port on our vertical axis. Mare Crisium is ten kilometers ahead."

"Why not the Sea of Tranquility for this project?" Davenport inquired as the Sea passed beneath them.

Rogers broke in, "Where would the fun be in that? We love a challenge." He slapped Martinez on the back. "Heroes don't exist in tranquility, do they, Marty?"

With hands shaking, Martinez continued to suit up. "I guess not."

The *Santa Maria* crossed the cold, lifeless moonscape. Nearing the landing zone, Lathem extended the eight-legged landing gear. Anderson shut down the thrusters, and the *Santa Maria* descended like a black widow trailing her silk behind her to the desolate, dusty regolith: luminescent from Earth but, in reality, a cold hunk of crust that regularly sucked light and warmth from the Sun. The metallic spider legs settled into a four-inch layer of dust upon impact.

"Houston, the *Santa Maria* has landed." Anderson could hear the cheers of exuberance from Mission Control. Even after a dozen trips to the Moon, touchdown was still a victory. For a brief moment, she allowed herself to feel like a hero, but only for a moment.

"Okay, gentlemen," the colonel ordered, "let's get it done."

Major Lathem shut down the main engines and cleared the exhaust pressure then released his harness and stood up. "Welcome to Mare Crisium, boys. This could one day be your home. Personally, I staked out a little ranch for myself the last time I was here."

The colonel smirked as she took her position in front of the large one-by-two-meter walleyed view window—a perch from which she could see three quarters of the ladder below and out beyond the horizon to planet earth.

After passing through the transfer chamber, Rogers and Martinez began descending the ladder to the lunar surface. "Wow! This is so awesome!" Rogers stood still at the foot of the ladder in the lunar dust, staring at the marbled earth resting low on the horizon.

"I've got to get a picture of this."

Davenport drifted over next to the colonel and reveled in the sight through the bubbled glass.

"Mr. Rogers, this is not a sightseeing tour nor a working vacation. Let's move along."

"But, Colonel, I need my camera. I'll bet you even money that I could sell a shot like this to *National Geo*. We are talking a cover shot. It would be serious boat money."

"There will be time for pictures later, Mr. Rogers. I need you and Mr. Martinez to get that lunar trencher out and fired up. No one goes home until we have forty meters of footer dug and poured around the first-stage perimeter and the foundation laid. Just follow the lines. You can thank Major Lathem and the crew of Survey I for the stencil work." The schedule allowed for two days of digging and one for pouring a foundation created by mixing bisphenal A and epichlorohydrin, which in turn creates a polar bond with the lunar dust, forming a solid base on which flooring would be attached.

The colonel watched Martinez hit the surface with both feet as Rogers moved away from the ladder. She remembered her first touch of lunar dirt: the feeling of a soft crunch reminiscent of wet snow, the wobbly knees of anticipation, and the exhilaration of adventure—she would never forget that moment. But today it was just work.

With one hand still holding the handrail, Martinez caught a glimpse of the earth. "Magnifico! Rog, I think I'll take that picture and send it to *National Geo* myself."

"Shut up, Marty."

"Gentlemen, you want to stow that conversation and get to work?" The colonel had moved away from the window momentarily, but she could still hear them over the cabin speakers. Everyone heard the reluctant "Yes, ma'am."

Turning from her command desk, the mission commander spied her pilot suiting up. "Major Lathem, what is first on your agenda?"

"I know what I'm doing, Colonel."

"By the book, Major."

"Colonel, I wrote the book."

"Humor me."

With a slight eye roll, Lathem droned his answer. "My first order of business is to pull core samples from sector C. After all the cores are pulled, Davenport and I will start laying out the grid for phase two of construction. We'll need to pull more core samples and set up the geophones just outside sector E. Do you want me to go on?"

"I want you to set up for the thousand-meter test as well."

"That's on my list, Colonel."

"Today, Major."

"After the break."

The colonel peered at the major. "That will be all, Major. Let's be about it."

Lathem grabbed his helmet from its snap hook and turned toward Davenport, "Eh, you comin'?"

"I'm comin'. I'm just having a little trouble with my shoulder clamp." His hands shook, and his breathing stuttered. The colonel pulled herself over to Davenport and secured his shoulder clamps for him. Eyeball to eyeball, Anderson stared into a very white face.

"Captain, you want to slow your breathing down a bit." He was almost panting. "Take a deep breath for me, Captain."

Davenport took two shallow breaths and blew them out hard. Colonel Anderson grabbed Davenport by the collar ring roughly. "I said a deep breath. Take it in through your nose and hold it for a two count."

Davenport closed his eyes and took in the oxygen. He held it for the two counts and exhaled slowly. "Again, Captain."

The next inhale was slower and more deliberate. "One more time." Color was returning.

"Good job, Captain." The colonel smiled big. "Now listen to me. You use up more O^2 when you're nervous. So keep an eye on your oxygen." The colonel tapped on his regulator. "It says you have eight hours. I doubt you'll get more than six. So keep an eye on it." Davenport's eyes still looked a bit glazed. "Do you understand what I'm telling you, Captain?"

Shaking his head up and down, he answered, "Yes, ma'am. Keep an eye on my O^2."

"Very well, Captain." Colonel Anderson handed Davenport his helmet and turned to Lathem, who stood at the hatch ready to go. Anderson lifted her right hand and touched the corner of her right eye with her index finger and then pointed to Captain Davenport. Major Lathem gave her an ungainly thumbs-up.

The colonel did a quick check of Davenport's lunar suit as the two men glided into the pressure chamber. "E-A, gentlemen. Environmental awareness: stay focused and pay attention to your surroundings." Anxiety still seized her soul.

Chapter Fourteen

The colonel sat transfixed by the sight of her crew. Like bulky players in some underwater ballet, they waltzed on the lunar floor. The two-step around the coring drill reminded her of her granddaughter's backyard play that she had attended exactly one year ago to the day, her fifty-second birthday. This present birthday brought no celebration. The thrill of adventure had left with the birth of her second grandchild. More mystery could be found in the tiny hand of a two-year-old than in the great expanse of space.

As she looked off to the horizon, the earth had settled just above a range of jagged peaks framed on each side by a tall sharp tooth. It looked like the bottom teeth of some savage beast waiting to devour her home planet. She rubbed her face hard and tried to dislodge the image by redirecting her attention to her crew.

Her focus came to rest on Major Lathem, who appeared to be working outside the grid area. Colonel Anderson referred to the grid documents in front of her.

Davenport stood upright. "Why are you setting up to pull cores from outside the grid area?"

My thoughts exactly, whispered the colonel to herself. "Good question, Captain. We will be pulling cores from a variety of places. But I'd like to pull these cores just outside sector C to make sure we are not on the edge of trouble." The five rectangular sectors were laid out candy cane shaped, with sectors D and E coming back and extending past A.

"But you're outside the entire grid."

"I didn't say we were going to build here. I just want to make sure we don't drift."

"I'm confused, Major."

"Trust me."

"No disrespect intended, sir, but shouldn't we pull the primary cores first?" The major sighed hard and glared at Davenport for a moment then looked back over his shoulder toward the colonel and the *Santa Maria*. Turning his head back toward Davenport, he cleared his throat.

The colonel started to speak but held back.

"Good point, Captain. Help me move the drill press over into the grid."

"Roger."

"Yeah, what d'you need?"

"No, I wasn't calling for you, Rogers. I was saying 'Roger,' as in 'okay.'"

"Well, then say 'okay.' I get confused easily."

"Yes, he does."

"Shut up, Marty."

The team settled in and worked for the next ninety minutes, being entertained by the banter of Martinez and Rogers. Putting up with the verbal jousting, Colonel Anderson marveled at their caustic wit. "Let's keep it friendly, gentlemen." Did they secretly like each other, or was she about to experience a major rift?

As Major Lathem pulled his third core sample from inside the grid, the colonel asked, "Davenport, what's your oxygen supply look like?"

"I'm good, Colonel."

"I want you to head in, Captain."

"I'll secure the equipment and catch up," Major Lathem instructed.

"Are you sure, Major?"

"Go on. I'll be fine."

"Want help with the core samples?"

"No. I've got to tag them first. You go ahead back. We're all headed in. Martinez! It's breaktime."

Martinez and Rogers had already shut down the lunar trencher. "We pushed through seventeen meters of trench."

"Seventeen whole meters?" asked Lathem.

"Shut up, Lathem." The words came out before Rogers knew what he was saying. An awkward pause put everyone on edge. Lathem quickly repositioned the drill to pull two quick cores.

Colonel Anderson broke the silence. "I hope you gentlemen will be picking up the pace. I don't want to be up here till Christmas."

"Sorry, Colonel. It is hard to find good help," Martinez complained.

"You've got that right," Rogers chimed.

"Whose idea was it to put these two guys together on the same team?" barked the colonel from inside the lunar craft.

"Yours, Colonel, but we're okay. We just feel obligated to harass each other ever since we became related."

"How are you two related?"

"Rog joined my family when he married my sister earlier this summer."

Martinez flashed his pearly whites at Rogers, and they gave each other a high five.

"Whoa! Did you feel that?" Martinez stopped dead in his tracks with his feet spread just wider than his shoulders and his knees bent. He lowered his head and turned it to the side as if he were listening for something.

"I didn't feel anything, Marty."

"I felt something like a humming in my feet."

Rogers looked at Martinez quizzically, as he had done a hundred times before. "Humming? Your feet are humming? Anyone else humming?" There was no reply. "I don't think your feet were humming."

"I'm telling you, my feet were humming."

"Maybe your oxygen is off, and your feet are falling asleep."

"Keep moving, gentlemen. I'll feel better when you are all back on board."

"My feet aren't falling asleep. That's more of a tingly feeling. This was a hum."

"Keep moving, Marty," pushed Rogers.

Davenport was in the transfer chamber by the time Rogers and Martinez were ascending the ladder. "All call, gentlemen."

"Davenport, reporting in. I'll be by your side in thirty seconds."

"Rogers here. I'm climbing the ladder."

"Martinez. I'm right behind Rogers."

A bloated pause sent chills down Anderson's back. "Major Lathem, you want to report in?" The colonel scanned the horizon.

There was no reply. Martinez stopped his climb and looked back around. "Hey, Sammy! Where are you?" There was still no reply. Martinez had taken one step down when the major appeared from around the far end of the lunar craft. "Where have you been, Major?"

"I'm coming. I had to stow and tag the core samples."

"How long does it take to stow the cores?" the colonel asked.

"I'm right behind Martinez, Colonel."

"Let's speak up when I ask."

"Yes, ma'am."

The crew settled in for a quick lunch and a six-hour sleep period. The colonel watched as the men dozed off. Martinez curled up in his berth, holding a picture of his bride. He was still smiling. Davenport looked like a nervous white cat. Rogers and Lathem both lay on their backs. The colonel offered a half smile and then drifted off to sleep, sitting up at her desk. The slight vibrations of a tremor rocked them to sleep. The next tremor would wake them up.

Chapter Fifteen

"Jack, you want me to do what?"

"Kim, we need information, and you are sitting on an encyclopedia of intel."

"No, I'm staring into the mouth of hell." The colonel opened up communication so that her team could hear the conversation. "Fifty meters from the *Santa Maria,* the grand canyon of rifts just opened up." Colonel Kim Anderson eased over in front of the view window and stared out at the rift that ran away from the lunar craft, a rift left behind by a moonquake measuring 9.7 on the Richter's scale. At its widest point, she estimated the rift opened the lunar surface over ten meters. One skinnier branch of the rift ran away from the *Santa Maria* at a forty-five-degree angle. "Jack, I've spent my life avoiding stupidity." Her head swirled as she turned toward her team in fear. "This can't be smart."

Her crew sat at their stations staring blankly. Only Major Lathem offered advice. "Let's go home, Colonel. I've got deep core samples that will tell us all we need to know." His dark and foreboding eyes caught the colonel's attention and then tied a knot in the back of her neck. Colonel Anderson shrugged in anxious pain.

"I say we start our preflight for the return, Jack."

"Listen, Kim, the worst is over. We have sensors all over the lunar surface telling us that calm has returned." The transmission was weak and distorted by static.

"It's the calm before the storm."

"I think the rift was the storm." Jack wanted to believe the worst was over.

"You don't know that. The next aftershock could strand us here."

"It's just one test. You're already there . . ." Jack paused. Anderson knew what was coming. "Colonel, we'll never have a better opportunity. We need you and your team to run the test and gather the information. For humanity, Kim . . . for your grandkids."

Martinez got to his feet, glanced out at the rift, and then back to Rogers. "We're explorers, guys. Let's explore."

The colonel watched the face-off. Rogers's jaw was clenched, the muscles in his face taut. He shook his head. Martinez flashed a big smile and nodded. "Come on, Rog. You're not scared, are you?" Rogers didn't move. "Let's go explore."

The tension in Rogers's face slowly melted into a smile of resignation. The colonel closed her eyes, "*Crap!*"

"Major, we can do this." Martinez encouraged. "Let's run their tests and then light the fires."

"Colonel, you still there?"

"Hold on, Jack." Anderson peered back at Lathem. "What do you say, Major?"

"To be frank, I still think the smart thing to do is to head for home. But no one has ever accused me of always doing the smart thing. I grew up fascinated by the thirty-meter tides of the Bay of Funday. Two weeks ago my cousin told me the ebb and flow had been reduced to less than a meter. The news reports are blaming lunar irregularities. Maybe it is all connected."

"I'm in." Davenport chimed before being asked. "Let's do it."

The colonel turned back toward the window. "I can't believe this is happening." She studied the ominous shadows cast by the jagged peaks framing the mare on two sides as they crawled to the edge of the rift—leering, snapping, and threatening. "This can't be smart." She keyed her mike, "Houston, this is Lunar Survey III aboard the *Santa Maria*. Do you copy?"

"I'm still h—"

"Come again, Houston." White noise filled the cabin. The colonel's eyes darted from one crew member to the next. No one exhaled as the colonel keyed the mike again. "Houston, do you copy?"

"I'm here."

"We are good to go with test." As the less-than-confident words came out, Kim's crew began to suit up in double time. "I repeat, we are good to go with test."

CHAPTER SIXTEEN

Jack Sooner, who had been fidgeting in the key communicator's seat behind a bank of monitors, jumped to his feet and jerked around, coming face-to-face with Colonel Thompson at Mission Control. "You happy now, Colonel?"

"This was your idea, Jack."

"You put me in this spot." Jack peered into the eyes of hellish arrogance.

Thompson wiped his nose. "It's the prudent thing to do, Jack."

"But is it the right thing to do? Prudent and right don't always lock arms."

"It's the globally responsible thing to do."

"Is it? Or are you playing some other game?"

"It is."

"So help me, Colonel." Why did he listen to this narcissist? Why did he allow the rocket off of launch pad 39-A? Rage boiled in Jack's gut. "I told you to bring them home. If we crash and burn, *we* will crash and burn."

"I know, Jack. It's all on file. You've made that perfectly clear. But leadership demands risk. Our planet needs strong courageous leadership, and we are going to give it to them." There was something wrong with being lectured on leadership by Thompson. "Besides, your own probes tell us the worst is over."

Not normally given to violence, Sooner marveled at his desire to coldcock the colonel. Maybe the trigger was Thompson's casual attitude in the crisis or his superior demeanor. Regardless, Sooner was glad his gun was not loaded. He would use his words. "To compare earthquakes on this planet with moonquakes on the lunar surface, based on available science, is foolish. We can't predict what might be coming."

"Jack, I think the test will show that the rift is an aberration in this sector. It's not the norm. This area will prove safe."

"You don't know that and I don't care, Colonel. It's over."

"The general is not going to flush a trillion-dollar project down the toilet without good cause."

"Good cause! What would he consider good cause?"

"If the geophone test does not reveal some sort of subterranean danger, he wants the space station back on schedule."

"I don't care. Regardless of what the test reveals, I want my team home."

"Run your test, Jack. Then bring them home. But understand: Survey IV is still on schedule."

Jack leered and wondered at the depth of ignorance. Thompson and Buchholz were both fools. Jack's mind started to climb the ladder of command. How could he trump an eagle and two stars?

CHAPTER SEVENTEEN

Commander Kim Anderson worked inside the lunar craft, trying to ensure interface between the primary computer and the GDCS (Geophone Data Collection System). The system included a geometric seismograph operating at 32 kHz with a trigger accuracy of one microsecond. For the last hour, the two systems had not been talking. The rest of her team was outside setting up geophones down the rift line. Two solar days and a lifetime of sweat had already been spent on the surface. With lips barely moving, the colonel said to no one, "We're setting off geophone explosives right next to the rift line on an unstable surface. Why?" She was having second thoughts. Colonel Anderson leaned over and peered out the walleyed viewing window.

"Major Lathem, what's it looking like out there?"

Major Sammy Lathem investigated the rift on all fours. With head bowed, he studied the rift then shook his head and said, "I don't know. It's probably two to four meters wide and there's no telling how deep."

Martinez froze next to the forward landing gear, catching the colonel's attention. "Did you feel that, Rog?"

"I did feel that, Marty. In fact, my feet are still humming."

"Let's go, Mr. Martinez. Let's get those charges and phones hooked up. We'll talk about humming feet later." Each geophone had a corresponding explosive charge for a maximum read.

Martinez, who was the lead lunar scientist, bounced across the lunar surface to Rogers, NASA's go-to geologist. "This was your idea, Marty."

"Let's move it, gentlemen. I don't want to be on this rock one second longer than I have to be."

Rogers connected the string of geophones that ran the two hundred meters down the rift line by pulling back the door on the gray, meter-high geophone junction box and plugging in the large cable.

"All fifty phones are in place," Martinez reported. "All we need to do now is hook the line into the external computer port."

The two men seemed to be swaying to some unheard music as they dragged the cumbersome ten-centimeter cable over to the lunar craft.

They disappeared from the colonel's sight. Fixing her gaze on Major Lathem, she waited for the voice of Mr. Martinez. This particular test was not on the itinerary. It had been discussed but not planned nor rehearsed. Kim was outside her zone of comfort. Martinez had the lead.

"I'm sliding the cable into place, colonel, but wait for the light," Martinez explained.

"I'm waiting."

"We are tightening the security locks." Two large four-inch screws held the cable in place.

The colonel listened to them breathe as she waited longer than she wanted to. "I still have no icon."

Martinez explained, "We'll get an orange indicator light down here next to the junction box first, and then the icon should appear on your computer screen."

"I'm watching."

"We have the light. Now, give it ten seconds, Colonel."

Anderson rubbed her neck for a ten count.

"I'm still waiting, Mr. Martinez."

"Don't jump the gun, Colonel. We'll never get the GDCS online."

The colonel closed her eyes and counted out ten taps on her forehead with her left middle finger. Then her eyes opened.

"There, I've got it. I have the icon."

"All systems are *go*." Martinez declared. "Now if the charges detonate correctly, the explosions will send vibrations through the Moon's upper crust. The phones should pick up the vibrations and convert the energy into a 3-D image which the computer will interpret, and then, *maybe*, we'll be able to figure out what woke up this sleeping rock."

"Rogers! Walk the line and arm the charges," directed Martinez. Rogers hopped, skipped, and jumped down the rift line, stopping at the distant charge.

"Use extreme caution," begged Colonel Anderson. "Monomethylhydrazine and nitrogen tetroxide are extremely volatile hypergolic chemicals."

Rogers opened the two slide valves and lifted the toggle switch arming the first charge. With precise timing, the two chemicals would be brought together into one explosive atmosphere, creating echo vibrations in the lunar crust. "Slow and easy, Mr. Rogers. Slow and easy."

"We're good, Colonel. I have done this before." He began working his way down the line, arming each of the geophone explosives.

"Mr. Martinez, I still don't have the GDCS up and running. I have the icon, but the system never opened up."

"Okay. Highlight the icon."

"Done."

"Right click on the icon and scroll down to Restart."

"Okay, got it. Uh-oh."

"What 'uh-oh'? There can be no uh-ohs."

"The screen went black."

"Wait for it, Colonel." Anderson grit her teeth hard. Her ability to wait was dissipating. Her focus shifted from the clock to the walleyed window and back to the screen. Nothing.

She began to hum as her eyes came to rest on the primary rocket control pad. The colonel quickly reviewed the lift off sequence, her fingers playing a piano that didn't exist. Then Anderson's heart clogged her throat.

"I've got a blue screen and the icons are coming back." Colonel Anderson heard a collective sigh in her earpiece. "I've got a box that says 'Loading GDCS.'"

"It's coming. Just give it time."

Anderson redirected her attention to Lathem who appeared motionless at the rifts edge. "Major Lathem, what's your status?"

"I need more light. Davenport! Grab the lunar candle on the aft landing pod." The two-million-candle-watt landing light had a quick release and a handle, allowing it to be used as a hand device.

Captain Davenport heard the request and headed toward the craft's landing pod. Martinez, appeared from under the *Santa Maria* with the flat lunar candle in hand and said, "I'll meet you halfway." Some fifteen meters from the rift, Martinez gave Davenport the spot light and quickly headed back to the lunar craft.

"Finally." The colonel clapped her hands together. "The GDCS is up and running. Mr. Rogers, how do we stand?"

"We are armed and dangerous." Rogers leaped up, playfully spinning out away from the charges. "And I am clear."

"Thanks, gentlemen. We are good to go."

The colonel turned her head and cracked her neck. "Mission Control, this is Survey III on the *Santa Maria*. Do you copy?"

"This is Houston. We read you loud and clear. What do you have for us?"

"Explosives set. Geophones are in place. GDCS is online.

"Roger, Commander. Wait for Chief Sooner."

"If one more person tells me to wait . . ."

"Kim, if everything goes south we won't be able to get to you," Jack choked up.

You're concerned now? Where was this concern three hours ago? Having second thoughts, are we? Colonel Kim Anderson adjusted the volume and spoke with calm clarity. "We're here, and we're set up, Jack. It's not like this test has never been run before."

"But never on top of a rift line in a clearly unstable area."

"We need the information."

"I'm sorry, Kim." Jack's voice trembled through the 186,000 miles of space. "I'm sorry I put you in this spot."

"It's okay, Jack. It's for my grandkids, remember. Besides, if anything goes wrong, we can lift off in less than five minutes—we're preset."

"Kim . . . I . . ."

"It'll be fine . . . give us the okay, Jack."

"Okay . . . okay." Jack took a deep breath. "God bless you and your team. You are good for test."

Chapter Eighteen

Slowly setting the digital timer for sixty seconds, Colonel Anderson paused before starting the countdown. Could the explosions trigger a bigger or more violent quake? Would running the tests seal their fate? She promised herself, again, that she would put in for retirement as soon as she got back, if she got back. Kim looked out the window for one last head count. She pulled and twisted on her hair and then hit the button in an anxious swat.

"Roger, Houston, we are at one minute and counting." Anderson moved over in front of the window. "Gentlemen, be alert. We are fifty-five seconds and counting."

Major Lathem lunar bounced over to Davenport and grabbed the light out of his hands and quickly bounced back to the rift with Davenport on his heels. The colonel watched the two men kneel on the opposite sides of the two-meter-wide crack.

"Be careful, Major."

"Just getting a front seat to the action, Colonel. We only get one shot at this."

Major Lathem eased down on his belly into the rift about a meter to obtain a better angle for viewing its dark recesses. Captain Davenport stood motionless, gazing at the celestial ball he called home. "Captain, the action is down here."

"What are we looking for?"

Major Lathem wrenched his head up at Davenport. "I don't really know. Just look. Look for anything. Just look."

Captain Davenport slowly bent one knee and allowed it to fall to the lunar surface. He bowed his head and fixed his gaze deep into the pit.

"Careful, Captain," the colonel admonished.

Rogers took his position next to the first geophone and Martinez stood in the long shadow of the *Santa Maria*, keeping an eye on the cable and the junction box. The team readied in position.

Having accounted for each of her men, Anderson pleaded with heaven. Shivers ran down her spine, and her ears buzzed and then popped. A profound breath slowed her heart; she slumped in the chair. "Five seconds, gentlemen." Kim's eyes riveted to the timer as the last five seconds ticked down in cold silence. Unable to hear the blasts through the vacuum of the lunar atmosphere, Kim grabbed the arm of her chair. She could see the bright flashes from the geophone charges. The controlled explosions sent the vibrations through the Moon's outer crust just as they were planned. Sweat seeped from her forehead. She wiped the perspiration with her sleeve quickly. Her eyes never left her team.

"Gentlemen, I'm getting a sick feeling."

Still unable to detect action at the rift, Major Lathem asked, "Colonel, are you getting any kind of reading?"

"Nothing yet."

"My feet are humming again," Martinez complained.

"We've all got that hum, Marty." Rogers took two steps back from the rift.

Lathem cocked his head. "I feel a slight vibration in my gut. No, wait. It stopped."

"I'm getting a lot of echo," Colonel Anderson explained as she read the computer data. "You're not going to believe this, but according to this readout, we're sitting on one gigantic cavity."

Martinez questioned, "Are you sure you're reading it right?" He headed for the port side of the *Santa Maria*. "Open the hatch. I'm coming in."

"Stay put, Mr. Martinez. I'm reading it right." Suddenly the craft began to shake violently, throwing the colonel back in her seat.

The Moon went into full quake. Lathem, still holding the lamp, slid headlong into the widening crack. Scrambling for a handhold, he began to frantically twist and turn. The rocks and ledges crumbled in his heavily gloved hands. Desperate, the major tossed the lamp and cried out for help. Captain Davenport could do nothing, having lost his equilibrium. He too slipped into the crack but managed to keep erect. He grabbed onto the rift rim, keeping his head and chest up out of the chasm. The two men stared at one another as death loomed over them like a summer squall. With nothing to hold on to, Major Lathem pulsed deeper and deeper into the rift. Trying not to be thrown into the control panel, the colonel screamed and then helplessly watched Lathem disappear into the darkened bowels of the lunar surface.

Panicking, Captain Davenport quickly began to inch his way out of the rift. "Move, Captain, move!" The walleyed window gave the colonel a front-row seat—terrifying and helpless. The rift seemed alive and hungry.

As the lunar surface heaved and twisted, the colonel watched the expanding rift shift into a collapsing rift. The split in the lunar surface began to close on Captain Davenport. His fiber steel suit would protect him against atmospheric exposure, but he would still feel the agonizing physical pressure. The giant vise crushed his body. Colonel Anderson heard his screams in her headsets. She opened her mouth but nothing came out. Terror muddled her mind.

The colonel's eyes widened as the growing rift snaked its way ferociously toward the *Santa Maria*. As the lunar surface split under the colonel, two of the craft's landing gear dropped down into the rift, causing the ship to slide and twist, jerking the geophone line loose and knocking Martinez onto his back and out of sight of the colonel. Horror gripped Kim's heart tighter when she saw a piece of the landing strut fly off.

Rogers, who stood some twenty meters down the rift line when the quake began, was knocked off his feet. His helmet hit a large rock on the way down, twisting his head to the right radically. "Mr. Rogers, are you okay? Mr. Rogers!" Shaking off the blow, Rogers began to crawl away from the rift parallel to the lunar craft.

"I'm okay, Colonel."

Then the rift began to splinter perpendicular to the main crevasse. One of the offshoots split the surface right between Rogers's legs. "Get out of there, Mr. Rogers!"

The gulf widened too quickly for him to respond, and he bounced down into the rift. Groping for a handle, he latched on to a small ledge, stopping his descent. Looking up, he spied the geophone cable sliding overhead. As the surface split at the far end of the rift, the lead geophone was pulled down into the abyss, dragging the rest of the phones behind. Rogers stretched out his long arm and caught the moving cable with his hand. The rift pulled the line so violently that his body erupted out of the crevice. Having lost his presence of mind, he forgot to let go once out and was dragged some thirty meters before he stopped abruptly with the help of a large boulder. The impact was brutal. Dazed, Rogers clung to the irresistible force.

"Mr. Rogers!"

"I'm alive."

"Hold on!"

The lunar surface continued to quake.

Colonel Anderson continued to knock around inside the craft. Her headset had been pulled off; and the earpiece, broken—where it went she had no idea. With her third attempt, she switched on the radio and grabbed another headset. Shaking her head in disbelief, Kim squeezed the mike.

"Houston! We are experiencing a massive moonquake. We have damage of unknown severity." Her hands trembled as she engaged the distress signal, a signal that would continue to broadcast until it was silenced or its two-year battery died. Kim took a deep breath, but her nightmare had only begun.

CHAPTER NINETEEN

Pandemonium reigned in Houston at Mission Control. The two-by-two-meter number one flat screen showed black snow. The twelve different monitors that surrounded the number one screen all presented fuzzy nonsense. The room heard only static. "What's happening?" Jack asked. Personnel scurried about everywhere—everywhere except in a small chamber just off the control room. The bloodred letters on the black door read:

"Military Personnel Only
Top Secret Clearance Required"

Two armed military guards, highly polished and razor sharp, stood on either side. Dr. Jack Sooner stood motionless in the center of the room. Finally, confusion gave way to determination and frustration gave way to training. "What's the situation?"

"We've got nothing, sir."

"Try again. Bounce a signal off of Delta." His stare jumped from one fuzzy screen to another. "Why have we lost communications? Did we lose an antenna?"

Five minutes later, they were still trying. "This is Houston Control, come in Lunar Survey III. I repeat. Come in Lunar Survey III." Meekerson, the young communications specialist, turned around and looked at Dr. Sooner in hopelessness. Delta did not help. Jack watched the young man's head sink to his chest as his arms went flaccid. Then the young man sat up quickly with a start. Jack turned just in time to see Colonel Thompson in his Versace suit exit the black door with red letters.

"Dr. Sooner, we just received word through the Omega Satellite System." Run jointly by the CIA and the NSA, the Omega system was an advanced observation instrument that could look down at a backyard barbeque or out into the corners of space. "The *Santa Maria* is down. Anderson has engaged the automatic distress signal." Thomas's swagger aroused Jack's suspicion.

Sooner shot an incredulous glare toward Thompson. "They never should have gone."

"General Buchholz wants you to prep just in case we need to bring them home. The code Anderson sent suggests that the ship is functional and life sustainable. But it may not be able to return in its own power. We need to move fast and be ready."

Mounting blood pressure on his frontal lobe pushed Jack to the edge. "Now, how actually are we supposed to do that? 'Beam me up, Scotty!'" Jack Sooner pushed his lower jaw out and rotated it. "We have no transportation." Their eyes locked. Chief Sooner studied the smug gambler-blank face and then shoved Thompson hard against the glass wall of his office. "We have no ship. We have no transport. We have no way of reaching the team. Look at this." Sooner grabbed Thompson's arm and jerked him over to a deck of six monitors. "What do you see?"

The first monitor showed launch pad 39-A, the second 39-B—citadel's willing but empty on the Florida coast. "You see an orbiter? No. There is no transporter." He tapped hard on the third and fourth monitors. "That's the Yeagar. That is the only chance we have." The Yeager, designed for the Aries VIII rockets, hung by straps in a maintenance hangar. Ten thousand of the thirty-five thousand heat tiles were not attached. "We are months away from any kind of launch. Oh, wait. Here are two possibilities."

Monitors five and six showed the old shuttle docks containing the Enterprise and Endeavor. "Haven't flown in years, but if we hurry we could get them launch ready in seven or eight months. I guess we could bring their bones back. So tell me again, how the hell are we supposed bring them home? Is he stupid? What's the old man smoking in those cigars?" Jack slipped off the edge.

Thompson never broke a sweat as Jack paced, threw pens and crumpled papers, and barked at anyone who got in his way. "Now we've got to call the families . . . What are we going to tell them? Your husbands are dead . . . No, no we can't tell them 'their husbands' . . . Their daddies . . . their grandma was killed in a terrible accident . . . They aren't dead . . . We have got to tell them that they are going to die. And there is nothing we can do but sit back and wait for them to die—to slowly run out of oxygen and suffocate. Maybe we could set up a video link so the wife and the kids can watch."

"You done, Chief?"

After accusing Buchholz and Thompson of criminal ignorance and reminding Thompson that he had in fact filed a formal "Protest of Warning" shortly after the *Hope*'s launch, he rested with head down and shoulders slumped. The Techs had turned off the hopeless white noise. No one spoke. No one moved. Jack felt the eyes of the room on him. He sighed hard, leaned against Meekerson's desk and let gravity pull his eyelids down slowly. "We have no way of bringing my team home. Oh, God what have I done?"

Noticing Thompson leaning against the glass wall just down from his door, the chief trudged toward his office. Ignoring the colonel, Sooner held at the door and addressed the room. "No one opens their mouth . . . please. We must contact the families first. I don't want the families to hear that their husbands are in a NASA-built death chamber from the six o'clock news. So until you hear from me, not a word."

Thompson, looking like a GQ model, smiled at Sooner with understanding. Sooner wrote it off as insanity. He opened the heavy glass door that led into his office and took a step. "Chief."

Sooner hesitated, tipping back out of his office. What more could go wrong? "There is another option."

Chief Sooner huffed. "What? What are you talking about?"

Thompson glided back over to the bank of six monitors. Under each monitor were four numbered buttons. He pressed the number two button under monitors five and six. Two opposing views of runway 33 at Cape Canaveral Air Force Base came into focus. The number five monitor showed nothing but an empty runway.

"What? I don't want to play games."

"Look at number six." Thompson popped a piece of candy into his mouth as Sooner moved quickly toward the monitor. With eyes narrowed under his wrinkled forehead, he asked, "What is that?"

"That, Chief, is our rescue vehicle. That is the X-102."

"You have got to be kidding."

"Chief, we are talking about a twenty-four-hour turnaround."

"I know what he's been doing."

"Captain Graham, one of your men has been sitting in the command seat." The chief stared at the X-102, hitting the zoom twice. "It was built to dock with Delta. It can carry nine passengers plus a crew of three. It has a cargo compartment large enough to carry the *Lewis*." Fully operational, the *Lewis* had not yet made its maiden voyage. But no one doubted its readiness.

Sooner looked at Thompson quizzically. "Chief, with a few minor adjustments, we load the *Lewis* with your probes, and"—his arms went up victoriously—"you are the hero!"

"We could do this—"

"No man left behind—"

"If they can hold on—"

"We have to try, Chief."

Dr. Sooner gave an affirming nod to Meekerson. "Send a message to Colonel Anderson. Put it in a loop and run it until we get a reply. Tell her the Cavalry is coming. Now, who will fly the *Lewis?*"

CHAPTER TWENTY

Heart banged. Chest heaved. Blood pulsed. Skin crawled. Head hummed. "I can't believe this is happening." Door opened. Hand reached. Foot stepped. Kim climbed. "Why did I say yes?" The ugly glared. Her hand slid. The ladder shifted. Her throat dried.

"Mercy." She forced herself to breathe slowly. If her men were calling, she wouldn't have heard them. Her labored breath drowned out her banging heart. She shook her head and blinked hard several times, trying to regain focus, and then continued her descent.

Colonel Anderson kicked up lunar dust for the first time on this trip. She stepped back from the craft to get a broader perspective. "Where are you, gentlemen? Mr. Martinez! . . . Mr. Rogers!" She struck the ladder handrail hard with the palm of her gloved hand. Still unable to spy anyone through the lunar dust cloud created by the quake, she yelled, "Where on this dirt pile am I supposed to find you men?"

"Ah!" It was Martinez. Severe pain dominated his response. "I'm behind you . . . under the craft . . . Help me . . . I'm pinned . . . My . . . my legs are crushed."

Moving quickly toward Martinez, the colonel looked like a spectator at the ping-pong tournament. Observing the large frame of Rogers kneeling next to Davenport, who appeared to be buried up to his chest, she asked, "How's Captain Davenport? Is he okay? Tell me he's okay." The words tripped out of her mouth in nervous succession.

"He's dead."

Martinez screamed in pain and began hysterically trying to free himself. "Oh, Jesus, don't let me die, don't let me die."

Rogers came in a lunar run. "Hold on, Marty. Take it easy. We're coming. We'll get you out . . . I won't let you die."

"You keep jumping around and rip your suit, you *will* die. Just slow down and be still." Colonel Anderson's instructions came out crossly. She realized her anger, but the expression seemed to channel her nervous energy.

Both Colonel Anderson and Rogers circled Martinez, assessing the situation. Mr. Rogers quickly grabbed on to the landing strut in order to try to move it. "Get a hold of the other side and let's see if we can lift it." Weighing in at 4,200 pounds on earth and under seven hundred pounds on the Moon's surface, they didn't need to lift the entire craft, just one leg.

The colonel bounced across to the other side and braced herself against the craft. She squatted down the best one could expect in a moon suit and prepared to lift the craft using her legs. "On three . . . ready?" asked Rogers. The colonel nodded. "One . . . two . . . three . . . lift." It didn't even rock.

Anderson studied the ship's supports. "The strut is wedged in the rift."

"Let's try it again," Mr. Rogers said, with panic rising. "One . . . two . . . three . . . lift."

The colonel felt a hand on her shoulder. She jerked her head around only to see an orange light scamper away. The colonel crept toward the light trail. *Must be a reflection in my helmet.*

"Where ya goin'?" Martinez begged. "Get this thing off me."

"Wait a minute." Colonel Anderson looked around the craft like a hungry hen in search of a worm after a spring rain. Finally she spotted what she was looking for. She headed over to the flagpole. "We need some leverage, Mr. Martinez."

"Hurry, just hurry!" Martinez ground his teeth together and clenched his fists.

"You're going to make it, Marty. The colonel's got a plan. Just hold on." Martinez and Rogers clasped hands. "I won't leave you, man."

Colonel Anderson pulled the pole out of the lunar rubble and bounced back to Martinez's side. Using the butt of the pole, she first tried to break up the rock that formed the lip over the foot of the strut. Striking the rocks over and over with all her might did little at first, but Colonel Anderson kept pounding. Beads of hot dread formed on her brow and then crawled down the front of her face. She paused to wipe, but wiping wasn't possible.

Mr. Rogers took up the task, driving the pole into the rock, twisting and prying. Finally, the lip gave up the fight and the strut was free.

"Let me wedge this under here," Rogers explained as he then worked the pole under the strut using the side of the rift as the fulcrum.

"Hurry, man. Hurry," begged Martinez.

"Calm down. This is going to work," the colonel explained.

Kaboom! An explosion of gargantuan proportions shook the surface, knocking Rogers to his knees and Anderson onto her back. The lunar craft pinched Martinez a little tighter.

As Anderson lay on her back, eyes stinging from sweat, she saw an unhelmeted face looking down at her. It was a male face as best she could determine—young with no facial hair, jaundice skin, and bright white shoulder-length hair. An orange light framed the head. The two dark eyes, kind but full of quizzical pity, stared at her. Was she hallucinating?

"Who are you?"

"It's me, Colonel." The face was gone, and Rogers helped the colonel to her feet. Anderson was disturbed. "Rogers, behind you at eleven o'clock."

Rogers turned around to see smoke and ash billowing from a rim peak of the Mare Crisium. "That makes no sense."

Anderson backed away toward Martinez. "Nothing on this trip makes sense."

"Get me out of here." Terror overwhelmed Mr. Martinez as he squirmed, twisted, and pounded on the strut.

"Mr. Martinez, hold still."

"Take it easy, Marty."

"I'm not ready to die."

With a serious aftershock, all three crew members started vibrating uncontrollably. Bam! Another peak blew. This one split a rift twenty-five meters wide right down the peak. A massive amount of steam vented. The team could see the lava flow. The two-kilometer rift glowed bright red. "This makes no sense," Rogers confessed in frustration.

"Reality doesn't require your understanding. Now, get me out of here." Panic seized control of Martinez.

"When I get the strut up, you pull him out." Rogers grunted and groaned as he lifted the craft up not more than two inches. As the craft eased off Martinez' legs, the colonel quickly pulled him free. Looking down, Anderson gasped. Martinez had one too many hinge points in his leg. Getting him inside would be a trick.

CHAPTER TWENTY-ONE

The doors swung open, and Colonel Frank Thompson watched General Lee Buchholz march through the black steel door into his Houston office like a conquering monarch. "Frank, have we circled the wagons?" The short fat man with an unlit cigar in his mouth took a seat in a leather burgundy wingback chair. His uniform fit tightly with the middle buttons bulging. The second from the bottom had already popped.

"Yes, sir. The X-102 is already being prepped at Kennedy, and my team is on the way." Colonel Thompson walked over to a four-by-six lunar relief map with the planned lunar outpost outlined in black. The *Santa Maria* was represented by a red pushpin.

"Snatch and grab, Frank. That's all I want. Just grab the cores, and get out of there."

"Understood. But Sooner wants probes deployed and more cores dug."

"If there is time, more cores works for me," said Buchholz. "Brief me on your team."

"I've pulled in Dr. Margo Street on science and—"

"Margo Street? Who is—?"

"She has her doctorate in geophysics and is renowned as an earthquake troubleshooter at Tectonics." Thompson moved back toward his desk but could feel the general's optical scalpel burning into his flesh.

"Don't screw this up, Frank."

"It is her hypotheses that we are working, General. She's good to go."

"If she is able to pull more cores, I want them."

"Understood. She'll cooperate."

"This is our last chance to gather cores." The well-chewed cigar in his mouth shifted from one side to the other. "You'd better be right." After a labored breath, he asked, "Who else you got?"

"I've got Dr. Kubo as chief engineer and payload officer." He was a tall Japanese fellow with thin black hair. Sunken eyes revealed years of insomnia, and a scar over his left eye created the illusion of danger. But nothing could have been further from the truth for this mild-mannered Buddhist.

"I know him."

"General, he's also our MD."

"I know. Now, what about the rescue team?"

"Captain Graham is on board. He brought the X-102, which is now being fitted for the *Lewis*."

"Excellent!" With hands in tight fists, the general raised them up to chest level.

Thompson rushed his response. "That wraps it up, sir." Thompson stood to his feet. "I'll alert you when the team arrives."

"Back the train up. Thompson, you're the lead dog. There is no argument there. You've got Graham on the X-102, and that's great, but who is going to command the *Lewis*?" Thompson sat back down, never taking his eyes off the robust general. "Don't even think about it, Frank. You've never even saddled up the simulator."

"I understand, General. I had Major Poole lined up."

"She's a good pilot. She's at least acquainted with the *Lewis*. Get her here."

"No can do, General . . ." Thompson felt the moisture gather under his left arm and trickle down his side. "She was injured in a car accident."

Thompson smiled and leaned back in his chair as General Buchholz shifted in his seat and then spun his cold cigar. He longed to strike a match. Buchholz offered two labored breaths before pressing his lips together hard in an unfriendly pucker. His eyes thinned. "I want Haistings."

"He's withdrawn, General."

"Frank, I want someone with experience. I want someone who has been to the Moon and back. I want someone who can command the *Lewis*." The general clamped down hard on his cigar with his back right molars. "And I want someone who can bring me my cores. Do you understand me?"

"Yes, sir."

"Do you have someone else who fits the bill?"

"No, sir."

"Then get me Haistings." Thompson opened his mouth to speak. Before any sound came out, the general pointed his stubby index finger in Thompson's face and said, "Convince him."

Thompson stared back blankly. "He won't go."

"For God's sakes, Frank! I'll get him myself."

The general stood to leave. "My jet leaves in twenty minutes. Be there in ten."

"Yes, sir."

Thompson opened his office door, and General Buchholz marched out of the room into the company of Bill Samson, NASA's press officer.

"What's the official story, General?"

"The *Santa Maria* is crippled, but not forgotten. For the first time in NASA's history, we are launching a rescue mission. Bill, I expect you to spin it well, make us look good . . . heroic."

"I can go to the press?"

"Double check with Sooner. Make sure the families have been notified first."

"One more question. What do you know about George Miller?"

"George? He was a good man. Why do you ask?"

"As press officer, I talked to George almost daily. Something's not right."

"I heard that it was a car accident. The police are investigating."

"The word is you've been asking around."

"Only as a favor to Jack Sooner. They were friends." Buchholz edged away.

"So what do you know?"

"I don't think they've found the guy yet. The car was stolen—no prints."

Bill scrolled down on his smartphone. "George was looking into some sort of connection between NASA and some lettered clandestine organization, and now he's dead. It's suspicious."

"Bill, don't go stirring up trouble. Let's focus on getting the team home. Now, if you'll excuse me . . . please."

Wondering what the press officer knew, Buchholz left the building in a hurry without looking back.

CHAPTER TWENTY-TWO

Colonel Anderson propped Martinez up against the craft to catch her breath and took painful notice of the landing strut's stabilizing rod's deadly stroke into the belly of the module. The perceived mortal wound magnified her feeling of despair.

She turned back toward Mr. Martinez. "You okay?"

"No. I think both my legs are broken."

"We'll carry you." The colonel pulled Martinez's arm over her shoulder.

"Wait. Where's Lathem?" Martinez tugged his arm loose. His eyes darted about, searching.

Anderson explained, "I don't know. He disappeared into the rift." For one horrific moment no one breathed. Anderson turned toward Rogers who had been at the rift checking on Davenport. Maybe he saw evidence of hope. Maybe? Rogers shook his head.

"Let's get you inside." Squatting low, Colonel Anderson grabbed Martinez's right hand with her left hand and pulled him laterally over her shoulders, slipping her right arm between his legs. She stood up straight. Taking two steps, the colonel lost her footing, and they fell against the craft. Hoisting him up again, the colonel carried Martinez around the craft to the ladder with great effort. She put him down at the foot of the ladder to get a better grip. At least that is what she told Rogers when the offer for help was made. "Just give me a second to catch my breath," she added with a huff. She took a quick look at the red rift. The magma flow moved slowly, but it moved their way.

Her mind began to spin as she saw Davenport slumped over like a wet reed. "Oh, God." Looking back over her shoulder, she spied Rogers on his knees. "Are you okay?"

"Yeah . . . I'm okay, just a little stunned." Rogers cleared his throat and pressed his hands against his chest. He stood to his feet and stumbled toward the lunar craft like an awkward college student with a hangover.

"I need my hand on the ladder." Anderson gave the instructions as calmly as she could. "Mr. Martinez, you've got to hold on to my neck. Do you understand?"

"Yes, ma'am."

After helping Martinez up, Mr. Rogers gently pushed the colonel aside and stepped in toward Martinez. "He's not only family, he's my friend." The colonel nodded in resignation.

Mr. Rogers pushed up the first step. With two of the craft's landing gear in the rift, the whole craft, including the ladder, now leaned to the right about thirty degrees. Scaling the ladder with two hundred and fifty pounds of man and equipment on his back became almost impossible, even on the Moon. Halfway up, Martinez lost both his consciousness and his grip and swung down toward the rift, knocking the colonel in the head. They both fell to the surface.

"Mr. Martinez. You've got to stay awake, and you've got to hold on," instructed Anderson.

Struggling for consciousness, Martinez tried again to attach himself to Rogers's shoulders. His legs, useless, dangled beneath them over the rift. Digging deep for strength, Andy Rogers gently grabbed Marty's left leg with his left hand and glided up the ladder. Slowly, painfully, they made their way up. The ladder shook a bit as Colonel Anderson began her ascent behind them.

The ladder seemed thicker; and the steps, further apart. Taking a moment to compose herself, the colonel reset her determination and wearily began the climb again. As she increased the weight on her right leg, her foot began to shake in a palsy quiver. The climbing stopped. She stared at her renegade foot, wondering if it would quit anytime soon. The ten seconds seemed like an eternity. The colonel pushed upward.

Having successfully scaled the ladder, they held Martinez up as they all squeezed into the pressure transfer chamber and waited for the green light in silence. The quiet was profound as thoughts of home rushed through her mind.

"Oh, sweet Jesus, please don't let me die," Martinez begged. His cry fractured the silence as the hydraulic door opened into the lunar craft.

"Is help coming?" Rogers asked expectantly. Help had never been sent before, but you can always hope. The colonel and Rogers gently released Martinez near the floor and removed their helmets.

"I hope so. I sent the distress message. Houston should know by now that something has gone terribly wrong."

Martinez sat up in agony. "Hope so? What do you mean 'hope so'? Have you talked to Sooner?" Colonel Anderson grabbed Martinez by the shoulders and laid him back down in a no-nonsense manner.

"Not directly. But we are broadcasting a distressed and stranded signal."

"Call him, now."

"Relax, Mr. Martinez." Kim stared deep into confusion. "Mr . . . . Martine—Marty, they won't leave us up here to die. They'll find a way to get us home." Anderson had no idea how they would get them home, but she would hope.

"We are going to make it, Marty." Rogers forced a smile. "NASA can't afford the bad press."

Martinez rolled his eyes. "Oh, sweet Jesus."

After removing their own moon suits, Kim Anderson and Andy Rogers began to carefully remove Marty's suit. Laying him flat on the floor, they released the shoulder clamps and pulled apart the primary seal. Unzipping the internal suit allowed the shoulder to open wide. "Now, how are we going to get him out?" asked Rogers.

The colonel moved to Marty's feet. "Mr. Rogers, grab him under the arms and hold him still. I'll try to gently pull the suit off."

Rogers dug his big hands under Marty's shoulders and tucked them up under his arms. Marty's face told a tale of pain and confusion.

"You ready, Marty?" The colonel's whisper calmed Martinez for the moment.

He shook his head, and a quiver went through his body. He grimaced in pain. Colonel Anderson started pulling the suit off. The first six inches went smoothly. Then it stopped. Straddling Martinez, the colonel moved up to his shoulders and began to work the suit down toward Marty's waist. Marty's arms were then removed from their sleeves.

"Colonel, he's shaking really bad." Marty's teeth chattered; his arms vibrated. His eyes glazed over.

Anderson urged, "Marty, try to relax." The colonel raised her head toward Rogers and said, "He's going into shock. Let's get this thing off him and get him covered up."

Rogers regripped Martinez's torso, and the colonel grabbed the suit at the boots and started pulling again. Once again, it slid well at first. Then it hit a catch that released a blood-curdling scream from Martinez. "You trying to kill me or what?"

"We hit a snag." Rogers ran his hand down Martinez's left leg, looking for the snag. "I think I've got it . . . Ooh . . . This isn't good."

"Now what?" Anderson's chest tightened.

Marty's eyes rolled back, and he checked out.

"Just pull the suit slowly, and I'll work the snag point," suggested Rogers.

They worked the suit off in ghastly silence. There was more blood than either imagined his clothing saturated. "Colonel, this isn't good." The tibia, the fatter bone in the lower leg, jutted through the skin about four inches below the knee. Frightened eyes stared at one another in disbelief. "Should we try to set it, Colonel?"

"Shhh." Martinez was still out. "Let's do it now."

"You've got to pull hard, Colonel. Pull as hard as you can."

Rogers maintained a firm grasp of Marty's shoulders as Anderson took hold of his left foot. After a deep breath, the colonel jerked the leg hard. The fractured bone disappeared into the mangled flesh. "It is not as easy as it looks," she said.

"There may be other issues, Colonel."

Anderson sighed hard. "For now, we'll put a dressing on him, shoot some morphine, and then pray for a miracle."

The colonel retrieved the medical kit and pulled a preset morphine syringe from its case. Quickly injecting the painkiller into Martinez's left thigh just above the knee produced no response. *Martinez is going to bleed out, and our doctor is dead.*

Martinez opened his eyes sluggishly and watched Colonel Anderson finish applying the dressing. "I need to make it home, Colonel." The words were soft and labored. "I promised."

"Shhh. Relax. Try to rest." She wiped the hair back from Marty's face.

The three stranded astronauts settled into the main cabin of the *Santa Maria* amid groans of pain and despondency, wondering if they would ever step foot on earth again.

Chapter Twenty-Three

He could see for miles. Major Bobby Haistings rolled his T-51 and banked into a cumulus cloud. Looking more like a stealth fighter than a trainer, the T-51 exploded from a cotton ball. The colors were spectacular.

After an hour of touch-and-go landings, the blaze orange sun still burned red at the core. The splinters of grenadine and rose that had reached out and touched the cool turquoise water below and the cobalt blue sky above had begun to fade. He had flown thousands of hours, but he never ceased to be amazed at an Atlantic sunrise. Rising early in the morning, Haistings often flew at sunrise on Sundays—it was a religious experience. A small glimpse of glory was there for the taking, and he took it. But the morning had slipped away.

Pushing the joystick away, the T-51 pitched forward. Nose aimed at the water, the two-seat trainer jet fell fast and hard. Abs taut and throat tight, Bobby swallowed hard and began easing out of the dive. Rolling to the left, his helmet bounced off the canopy just before he leveled out and pulled the stick into his gut. Pitching up at a forty-five-degree angle, Bobby blasted through a low, lone vapor patch. After three complete rolls, he steadied the aircraft at ten thousand feet, and the T-51 chased south, down the coastline eight hundred meters off the beach.

The recent rains purified the air; it was cool, crisp, and clean. His mind drifted to earlier days—rambunctious days of living life on the edge of sanity as one of NASA's test pilots who pushed aircraft to their absolute limit. He rolled the aircraft to the right and caught a glimpse of the Florida coast—sandy beaches and clear emerald waters. *I think I'll take Carol and Stacy to the beach today. It looks clear again.* Bobby envisioned a day at the beach as a relaxing day with cool drinks and a warm breeze. However, deep down inside, he knew it would be a messy day of lotions, lunches, and lounge chairs amid complaints of itchy, sticky sunburned skin.

"Whoa! What was that?" Colored lights flashed around him. His head bobbed around the cockpit, trying to see. Multi-colored lights streaked past him. He had seen these lights before but never so many.

"Whoa!" Another one flashed by within an eyelash. "That was close." Then the supposed super-heated meteor paused. *What's going on?* The lights' leading edge stopped and turned toward Bobby and then ducked behind a cloud that Bobby flew by at four hundred miles an hour. Bobby turned to see, but the luminary was gone. It looked like a translucent bronze face, a familiar but unknown bronze face. Bobby shook his head and stretched his neck. "I have got to cut down on the coffee."

Then thousands of lights, star shaped with sharp barbs, began to fall from space. "A meteor shower?" Bobby prepared to take hits, but none struck his aircraft. It rained lights, yet their paths didn't cross. "This is really strange." The lights didn't fall into the ocean as Bobby expected; they congregated into a ball directly in front of his aircraft. The ball slowly grew in circumference and brightness until it was about three inches in diameter on the horizon and as bright as the headlamp of an oncoming train. Bobby banked hard right, but the ball of light maintained its position. He pushed left with the same result. Regardless of Bobby's heading, the nebula of light stayed directly in front of his craft.

Then the sphere of sharp light rushed at the T-51, exploding in the cockpit. Dazzling light filled every nook and cranny. Bobby saw nothing but bright white. Blinded by the brilliance, Bobby felt cold hard pain in his chest, and then a cool chill ran down his legs. A high-pitched buzz tickled his ears, and then it all disappeared.

Bobby found himself over land, heading west and staring at a three-quarter moon a half inch above the horizon. "What was that about?"

Whatever it was, it lived outside his box. Bobby banked left until he had a due east heading. The Florida coast came up fast and looked familiar.

Radio transmission broke in. "Yankee 0-1-9er this is Cape Canaveral tower. Do you copy?"

"This is 0-1-9er, I copy."

"Major, we need you to cut your flight short this morning and head for home. There will be a car waiting for you on the hard deck."

"Roger, I'm headed home."

Unsure of the reason but glad to be going home, Haistings banked hard left and dove toward the ocean, looping around and pulling up just over the water. Bobby began to wonder if his family was okay. The more he thought about them, the more anxious he became. He kicked in the afterburners and raced to the base, keeping one eye open for strange lights.

Major Haistings passed the base on the right, extended his flaps, and eased up on the throttle. Banking hard left, he pulled the landing gear knob down. Nothing happened. There was no drag. No green light appeared in the handle. No door opened, and no gear extended. He pulled the knob up and down again to cycle the gear. Still no green light appeared. But a disturbing "thunk," followed by a small amount of wind draft, would test his skills.

"Yankee 0-1-9er, you're clear to land on runway 1-3."

Cleared but not ready, Bobby alerted the tower to his situation and requested a flyby. The tower approved the look. Bobby flew by tilting his right wing, revealing his underbelly. The next call from the tower was not good.

"Yankee 0-1-9er, your gear is in transit. I repeat. Your gear is in transit."

"Roger, tower, I am unable to lock them down. Bobby cycled the gear two more times only to have some mysterious hand stop it in transit.

Two pumps on the manual landing gear handle and the handle froze. Now it was stuck in transit. Bobby knew within minutes that word would spread to the duty officer who would coordinate with Lockheed engineers and other squadron pilot—everyone deliberating on his best course of action.

The T-51 protocol called for a belly landing on a foamed runway when one or more landing gear could not be extended. Bobby reviewed his emergency egress procedure in his mind and confirmed with the tower that he would wait for foam.

Some emergency button had to have been pressed, as multiple fire engines scrambled for position. Bobby eyed two ambulances and hoped they would not be employed.

Bobby made one more pass. The tower indicated that his left gear was not fully retracted. Anticipating a pull to the right, Bobby set up his final approach down the left hand side of the runway. Favorable winds blew in his face.

The fire engines sprayed the runway with the thick slick foam used to cushion the impact and eliminate sparks, with hopes of saving the pilot and the craft from fire. As the emergency crew completed the foaming, the rescue vehicles framed the runway at the top end. Bobby dumped his remaining fuel over the ocean and began to bring his aircraft down on fumes.

"Yankee 0-1-9er, you are clear to bring your craft down. Good luck."

At thirty feet, he fuel chopped the engines and brought the plane down on its belly, skidding and weaving two thousand feet down the runway. The foam eliminated the sparks but elongated the slide. The T-51 pulled hard to the right and skidded past all the rescue vehicles and off the runway. As he slid into the grass, he plowed through the fence that surrounded a small ballpark. The early morning players who had gathered at the fence to watch the excitement scattered. The craft tore through center field with emergency vehicles in close pursuit. Still pulling to the right, the T-51 plowed over third base and was captured by the fence protecting the dugout.

Bobby egressed in a hurry and ordered everyone back from the craft as the twin engines were bathed in fire-suppressant foam.

Slicing through the crowd, a young lieutenant armed with a pistol grabbed Bobby by the arm and ushered him toward the black SUV. "Major, I have orders to bring you into HQ."

CHAPTER TWENTY-FOUR

With the sun still shining through newly formed clouds, a light rain wet the windshield and trailed backward on the side windows. The nervous nineteen-year-old driver, who didn't need to shave but every other day, turned the wipers on. Bobby's breathing slowed as he unzipped the calf pocket of his flight suit. Pulling on the zipper tongue, he shuffled the two sides of the zipper again. Up and down, he tugged at the pocket. His mind drifted.

He was eleven years old. Holding to a rock about thirty feet out in the surf of New Smyrna Beach, Florida, his hot tears mixed with the cool rain—his whole body shook. The beach was deserted except for the emergency vehicles streaming onto the beach with lights flashing and sirens blasting.

The wind was up, and the surf was high. For the last couple of years, Bobby and his brother, Lance, had endured the arrogant boastings of the Maxwinnie brothers. Frank and Simon were notorious at Beach Head Elementary. One and two years older than Lance, respectively, Frank and Simon, ignoring the warnings, dared the waves of a storm. "You gotta surf the storms. That's when the big waves roll in." They were kings. But they moved up into junior high and now ran with a different crowd. Lance wanted to step into their shoes. He wanted the other kids to know him, especially Sarah. She was the first to wear makeup and a bra—a real one. Lance knew that if he could just catch one wave in a storm, Sarah Maxwinnie would turn her head his way.

The flags flapped hard as gale force winds whipped the rain horizontally across the beach. With their toes digging into the cool wet sand, Bobby and Lance leaned like statues, watching the waves crash against the sand.

Bobby turned toward Lance, who bent over and velcroed the safety line to his right leg. Bobby buried his smile in his fear and yelled, "Lance, don't go!" The wind and the waves bellowed in his ear. No dog barked; no fish jumped; no bird flew. "There's bad mojo out there."

"Just one, Bobby. I can do this," Lance said, convincing himself.

"I'm scared, Lance."

"Me too."

"Then don't go out there."

"Courage is not the absence of fear. It is the overcoming of fear. I'm going to push through." He sounded just like their dad.

Lance jumped on his board and began to paddle out past the break. The waves were tight, making the paddle-out more difficult. He made the break on his second try. He turned around quickly to catch the first wave possible. It didn't matter how big. Ten seconds on both feet was all he wanted.

The wind-whipped swell rushed toward him with a fury. He paddled hard and then snapped up on his feet. It was everything he had imagined. "Oooh! Weee! I'm surfing the storm!" It was the biggest wave he'd ever been on top of by far. The strong wind pressed hard against his back. The rain slammed against his head.

Bobby jumped up and down in the ankle-deep surf, yelling at the top of his lungs, "Yeah! Yeah! All right! Lance, you're surfing the storm! You're the man!"

Then the bottom fell out, and Lance did a face plant into the churning water. Bobby waited for Lance to surface. "Where'd you go, man?" His eyes darted up and down the beach. "Lance, where'd you go?" Bobby began to panic. Then the board popped up. "Lance!" He saw a hand and exhaled hard. "That was close." Then Lance's bloodied head surfaced. His eyes fixed on Bobby and screamed for help, but no sound came out of his mouth. "Lance!" He disappeared again.

Bobby took two giant steps into the surf just as Lance popped up again, screaming for help. Coughing up the salty foam, he thrashed wildly. Caught in a rip current, he was dragged back under the water. Bobby turned to run for help. Barely out of the water, he did a one-eighty and ran back into the water. There was no time to get help. "Oh, Jesus, what do I do?"

He ran into the surf and dove in where he had last spied Lance. With eyes wide open, he searched, arms and legs flailing around, desperately wanting to feel flesh. He found nothing but churned water and sand. A large wave picked him up and sailed him onto a rock. The current had carried him more than a hundred yards up the beach from where he had entered the water. Fear would not allow him to let go of the rocks. Search and rescue had to save Bobby. They found Lance's body two days later. Bobby would never forget the look on his brother's face as he went under for the last time. He had nightmares for years. The counseling helped only a little. The tragedy would affect every future decision.

CHAPTER TWENTY-FIVE

Arriving in front of the headquarters, the car door swung open quickly, jerking Bobby from his memories. The armed lieutenant jumped out, and General Buchholz slid in next to a very surprised astronaut. With a freshly starched shirt, clean shave, close haircut, trimmed eyebrows—he hadn't trimmed his eyebrows since his daughter got married—and a breath mint, the general extended his hand to the major. His cigars would stay in his coat pocket.

"Good morning, Major. I'm General Lee Buchholz." They had met before, but it had been over a year. The general had added a star and three more medals that decorated his left chest. Bobby had exchanged two silver bars for a gold oak leaf.

"Good morning, General." Bobby didn't bother mentioning their earlier meeting. "Major, while we don't know each other on a personal basis, I know your record. I have been very impressed with your performance reports. Your commander tells me that you are one of the finest . . . a part of the elite." Bobby wanted to roll up his pants; his shoes were lost. "What can you tell me about the *Lewis?*"

"Yes, sir. The *Lewis* is a new generational lunar craft. Equipped with two fifty-thousand-horse-powered GE jets, it has twice the speed, twice the range, and twice the payload of the *Santa Maria*. Functioning more like a Harrier jet than a fixed wing or helicopter, the *Lewis* has a slick VTL, a smooth transition, and a Mach 4 cruising speed in earth's atmosphere. It is a spectacular ship. It has a hydraulic robotic boom arm with micro adjustments. It can drill a core sample, pick up a lunar rover, or screw a lid on a mustard jar."

"That is quite the ship."

"Yes sir, it is. I believe the *Lewis* will take us to the next level in lunar exploration. Lunar and beyond. I think—"

"You helped to develop the *Lewis*, didn't you, Major?"

Bobby's cheeks flushed. "Yes I did, General." Bobby wiggled in the seat. The SUV seemed smaller as the rain beat down louder. "Begging your pardon, General. May I ask what this is all about?"

"Major, I understand we have a dozen in training right now, is that correct?"

"Yes, sir, that's correct."

"How many have completed the training?"

"None yet."

"How many would you trust to command the *Lewis* today?"

"General, we don't have any astronauts ready to command the *Lewis* at this time."

"Except for you, but you are doing the training."

"That's correct. Sir, where are we going with this? We both know all this information." The general sat still, staring at the back of the front seat like a nervous prom date. "General, you know I've put in my paperwork to transfer out of the active astronaut program. That's why I'm training."

"The *Santa Maria* is in trouble."

"I'm not flying in space anymore."

"We are receiving a signal indicating that she's life sustainable but not flyable. I need you to bring her back."

Bobby's heart plummeted deep into the upholstery. "I'll support you any way I can, of course. But I'm done with space travel."

"Major, I hate to put you in this position, but you are the only hope your fellow astronauts have."

Bobby couldn't believe what he was hearing. How could NASA put itself in this position? The sidewalk cleared as the rain came down harder. Lightning struck the utility pole on the other side of the street. Everyone in the vehicle jumped. The air was ionized;

each man sat straight up. Bobby was suddenly aware of every hair on his body. He stared at the back of his hands and thought of his lightning conversation with Carol.

"General, there is a reason I joined the air force and not the Coast Guard."

"I've read your psych file. I know about your brother. I understand."

"I don't think you do."

"You need to put it behind you, Major. You're the only astronaut we have who has not only been to the Moon and back but is also trained on the *Lewis*. By your own admission, the *Lewis* is the only lunar craft we have that can transport a team to the Moon, double up and bring the two crews home—that's assuming we still have a full crew on the Moon."

"What about Graham? He'll be better than me in a week."

"We don't have a week. But Captain Graham is on your team."

"My team?"

"Your team, Major. You will be in command of the rescue. Colonel Thompson will command the overall mission."

"Colonel Thompson?" Like a sharp stick in the eye, just the sound of his name made Bobby's head hurt. "General, I don't do rescues."

"Your word will be law once you launch from Delta.

"I hear you, but—"

"Lives are on the line here."

"But, General—"

"We want you to try. If you can recover the craft, that would be icing on the cake. If you have to take it apart and bring it home in pieces, that is fine with me. But the number one priority is the crew."

"Yes, sir."

The general put his hands together as if he were going to pray. "We estimate that they have enough supplies and oxygen to last five more days. If all goes well, you will be there in four. There is, however, one more piece to the puzzle." This was the part Bobby dreaded most, the proverbial "but": "It's yours free, but . . ." and "I'll have it to you on Monday, but . . ." The *buts* always suck the fun out of life.

"And that would be?"

There was a long pause. The general studied Bobby's face. Bobby knew he wanted a good read.

"Major, we have think tanks around the world working 24/7 running different scenarios, but we need hard data."

"Regarding?"

"The lunar surface. Some think it may be breaking up, and that would be catastrophic."

"So what would you want me to do?" Bobby asked in resignation.

"You? Nothing. You get the crew and the *Santa Maria* and bring them home. However,"—Bobby took a cold breath in anticipation—"I want to send a geophysicist up with you. We need probes deployed and cores drilled. She'll be on her own."

"I can't babysit some wannabe astronaut."

"She won't be your responsibility. Her timetable will be directly connected to yours. If you can't free the *Santa Maria*, cannibalize what you can and head for home. Either way, when you say go, you go."

Bobby couldn't think. Too much data was streaming through his neurons. His thinker locked up. A deep nauseating pain began at the base of his skull and ran straight through his head to his left eye. He closed his eyes tight and pushed air out his nose hard.

"Time is of the essence, Major. Five lives hang in the balance of your time."

Bobby turned away in disgust. "Take me to my car." Bobby knew what he had to do next.

CHAPTER TWENTY-SIX

After another dose of morphine and three milligrams of Lunesta to help Marty sleep, Colonel Anderson and Mr. Rogers suited up to bring in Davenport's body and search for Major Lathem. Sam Lathem's biotransmitter was still broadcasting. Wherever he was in the rift, he was still alive. They had to search for him.

Anderson grabbed the lunar candle from the forward strut and strapped it to her wrist and then waited for an aftershock to stop. The colonel wanted to stage the work around the persistent trembling coming every twelve to twenty minutes. As the lunar surface returned to calm, Anderson and Rogers moved away from the ship slowly, having attached a hundred meters of safety line. Lathem slid into the crevice about eighty-five meters from the *Santa Maria*. The extra twenty-five feet would allow for some mobility.

Anderson's breathing was labored, and her movement was stiff. Rogers watched as the colonel stumbled over a shallow ditch adjacent to Davenport's remains. "Relax, Colonel."

"I'll relax when we find Lathem alive and get him back on the ship."

"If he's alive, we'll find him."

Having brought a small spade from the equipment locker, Rogers began to dig around Davenport's life-support system. When the rift closed, Davenport's body was crushed down to less than half its size. Breaking up the lunar surface and digging him out would take some time.

The colonel moved down about seven yards to where the rift was about a meter and a half wide and too deep to see bottom. As her memory served her, this was where Lathem slipped in. With the lunar candle blazing, she searched every ledge and outcropping, looking for some sign of life. She saw nothing.

"Major Lathem, can you hear me?" No response. Her hope in a response was fading fast. Lathem's vitals were barely perceivable. But she wasn't ready to give up.

"How are you doin', Rog?"

"I'm making progress. Weightlessness is one thing, but lunar rock is rock." He continued to pound and break up the stones and heavy dust around the body. He drove the four-inch blade six or seven inches into the rubble then twisted the handle and pulled it down, which pushed the loose gravel up. With a quick flick, he moved some of the rock off to the left. Again and again, he repeated the process, creating a trough around the crushed astronaut.

"Want some help?" The colonel moved back toward Rogers.

"I think I just about have it."

Blam! Another peak blew. The surface jerked and shook the two living astronauts to their knees. The rift started to spread again, and Davenport's body began to slide. Rogers stretched across his trough and took hold of Davenport's shoulder harness. He held on until the shaking stopped.

"We need to pull him out now, Colonel."

Kim moved quickly over to Davenport as Rogers stood to his feet, not letting go of the body. They pulled the body free and laid him flat about ten feet from the rift line.

Turning back toward the rift, Rogers asked, "Did you see anything, Colonel?"

"Nothing. But there is a bend in the shaft. I want to go down and take a closer look."

"Let me go."

"No. If you get into trouble, I can't pull you out. But you can pull me out."

The look on Rogers's face said he didn't like the plan but it made sense. "True enough."

The two astronauts moved back toward Lathem's entry point. Rogers found two large embedded rocks to brace against. They were about shoulder width apart, giving him a solid position. He ran the colonel's safety line around his back and prepared to belay her down into the rift.

"Belay me down after the next aftershock." The colonel stared down into the rift again. "Give me thirty feet. If I can't find him, I'll come back out."

"Any more than ten minutes, and you'll be pushing your luck."

"Ten minutes."

Eleven minutes later, the next aftershock was over and Anderson's head disappeared into the rift. Three meters in, she paused to look around. The crevasse zigzagged down, dropping away from her feet. "Give me two more meters."

She dropped to a ledge and to what looked like the mouth of a cave, where she spied the handle of Lathem's lunar candle.

Rogers watched as lava oozed from the most recent peak that popped. "Come on back up, Colonel."

"Just another minute."

Rogers's heart jumped as he perceived a shadow moving over him. Snapping his head, he looked up. He saw nothing that could have caused a shadow.

"No, really, Colonel, come on back up."

"I found something." Picking up the handle and recognizing it for what it was, she flashed her candle deeper into the cave. In the far corners, the floor looked shiny, almost wet.

Her foot slipped, the candle struck the cave roof, and Anderson clawed for something to grab. The most violent aftershock came early. Being shaken deeper into the dust-filled cave, Anderson abandoned her lunar grab points and began a hand-over-hand climb up the safety line.

Rogers held on. The rock under his left foot gave way and tumbled into the rift. With his right foot firmly planted and his left arm around the boulder he had been leaning against, he held tight. His bicep burned as he pulled with all his strength. Then the line went limp, and she was gone.

CHAPTER TWENTY-SEVEN

Bobby whipped into the driveway of his light orange brick home, hopped out of the antique Mustang, and rushed to the door. The knob held its locked position. He fumbled for his keys as he noticed the light yellow paint chipping around the door jam. He finally managed to get the door opened. Stepping over the threshold onto the Spanish tile, he moved through the entryway and paused in the living room. "Honey, I'm home."

Looking around quickly, he found no one. Moving fast into the kitchen, he found a note on the refrigerator door, held on with magnetic lips: "Gone to the supermarket. Back before church."

Bobby flew out the door and steered his ride to the only store Carol shopped. Time ticked on. Marching across the front of the store, he examined each aisle in search of his wife. There she stood, in the meat department with their little girl, Stacy. Bobby hesitated.

"What are you doing here?" she asked.

"I got called in."

Carol froze in her tracks. Stacy danced around and pulled on Carol's skirt. "Mommy, I gots to go."

Squinting her baby blue eyes, Carol asked, "What's up?"

Bobby scratched his head and started to speak. Suddenly, he had to go to the bathroom. It's funny how a five-foot-three-inch woman can make a six-foot-one-inch man shake in his boots.

"What's up, Bobby?"

His throat dried; his tongue thickened. "They want me to fly."

"Define fly."

"Moon trip."

She threw a steak into the basket, breaking the eggs without a twitch. She then pushed the cart with a wobbly back wheel down the aisle, ignoring Bobby. Life was too uncertain for promises.

Stacy held herself with her dress hiked up and danced about the store, crying, "Mommy, I can't hold it any longer."

"Why didn't you go before we left?" Carol snapped.

"I didn't have to."

"Well, try to hold it." Carol snatched Stacy's hand into hers and walked off to the frozen food department without another word. Bobby pushed the cart behind them.

"What happened to 'You couldn't pay me to be up there right now'?" asked Carol.

"I don't have a choice."

"You always have a choice," she replied.

"Carol, the *Hope*'s in trouble." Their eyes locked; their breathing stopped. "They can't get home."

Carol covered her mouth. "Oh Jesus." Her neck blotched red.

"Shhh. It's hushed right now."

Bobby leaned down and pinched the tip of her left earlobe with his lips and then said, "It's a rescue mission."

"Oh, Bobby." Her voice was soft and airy.

"They can't get home on their own."

Carol whispered, "When are you supposed to leave?"

"I need to be ready in an hour. The clock is ticking. Life support's limited."

"Bobby." Like a cool mist, she leaned into her man. "I understand."

"Mo-o-o-meee! I really got to go."

Carol motioned for Bobby to follow as she grabbed Stacy by the hand and walked briskly to the customer service window, where she cut in front of a short, stout elderly woman who was trying to return a box of hair dye. Carol interrupted the ensuing conversation. "I'm sorry. Ma'am, do you have a bathroom we could use?"

The lady behind the window had dropped her head to read the sales report on the counter and replied without even looking up, "No, ma'am, we don't."

"Ma'am, we need to use your bathroom," Carol insisted.

"I'm sorry, we don't have one," whined the lady from beneath her tweezers-plucked eyebrows and heavy makeup. While this lady looked like she never used a bathroom, Bobby knew differently.

"Let me put it to you another way," Carol explained. "My little girl is going to go to the bathroom in your store. Where would you like her to go?"

"Right this way," she replied as she scooted off her stool and opened the door.

"I'll see you at home, Carol." Bobby left the cart next to the customer service window and headed home to pack a few personal items while Carol and Stacy quickly finished their shopping. *I should make sure Carol knows where my will is and all the insurance papers. She should pay off the house and then invest the insurance money. I wonder if she'll move to Tampa to be close to her folks.*

"Here, let me help," Carol offered.

Bobby jumped, dropping his toothbrush on the floor.

"Are you okay?"

"I have to be."

Bobby shoved his flight bag onto the floor, and they both sat down on the edge of the bed. Bobby gently took Carol's hand and began to caress it with his long slender fingers for what seemed like hours. Bobby felt her hands begin to quiver and calmed them by pressing them firmly against his chest.

"Carol, you need to know something."

"Don't even say it."

"I have to say it. The risk is great."

"You've faced greater risks."

"No, not really. If it were just up and back, picking up a crew, that would be no problem. But the crew's in trouble. The Moon's quaking."

"What does that mean?"

"I don't know. They're sending some scientist from Tectonics to do research. But Carol, if something happens . . ."

"Nothing's going to happen."

"But if it does . . ."

"It won't."

"Stop . . . Listen."

"No. We'll talk when you get back."

"I may not make it back."

"Why are you doing this to me?"

"Because I'm not a hero, Carol."

"You're my hero, Daddy." Stacy ran to her daddy and buried her head in his lap.

Carol tried to fight back the tears. "You're my hero too." The valve turned, and the tears soaked her face. She couldn't stop.

"What's wrong, Mommy?"

"Nothing, pumpkin. Your daddy is just going on a trip."

"Why?"

Carol knelt down with great compassion. Gently taking Stacy's hands, she said, "Do you remember Mommy's friend, Miss Kimmy?"

"Uh huh."

"Well, she and some men are in trouble," explained Carol. "They're stuck on the Moon. And your daddy has to go and get her and bring her home."

Stacy blinked a couple times and scratched her nose. "How long?"

"Just a couple of days," injected Bobby. "I'll be back, I promise. Now run along, and let your mommy help me pack."

Carol embraced Stacy before the little one scampered out of the room.

"I just want you to think through the possibilities." Bobby picked the conversation back up.

"I have thought it through. Many times." A smile blossomed on Carol's face. "Bring Kim back, Bobby. Bring them all back."

He hugged her tight; their lips touched ever so softly. Five minutes later, Bobby walked out of the bedroom to find Stacy in front of the TV. The shoes and the socks were off for her methodic hunt for toe jam. "Save some for me, Stacy." She ignored her daddy.

Carol stood next to the large picture window, reading the newspaper. The sun shone in brightly through the open mini-blinds, giving the pastel living room freshness. Carol looked ravishing. Her silhouette showed through her light cotton sundress that she now wore. He wanted her. But there was no time.

"Carol, I've got to depart the pattern, and you need to put a slip on." The words came out in one breath. Carol smiled understandingly and headed for the bedroom. She emerged shortly and met Bobby coming in from the back.

"I barred the back screen door. Make sure you keep the place locked up."

"I always do . . . We aren't the ones to worry about, Bobby."

"Just do me a favor and keep the stick in the sliding door."

As they stepped out on the small porch, Bobby and Carol noticed the dark clouds to the south heading their way. "Will you still go if that mess blows in?"

"Probably. We just don't have the luxury of waiting. We'll look for an envelope and try to squeeze by."

Carol jumped behind the wheel as a clap of thunder sent Bobby to the roof. He reached up and nervously refastened the ragtop's right forward lock, twice.

Carol reached over and squeezed Bobby's hand. "We'll be fine. You take care of yourself."

The wind kicked up, and the sky opened its mouth, sending a torrent just as they entered the base.

"We saw the strangest thing on the way to the market this morning," Carol said.

"An angel, Daddy. We saw an angel."

Bobby looked over at Carol with confusion tattooed on his face. Carol smirked, "Did you see the meteor shower this morning?"

"Yes, I did."

"They were flying over the car, heading for the ocean." Carol motioned with her hand, wiping it from behind her head out toward the windshield. "They were really low. One meteor looked like it was pacing with our car."

"Really." Bobby's tone communicated doubt.

"I'm telling you, it moved over the sidewalk and just in front of and above the hood. Right there. Carol pointed toward the right front headlight.

"A sparkler, Daddy. A sparkler with lips."

"Lips?" Bobby's expression begged for help.

Carol shook her head. "It seemed to smile at us, Bobby, and then it was gone."

Bobby's mind went to his own encounter with a flying smiling face, but he thought it best to hold that story until he returned.

"Angels, Daddy. The angels are watching over us."

As Bobby, Carol, and Stacy pulled up to the headquarters building at Cape Canaveral Air Force Base, the windshield wipers beat quickly against the glass. "I pray they keep watching over you."

Visibility was less than twenty yards. Bobby looked around the floorboard for an umbrella but found nothing. He grabbed the newspaper from his flight bag. "Carol, be careful in this rain."

Turning to Carol, they embraced, not saying a word at first. Would this be the last time he saw her—the last time he held her in his arms? Would he gaze into her eyes again? Uncertainty flooded his mind. "I love you, baby." Bobby wiped a tear from Carol's cheek and kissed her with two quick pecks followed by deep impact. "I'll be back."

After kissing Stacy good-bye, Bobby, dressed in his gray flight suit, leaped out of the car in a hurry and ran to the door with his newspaper hat. A young soldier opened the door and saluted.

"Kind of wet out isn't it, sir?" the sergeant asked.

"Just a tad."

Carol drove off in the pouring rain with Stacy waving in the window. Bobby watched them until they were out of sight.

Bobby gazed up at the strange grayish yellow sky as a meteor blazed by. The air seemed thick and haunting.

"The Truman Room, sir."

"Excuse me?"

"Your meeting is in the Truman Room."

"Thank you." Bobby released the panic bar and quickly entered the building, wondering what lay ahead. Surely there was more to the story than he knew.

Chapter Twenty-Eight

"Colonel! Colonel Anderson, can you hear me?" The voice seemed distant but on the move. Closer and closer, louder and louder, the voice came until she realized it was Rogers in her earpiece.

"I'm here." Reality came into focus for Anderson, who had had the wind knocked out of her from a ten-meter drop. She lay on a ledge about three meters below the main shaft that had leveled off into what would be considered a cave. The shaft that she now lay in did not exist before the last quake.

"I'm okay." She looked up to see Mr. Rogers peering down into the dusty bowl.

"There you are. After the safety line snapped, I couldn't do anything more than hang on until the shaking stopped and the dust cleared."

"I need to get out of here before the next aftershock."

"I understand, but don't try to climb."

"Do you have a better plan?" The line broke below the lip. Anderson did not have enough line to reach up and out, and Rogers didn't have enough line to reach down.

Rogers pondered the situation. "I'll unhook my safety line from the ship and send it down."

"Is that a good idea?"

"It's the only one I have at the moment. If you try climbing and snag your suit, there's no helping you."

"Make it quick."

As Rogers moved back toward the ship, Anderson found her lunar candle and used the time to investigate. Dark lunar rock, shinier than expected, covered the opposite wall. One vein had the appearance of shiny coal. She followed it up only to discover it ended in the floor of the shaft that was above her. She then followed it down. The vein and crevasse sank far below her field of vision.

Working the light up the adjacent wall, she found another opening, another shaft smaller than the first, running down and away from her. With one hand on a lunar grab point, Anderson leaned out to look down the shaft as far as possible. Something white caught her attention. It looked out of place but familiar.

There on the floor, surrounded by loose rock, appeared what looked like a sole, the bottom of a moon boot. Anderson repositioned herself and looked again from a slightly different angle. No moon boot appeared. She saw rock, dust, and then a shadow. Anderson jerked back. *Did I just see something move?*

"You ready, Colonel?" Rogers was back and none too soon for Anderson. He lowered the safety line. "Time is ticking."

Anderson disconnected her safety line and attached Rogers's line to her harness at the D-ring. "I'm ready. We'll need to work together. I don't want you to drag me up the wall."

"No, don't want to do that. So as I pull you up, lean back a bit and walk up the wall. You're not heavy. We just need to work together and find a comfortable pace."

"On three . . . One . . . two . . . three." Anderson pushed back and began her ascent. Two steps up, and she saw an orange glow coming from the first cave. As she passed it, she yelled, "Stop!"

Anderson twisted around to look down the cave. Her ears popped; her eyes widened. "Let's go, let's go!" Hot molten rock filled the cave and headed her way.

Rogers pulled, and Anderson hopped out of the rift in half the time anticipated. "We have a lava flow in the rift," declared Anderson.

They took hold of Davenport's body and dragged it toward the *Santa Maria* in a hurry. Glancing back in the direction of the rift, Anderson saw no lava. She hoped that it was diverted down the other shaft. She supposed it was just a matter of time.

Having placed Davenport's body in the equipment locker, the two astronauts returned to the safety of the ship. Sitting down at the control console, Anderson reengaged the manual distress signal on a different frequency. "I think our window of opportunity just got smaller."

CHAPTER TWENTY-NINE

Major Bobby Haistings quickly walked the length of the vacant hall, hearing his hard soles rhythmically strike against the highly glossed tile floor. Following the red painted line on the floor would take him to the command section. A right and then a left brought him to a T; turning left at the top of the T, he approached the Truman Hall. The black steel door stood out in the military gray corridor. Bobby couldn't see the airman running the buffer, but he could hear the motor and smell the new wax. The lack of other personnel created a surreal scene and a queasy feeling in the pit of his stomach.

"Sir, I'm going to need some ID today," requested the armed guard. His partner didn't move except to raise his weapon to an alert position. Eyes forward, shoes polished, creases razor sharp—this was the A team. *This is a rescue mission, not espionage.*

The guard examined the picture very carefully and then announced, "He's clear."

Bobby clipped the pass card onto his left chest pocket zipper tongue. The guard said, "Thank you," and then turned toward a keypad and punched in a five-digit code. A loud buzz was followed by a metallic clunk, and the door opened into a narrow hallway. Bobby found two doors on the left and one on the right—there were no markings on any of them. The hall turned left at the end. He followed the hallway, passing a glassed bulletin board on his left. In the far reaches of his peripheral vision, he caught a reflection that was not his. Bobby stopped suddenly, looking left and then right, only to find the hallway empty.

"Carol's story is messing with my mind."

Now, staring down the passageway, he made himself acutely aware of his side vision. Seeing nothing, he took a couple more steps before stopping again. He heard crying, or was it the whine of the distant buffer?

Prodigious dread rippled through his body. "What is this about?" Bobby shook his whole body and then pushed down the hall. The second right brought him to a door marked Truman in gold raised letters.

Bobby entered the dimly lit room to find the rest of the rescue team and ten support personnel jammed into the small briefing area. He spied an open seat next to his old friend, Rocket, and took it quietly.

Thompson alerted Buchholz of the team's arrival. The general marched through the door and took his seat at the front of the room. The team had no chance to get to attention before Buchholz motioned them to be seated. Thompson remained standing and addressed the group from the podium.

"Please open your notebooks." Bobby observed a small, one-inch-thick three-ring binder in front of each team member. Burgundy in color, it had NASA's raised seal on the cover. "Inside you will find the rescue plan laid out step by step." Bobby nodded his approval.

"Hold that order, Colonel." Addressing the room, the general continued. "I'm General Lee Buchholz, and you ladies and gentlemen are about to embark on a mission of extraordinary significance." Bobby's lips cracked into a nervous smile at the general's attempt to add drama with slow syncopated speech.

Buchholz cleared his throat. "As I am sure you are aware, we don't usually risk human lives for deep space rescue!" The astronaut group was the only group that will not risk a rescue. Every astronaut knew it. They all signed releases prior to joining the group. "However, that policy was based on the impossibility of rescue. Today it is possible. We have been in contact with Colonel

Anderson and are receiving one automatic distress signal and one manual input distress signal." The manual input signal had to be reset every six hours. "We know we still have at least one team member alive. We are hoping for more. We are going to get this team back." Exuberant chatter filled the room.

"However, not only are we launching a rescue mission for the first time in NASA's history, but we will be bringing back information from the lunar surface that may save humanity from extinction."

Now we've crossed over into melodrama.

"Such as?" With eyes unblinking, Bobby focused squarely on the general.

"Major, the Moon may be breaking up." Dr. Margo Street dove into the conversation without testing the water. Her sweet but confident voice drew all eyes. "As you may know, any major shift in the Moon's orbit or mass will alter the continental makeup of the entire planet." She captured the room's attention and herded it into her own corral. "The entire ecosystem is at risk. Major, humanity is at risk. We need to find out what's going on."

Bobby swung around to come face-to-face with the dark-haired beauty.

"I'm Dr. Margo Street."

"Funny, I don't remember the name."

Thompson stood to his feet. "It's my call, Major. Dr. Street is a highly qualified geophysicist with Tectonics. It is her lunar hypothesis that we are working."

Bobby smiled lightly at Street. "I apologize if I'm coming across as rude, Dr. Street. But you must understand: this is not a training mission. This is a first of its kind rescue mission on an unstable lunar surface." His eyes drifted back to the notebook. "I don't know what we are getting into. I fear for the crew of the *Santa Maria*. I fear for us. I don't know what you've been told, but it's going to be luck and a prayer for any of us to survive." Bobby's eyes lifted slowly, finding a friendly set of eyes staring back at him. "Dr. Street . . . I just want to make sure you understand what you're getting into."

"I understand."

"Are we finished, Major?" The general closed his folder. "Get on with the briefing, Frank."

After explaining the division of labor and responsibilities, Thompson outlined the big pieces. "We are presently loading the *Lewis* onto the X-102."

"Major Haistings will command the *Lewis* and the actual rescue operation," added the general, with a bead on Thompson.

Thompson sighed and continued. "Upon arriving at Delta, Dr. Kubo, Major Haistings, and Captain Graham will need to deploy the *Lewis*." Thompson paused to allow the team to watch an animated demonstration of the deployment on a 3-D imager. "It's jerry-rigged, but it will work under the circumstance."

Dr. Kubo added more narration. "There are sixteen shipping straps securing the *Lewis*. Let's make sure we get them all."

"Major Haistings, I want something to show to Congress," barked Buchholz. The air got heavy as the team shifted in their seats. "I need that lunar craft. Can you bring it back?"

"I'll do everything I can to get the crew and craft back."

Thompson stepped up. "We are on the clock, people. Lunar positioning will close our Delta launch window Tuesday morning at 1047 Zulu. If we miss the window, the team is dead. I don't plan on missing it. My target launch from Delta is 0900 Zulu."

Bobby looked at his watch, noting the day and the time, and then listened for another crack of thunder. "Our first launch will be high risk," Bobby said.

Rocket leaned in toward his friend. "If we can take off, I can fly us out of danger."

"Upon establishing lunar orbit, we will photograph the lunar surface and launch twenty-seven thousand data probes, spread equally around the northern and southern hemispheres as well as around the lunar equator," explained Thompson.

No bigger than a thumbnail and encased in small pods, the probes would be propelled by small rockets and dispersed in a fanned pattern. Then, six hundred meters above the lunar surface, the pods are engineered to explode and further scatter the probes.

"There is an open plain here." Picking up a laser pointer, Thompson directed the beam to a detailed moon map that appeared on a flat screen behind Dr. Street and across from Bobby and Rocket. The stranded *Santa Maria*'s location was indicated by the red letters "SM." The landing zone, marked by the letters LZ, had been established about one hundred meters from the *Santa Maria*.

"Now, along with the craft and crew, we must retrieve the computer's hard drive. If nothing else, get the computer information. There are also two key core samples that we need. One is marked H21, and the other is H121. We are hoping they will tell us something about the stability of the substrata."

"While we attempt to recover the craft, Dr. Street will be given ten hours."

"Ten hours!" Street interrupted. "I thought I had two days."

"You get ten hours."

"I need two days. I want to examine the rift, take samples, and drill cores. I want to collect lunar lava. What am I supposed to do in one day?"

"The longer we're on the surface, the greater the risk. I'm not willing to take that chance. You get one long day. Do I need to find someone else?"

"I'll take the day," Street accepted. "I don't know what you expect me to do in ten hours."

"I don't care. Just gather as much information as possible," Thompson instructed, with priggish impatience. "You get ten hours, do you understand?" Thompson asked.

Bobby and Rocket exchanged glances. Ten hours was a blimp in time, a hiccup. Surely he couldn't be serious. Did they really want to recover the *Santa Maria* or just pick up the crew?

"I'll get the information," Street muttered.

"All right, ladies and gentlemen. Start your preflight. As soon as we have a break in the weather, we're gone," Thompson declared confidently just as a peel of thunder shook the building. "You're dismissed." Thompson glanced at Buchholz, who sucked on his unlit plug.

As the room emptied, Bobby and Rocket stayed seated, reviewing their notes. Dr. Street stayed to study the moon map. Bobby watched as she closely studied the shadow regions around the Mare.

"What about an air bag system?" Bobby asked Rocket. Airbag systems had been used for years in every major city. They were standard equipment on most Fire and Rescue vehicles. Made of Kevlar and canvas, they were stuffed under and between crushed vehicles and then inflated at a prescribed rate.

"What's an air bag system?" Margo queried, with lips twisted.

Rocket quickly explained the system in more detail than was necessary. He looked at Bobby for confirmation.

"Thanks for the update," Bobby opened.

"Film at eleven," Rocket closed, with a nervous laugh. He reeled it back in and gave a smile, tipped an imaginary hat at Margo, and then said to Bobby, "With only ten hours, we've only got one shot at this. Let's find an air bag system."

Bobby watched Rocket and Margo exchange nervous smiles and stares of interest.

CHAPTER THIRTY

Thompson passed the command room and saw Buchholz standing in the middle of the room, puffing on his unlit cigar and staring at the X-102 on a seventy-two-inch monitor. Steam rolled from the X-102 as blast pad 9-A held it in place. NASA technicians loaded the liquid oxygen. Thompson coughed, startling Buchholz, who jerked around, knocking over a cup of coffee on the desk behind him. Thompson dodged the perturbed darts that Buchholz threw, accusing him of spilling his coffee. He shook it off as Buchholz looked at a young airman and said, "Clean it up."

Without another thought about the coffee, Buchholz moved in close to Thompson and said, "I want those cores." The words came out louder than he had planned. He looked around the room. They were not alone. He gnashed his teeth. Thompson squared his jaw. Buchholz would never blame himself if he could find someone else to blame.

Dr. Kubo sat at a computer terminal. He had been watching a 3-D animation of the *Lewis* until he was sprinkled with coffee. He noted the general's consternation and then turned back to the computer screen.

Buchholz motioned Thompson to come closer. "I want those core samples. In fact, I want five. We need to make this trip worth the risks."

"What about the *Santa Maria* and her crew?"

Buchholz grabbed the fabric of the G suit on Thompson's left arm and pulled Thompson's ear down to his mouth. "I don't give a rat's hair about the *Santa Maria* or its crew. I want those cores." His breath was hot and smelled of coffee.

"We could get burned."

Buchholz ignored Thompson's concern. "Let Street gather the information. Just get me those core samples. Put them in my hands." Buchholz surveyed his immediate surroundings again. Dr. Kubo looked his way with interest and concern. The general turned his back on the doctor and moved Thompson toward the window. He whispered, "We're controlling all transmissions from the lunar surface. So what happens on the lunar surface will be up to your own imagination."

There was a ghastly tone in his voice. Thompson understood exactly what he meant. "What about the doctor?" asked Thompson. They turned toward Dr. Kubo, who was once again looking their way.

Buchholz grimaced, "Whatever is necessary." With a new surge of power and authority, Thompson exited the room and paraded toward the X-102 with a fresh spring in his step.

CHAPTER THIRTY-ONE

Aboard the *Santa Maria*, Lunar Survey III gripped life faintly. Martinez, propped up against the aft bulkhead, shook like a beach bum on a frozen lake. Partially covered with standard-issue air force blue blankets, his teeth chattered and sweat dripped from his mustache as he squirmed in pain. Both legs discovered broken, he lay still as his flight suit, soaked with blood from the thigh down, clung tightly to his skin. With a tourniquet located just above the knee on each leg, Martinez required constant attention. Colonel Anderson, the mission commander and stand-in medic, would loosen the wrap every few minutes, hoping to keep the blood circulating. However, each time the tourniquet was loosened, blood oozed from the compound fracture on the one leg and the three-inch bone-deep gash just below the knee on the other leg. It looked futile. It felt useless. What more could she do? What more could anyone have done? Should she try to set the other leg or just keep shooting morphine?

I'm not a doctor, the colonel complained to no one but herself. *What was I thinking? The risk was too high. I knew that. I have killed us all.* The mutterings of madness slipped from her lips in a melody of discord.

Glancing briefly at Major Lathem's duty station, the colonel's head fell and her eye twitched. *That's all I need.* She reached up with the middle finger of her left hand and tried to hold it still. Should she go out again to search for Lathem? What would be the point?

"Do you think Lathem is still alive?" asked Anderson.

Rogers looked up at the monitor. Lathem's biotransmitter was flat. Then there was a blip. A heartbeat? It went flat again, followed by two more blips and then a long flat line.

Anderson offered, "Could be a malfunction. His biotransmitter may be shorting out."

"Or it could be a malfunction hiding his viability."

"He's been out there a long time. He'd be out of oxygen."

"Under normal breathing," explained Rogers, "that would be true. But if he is unconscious his breathing may have slowed considerably, extending his life."

"Wishful thinking, Mr. Rogers. I like it, but it is not likely." Another blip caught her attention. "I still think we've lost him."

Her conclusion did not quiet the questions in her heart. Should she search again? Why? To take his body home, of course. It would expend a lot of oxygen. For what? A colleague, a fellow explorer. She had not only trained with him, but she had flown with Major Lathem before. Besides, all astronauts are cut from the same stone. Once you have strapped on the harness and felt incredible g-forces give way to the weightlessness of space together, you're family.

I can't go out. I need to stay with the living. The rescue team can help recover Lathem. The questions kept coming, crowding her mind. She dug a hole in her soul and climbed in. Whipped, with her face rubbing canvas, she wanted to throw in the towel, but there was no towel to throw. If only she could shut out the moonscape. It growled, it snarled, it clawed its way toward the crippled craft.

Martinez grabbed the colonel by her lapel as she tightened the tourniquet once again. "We are going to make it, aren't we?" The terror in his eyes burned deep into Anderson's wounded spirit.

"Oh God, I wish someone would shake my arm and wake me up." Her hands trembled as she pulled Martinez's hand from her suit.

"Just try to relax." Martinez rolled his eyes low. "And try not to move." That was sometimes difficult. Periodic tremors—aftershocks—bounced the crew around like an amusement park ride.

One earlier tremor had caught Rogers crossing the cabin, and his large, size-thirteen boot had come down heavily on Martinez's right leg, just below the gash. The colonel had never witnessed blood actually drain from a man's head. The head-to-the-bulkhead thud made her nauseous. When Martinez regained consciousness, revenge banged in his heart.

Rogers would have apologized profusely, but how do you voice regret for sending your brother-in-law on a short trip to hell and back? So after patting his own chest hard, he pushed out "sorry" and then retreated sheepishly to the control console on the distant side of the four-meter cabin. It was more of an oval. He just wanted to stay as far away as possible. Mr. Rogers tried to hail Mission Control or Delta or anyone who would respond.

Colonel Anderson found Rogers still sitting at the console an hour later. She slid down next to him, looking for some encouragement. Communication should have been reestablished hours ago. Delta had cleared the earth seven hours previously. There was no good reason for the silence, not in her mind anyway. Had they been written off? Had Buchholz cut his losses?

A graveyard came to mind. Not just any graveyard: it was an unkept, overgrown graveyard. The colonel was sixteen years old—she had just begun to dream of space flight. Her family was on a vacation in Rochester, Minnesota. They had gone biking along the Root River trail. Southeast Minnesota was known for its endless bike trails through rolling hills and quaint little towns. On this particular ride, she and her sister had stopped under a large oak tree that was perched precariously on the bank of the river. Half of the large tree's roots were exposed—the soil had been washed away by years of erosion.

"Hey Kimmy! Come look at this." Amber had wandered up the hill on the other side of the trail. "There's an old graveyard up here."

Kimmy scampered up the hill to investigate. Amber had stubbed her toe on the marker. It's the only way anyone would have found them. The brush was over three feet high. On the surface, you couldn't see any markers. Kimmy and Amber began to stomp down the grass and the brush. They found twenty or thirty markers before Kimmy found a very large piece of granite lying on its back in the center of the circle of markers. Engraved on the granite slab were the words "We will Never Forget You." Kimmy looked at Amber and said with a smirk, "Guess what? I think they forgot."

And it all came rushing back. They forgot. She wanted to hit someone. "I will not just sit here and wait to die."

CHAPTER THIRTY-TWO

"Rescue One, the lightning has moved out of the two-mile window. We are at T minus 2:47, 46, 45."

"Roger, control, we are good for launch."

The team cleared for launch two hours previously and then had paused, waiting for a weather window. Each crew member sat securely in their seat. Major Robert Haistings found some humor in watching a grown man sulk. Thompson wanted the command seat—he was the Mission Commander. However, on the X-102, the Command seat belonged to the pilot. Captain Steve Graham held the controls, while Colonel Thompson observed everything closely from the copilot's seat. The learning curve would be steep, but he would try.

Lightning flashed and thunder boomed. Most teams had months, sometimes years, to get to know one another and understand how each other worked. The many unknowns complicated the rescue in Bobby's mind. The *knowns* exacerbated his anxiety.

Bobby knew Thompson as a narcissist who had squirmed his way into NASA with the help of wealthy parents with Washington connections. Rumor had it that he had been written out of the will recently. That complicated his motivations. A well-known womanizer, it didn't surprise Bobby that Thompson would pick an attractive woman for a science officer. But he feared that the presence of a gorgeous woman could hamper Thompson's already questionable judgment. The longer he stared at Thompson, the greater his unease.

Rocket, on the other hand, was the best wingman Bobby could have hoped for. They had history together. Rocket followed Bobby across the stage at the same high school two years apart and served as best man at his wedding. Meeting the summer before Bobby entered the ninth grade, Steve, who had not yet acquired his cool nickname, filled a void in Bobby's life. Rocket was the friend who stuck closer than a brother, but while Bobby had never even seen the X-102 up close, Rocket had never stepped foot in the *Lewis* simulator. Any help in either direction would be limited. There was no backup, no plan B, and no room for mistakes.

Traveling to the right, Bobby's eyes found the menacing face of Dr. Kubo, who sat directly across the aisle from Bobby and behind the colonel, with a deck of computer monitors in front of him. Serving as flight engineer and loadmaster, he kept a close eye on his cargo. His jacket was impressive albeit thin. Dr. Kubo had done his homework and endured the training. Although green as a baby fern, he was next up, and he deserved to be on a mission. But was this particular mission a good idea? All-star games always disappoint because of a lack of team history. The sum of individual effort is never as great as the team. This team had no history, and Dr. Kubo had no team play. For Rescue One, the learning curve was a cliff. Doubts continued to mount.

A complete unknown, Dr. Street baffled Bobby's mind. Untrained and untested, Street appeared as a disaster looking for a place to happen. Could she function in weightlessness? Could she handle the *g*-forces? Would she lose the contents of her stomach? Unlike the old shuttle systems, which pulled only three or four *g*'s, the X-102 was more like an F-18 pulling eight or nine *g*'s. This could get ugly fast. Her eyes flit as she sprinkled the cockpit with a hesitant smile.

Bobby figured she was about five feet four inches tall and no more than one hundred and twenty pounds. If memory served him, she had the physical makeup of a gym hound. Physically, she would survive. But was she mentally prepared? They were all about to find out.

The silence was broken by Rocket, who asked Margo where she was from.

"Roswell, New Mexico" was the reply.

Rocket flinched. Bobby smiled. This would be fun. "Why couldn't she have been from Sibley, Iowa?" Rocket mumbled as he worked the foot pedals, rotating the rudder side to side.

"Really? Are you into the whole extraterrestrial thing?" Bobby asked.

"I'm not obsessed with it."

"But you believe in the possibility?"

"Hey, Bobby," Rocket barged in, "you know there are whole departments in major universities throughout the world dedicated to the possibility of extraterrestrial life?"

"So when did you join the ET fan club?"

Rocket set the flaps to their takeoff position. "I'm not saying I believe in extraterrestrial life. I'm just saying that believing in the possibility or looking for life beyond earth's atmosphere doesn't make a person ignorant."

"Thanks, Rocket." Margo tried to tap him on the shoulder but her harness hampered her reach.

Bobby sighed hard and asked, "Dr. Street, why are you here?"

"Call me Margo."

"Okay. Margo, why are you here?" Wanting to peel back the romance of space travel, Bobby went on to explain the extreme danger.

Margo was undaunted. "As a geophysicist, my primary attention falls on the Earth's tectonic plates." She pulled on her collar. "I'm an earthquake specialist. But we also study the Earth as one of many planets."

Bobby floated a quizzical glance. "An earthquake specialist is interested in interplanetary research? How does that work?"

"We are all connected, Major," Thompson offered.

"I understand," Bobby persisted, "but why did you enter into the AAP? I mean, the Active Astronaut Program is not something one enters on a whim. NASA is no place for dabbling."

"It was the one thing my father said I couldn't do." Margo looked surprised that she had actually said that out loud.

The cabin remained still as Margo told of an eccentric relative on her mother's side who filled her summer childhood days with stories of UFOs and Area 51. Margo's father wrote him off as an uneducated quack. Every opportunity to belittle was taken. Dr. Street, the senior, supported the space program believing that solid research could be accomplished. But that kind of research was not for his little girl. She could be anything she wanted within reason. But she should leave space exploration to the best of the best—an elite club of which Margo could never join. She just didn't cut it.

"I joined the club. And the intel that I will bring back will be the most significant intel of the millennium."

"Rescue One, the clouds have moved out of the two-mile window." It was back to reality. "We are at T minus 2:47, 46, 45."

"Roger, control, we are good for launch." Thompson's voice dropped an octave—he would at least sound like the alpha male.

Margo swallowed hard and tried to corral the monarchs. Her face turned pale, and her skin was viscous as every ounce of blood headed south. Her confidence seemed to have slipped out of the escape hatch with the ground crew. Bobby worried that Margo's reaction would get unpleasant.

As the main engines fired, Margo puckered her lips, expelled three fast pants and whispered to herself, "I can do this." Gripping the console and pushing hard against the headrest, she braced for takeoff.

"Three . . . two . . . one . . . and we have takeoff." The thrust sucked the air from their lungs. "Good luck and Godspeed, Rescue One." Bobby knew they would need more than luck.

Chapter Thirty-Three

Kick, stroke, kick
Kick, stroke, kick
Faster, faster.
Kick, stroke, kick
Kick, stroke, kick
Faster, faster.
Kick, stretch, pull!
Kick, stretch, pull.
Follow the bubbles,
Follow the bubbles.
Kick harder.
Stretch further.
Kick.

Earth and Moon worked together, pulling the water from the near-deserted beach just to the east of Washington, DC. Sand crabs scrambled through the shards of light, leaving just a hint of a wake in the salty water. Moon smiled brightly at her work. The table was set. She released the angry clouds, which rushed in, growling at anyone who dared to venture onto the beach.

Two took the hidden dare. Intoxicated with love, the honeymooning couple was lost in each other's arms when the tsunami struck the beach at 150 miles per hour. The hundred-foot wall of liquid death rushed over the land, crashing into the Chesapeake Bay, where the Earth said, "No further."

Stroke, stroke, str . . . o . . . ke
Follow the . . .
Kick.
No one survived the attack.

*　　*　　*

Car seat secured, seatbelt fastened, and gas tank filled, the Mustang kicked up its feet and splashed through the downpour as Carol and Stacy headed home after the cake was eaten and the presents were opened. Carol had left her sister Megan's house just before 6:00 p.m. She wanted to get home before dark. Leaving St. Cloud, she worked her way toward Highway 192. Nervously slowing down, Carol approached a low bridge covered with floodwater. She stretched her fingers on the skinny antique steering wheel, took a deep breath, and watched a small SUV motor across the bridge. Carol pressed on the gas pedal abruptly, wanting to get across quickly. They were no more than halfway across when the wall of water hit. The Mustang scraped the guardrail. The creek water sloshed against the lower part of the window before Carol could gasp. Terrified, Stacy began to scream as Carol desperately tried to restart the car. Not even the starter motor cranked.

"Come up here with me, Stacy." Her voice was calm but shaky. Carol helped Stacy climb up front as fast as she could and hugged her up close.

Stacy laced her fingers and closed her eyes tightly. "Please help us, Jesus."

Boom! Both Carol and Stacy screamed and tightened their grip on one another. The flash of lightning and crack of thunder were incredible. The air seemed supercharged. Carol could feel the fine hair on her wrist. More flashes followed, with many different hues of color. One bizarre streak of light flew across the hood of the car; the floating specter didn't look like lightning at all.

"The angels are back, Mommy."

"You think so, sweetie?" *I think we are in the middle of a meteor shower.*

"It's pretty."

Distracted for the moment, the girls were captured by the light show. Carol was unsure of how much time had elapsed, when outside voices startled her back to reality.

"You in the car, are you okay?" Two police cars and a rescue vehicle from the fire department positioned themselves just above the water level on the road.

Carol praised God amid a burst of tears. She cracked her window just a bit and yelled back, "We're okay, just get us out of here!" Her heart pounded in her throat; her hands dripped clammy as she wrestled off the panic. *Breathe, Carol, breathe.* The water soaked her knees and threatened her seat. Her body began to violently shake. Carol wasn't sure if she was cold or scared beyond words.

"Just sit tight. We'll come to you," the policeman instructed. As Carol responded with a nod, the current picked up and pushed the Mustang sideways down the guardrail. She could hear the scrape. For some odd reason, the first thing that popped into her mind was "Bobby is going to be ticked when he sees that mark." Her mind did a quick survey of past scrapes. His frustration would quickly turn to delight with the realization of another Mustang project.

The railing began to give way; pressure bolts exploded like popcorn. One by one, the posts pulled up and out of the soggy ground. The passenger side wheels slipped off the pavement. The car now sat at an angle, allowing the angry rivulet to get underneath the car, rolling it over on its side. Stacy screamed again and Carol grabbed her and lifted her up, bracing her against the steering wheel. Water flowed into the car.

"Get us out of here!" Carol shrieked.

"Just hold on!" the policeman yelled. Another company of Fire and Rescue with a swift water team had just arrived. Red and blue lights flashed as white hot meteors the size of golf balls peppered the torrent. Three ripped through the convertible top and burrowed into the back seat. Carol shielded Stacy with her body. The bystanders took shelter—meteorites had killed over ten thousand people worldwide in the past seven days. Fire and Rescue pulled back to work under a cover with one eye to the sky. Carol prayed for mercy.

The meteor shower was brief. The animated captain stepped out from his shelter, yelling louder and pointing more aggressively. Carol watched as a rope was secured to a crossbow bolt and shot across the seventy-foot span, which the creek had now become. Another engine had arrived on the other side of the now class 3 rapids. The tailboard from the second engine, positioned on the other side to receive the line, waved the all clear just before the shot fired. Retrieving the bright orange bolt from the palm tree into which it had lodged, she fastened it securely to the same tree. The line now stretched across the creek with its parabolic peak sloshing against the overturned vehicle.

Having a harness already on, a young lieutenant hooked himself on to the span line and began to swim out to the car. As he got close to the Mustang, Carol pushed her horrified daughter out of the window amid screams of, "No! Mommy, I want to stay with you!"

Carol didn't listen. The fireman grabbed Stacy, who then latched onto his neck for dear life. He had to pull her back just a smidgen to secure a safety line on over her head and under her arms. He then explained to Carol that he would be back shortly. He fought the current back to the bank with the help of two other rescue personnel who pulled on another rope fastened to his harness. When they were about ten feet from the shore, the railing broke loose and the car swept over.

Stacy screamed, startling her rescuer, who slipped back and dropped her. The little wet girl slipped out of the harness, splashed into the strong current and disappeared under the water.

With a step and a splash, the captain who tended the span line went in after Stacy. He came up quickly, with the little girl in a hair-curling squeal. The captain and little girl swept through the white water.

Seeing a low-hanging branch, the fire captain positioned himself and Stacy to pass by under it. Holding Stacy with a death grip in his left arm, he reached up with his right and hooked his elbow around the branch. He heard a pop. The disturbing roar that came out of his mouth sent Stacy up over his head and into the tree.

Terrified, Carol struggled to get out of the Mustang. The car kept rolling over and over. The water actually cushioned the tumble. If it wasn't life and death, it might have been fun. However, tossed around like a rag doll, she lost her up and down perspective. Water quickly filled the cabin—no air pocket was left. *How much longer can I hold my breath?* Her chest began to burn. Thoughts of Bobby and Stacy scurried through her mind. The shaking stopped. A strange calm came over her. The terror of the earlier moments had subsided. Maybe there would be time for panic later. Maybe her adrenaline had kicked in, helping her to stay level headed. She had heard of such things. She wasn't sure. She didn't care. Carol looked up and could see daylight. The rain must have stopped. Groping for the light, the burning turned to a sharp pain. "Jesus, is this it?" Carol could smell Stacy's hair and taste Bobby's aftershave. Warmth enveloped her. Death was sweeter than she had imagined. She looked behind her to see if Stacy would followed.

CHAPTER THIRTY-FOUR

With teeth clenched and vision blurry, the fire captain told Stacy to stay put in the tree and wait for help. But the little blonde had had enough. With one petite foot in front of the other, Stacy stepped over small shoots and broken joints, keeping a firm grip on the overhead branches. The water level continued to rise, capturing the branch in its teeth and bending it downstream. The branch bounced a bit as the captain repositioned himself more in the branch than under the branch. Stacy's foot slipped; she screamed and headed for the water. The captain launched his body sideways, positioning his right foot under Stacy. Maybe she could grab his leg. With Lilliputian fingers tightly wrapped around the overhead limb, she sprung back up onto the main branch. Eyes wide open and focused on her next step, Stacy paused, took a breath, and continued. She climbed through the leafy branch, ignoring the captain's urgings, and ten steps later, she stepped out onto the muddy bank.

The rain beat down harder than Stacy had ever experienced. She turned around and stared through the sheets of water at where the Mustang should have been. Then she followed an old branch that whipped through the newly formed rapids. When the branch vanished, her eyes exploded with horror. She took a big gulp of air and let out a deafening shrill. "Mommy!" She strained through the haze, longing to see the car somewhere down the creek. She saw nothing. A giant man scooped her up and carried her away from the water and then handed her to a female with a pretty smile and shiny earrings. She carried Stacy to a large square truck with flashing lights, wrapping her in a blanket along the way. She would wait, cold and bewildered.

Soon the door on the square truck opened unexpectedly, startling Stacy. "The rain stopped. The sun is shining. There's a big rainbow." He beckoned to Stacy to take a peek. Stacy recognized the big man as the one who had carried her up from the river. "Do you want to see the rainbow?" Stacy leaned forward and peered out of the door. She smiled.

"Do you know where your daddy is?" asked the pretty smile. She looked too young to be a professional, but her face was friendly. Stacy did not respond. The pretty smile continued to talk. Stacy could see her lips move but didn't hear anything else. Another blanket was brought and wrapped around her. And the big people kept talking in a buzz.

Stacy closed her eyes and curled up under the blankets. Big people would occasionally stroke her hair and say things to her, but Stacy paid little attention. Still huff huffing, she returned only a blank stare. Finally Stacy stopped shaking and made one simple request: "Find my daddy."

"We are trying, sweetheart. We're trying." The pretty smile with shiny earrings introduced herself. "My name is Heather. What's your name?"

"Stacy."

"Stacy. That's a pretty name. What's your last name?"

"Stacy Haistings. I want my daddy!" Her voice was soft and timid.

"Do you know where your daddy is?"

"He's an astronaut."

Heather turned toward the big man at the door and nodded as he wrote on a piece of paper. "Contact the Cape," she said, "and find Mr. Haistings. He'll want to be with his little girl."

Chapter Thirty-Five

"This is Delta, go ahead." Morgan's voice pierced the cabin. Colonel Anderson almost severed her spine reaching for the mike. The silence had been debilitating, stripping the crew of any hope. All confident expectation vaporized with the failed recovery of Major Lathem. The colonel had been secretly waiting for the next disaster. Now, with actual voice contact, hope returned.

"Delta, we need help! We have casualties. I repeat. We have casualties!" The words were fast, furious, and loud.

"This is Captain Morgan. Good to hear your voice, Colonel."

"You can't believe how good it is to hear yours. I thought you had forgotten us."

"Negative, ma'am. You are not forgotten."

"Where have you been? Why the break in communication?"

Answering her question quickly, he said, "Satellite issues. We lost two in a meteor shower. We've rerouted, but electrical storms are playing havoc." Then he requested, "Say again your count."

"I have one man dead and one missing."

"Life support status?"

"We have five days of water and food and just over three days of oxygen and power."

"Roger, Commander."

"Do we have any hope?" Why did she ask? The colonel knew the status of every ship in the fleet. She also knew they were a good forty days from any launch. There was no way her team could survive for another forty days. If she honestly thought about it, they were as good as dead. She needed to hope, even if it was illogical. "Captain Morgan, lie to me. Please, don't tell me no one's coming."

"Ma'am, a rescue team is coming. NASA has appropriated the X-102."

"The X-102?" The colonel's mind rifled through mental files. The X-102 sounded familiar. Newspaper clippings flashed through—a web article on the concept ship.

"Yes, ma'am. The X-102 is a commercial craft developed by TopAir International."

"I have read a few articles on the concept craft."

"Not just a concept any more. The X-102 will bring the team to Delta, where they will launch the *Lewis*. They should be at your doorstep in less than seventy-one hours."

Colonel Anderson's loud heartbeat pushed the oxygen-rich blood coursing through her body. Her head began to spin. She glanced up at her oxygen counter, trying not to overreact. "When do they launch?"

"They've launched, ma'am. If all goes well, their ETA is Thursday morning at zero seven hundred hours."

Colonel Anderson's body vibrated with excitement. Her exuberance should have charged the *Santa Maria*. It did not. Rogers looked up in anxious suspicion.

Amid great static, Morgan filled Anderson in on the plan and on the team that was coming.

"Bobby. Of course. He's the only one who really knows the *Lewis*."

"Yes, ma'am."

Colonel Anderson again looked at her oxygen supply counter, which read eighty-one hours, three minutes, and twenty-nine seconds and counting down. "We have a ten-hour window to play with."

"We can't promise future contact . . . will try to update you." The transmission was becoming more garbled.

Anderson fine-tuned the gain. "Try, Captain. We need the hope."

"Stay alive, Colonel."

"Come quickly."

She ended the transmission and turned back toward Rogers. "We'll be cutting it close." Rogers gave no confirming indication. "Mr. Rogers, do you understand what I'm saying?" Thirty seconds of blank stares followed.

The colonel snapped her fingers in Rogers's face twice. He responded through glassy eyes, "The hope is thin. They will never make it. They aren't coming."

"I prefer to believe they are."

"You can believe what you want. I'll believe it when I hear Bobby Haistings's voice coming from the *Lewis*."

Colonel Anderson returned to the communication desk and examined the oxygen counter again by tapping it three times. "Come on, Bobby. We are counting on you."

CHAPTER THIRTY-SIX

"This is Rescue One aboard the X-102 requesting docking instructions." Thompson was all business.

"This is Major Morgan, we read you loud and clear, Rescue One. You are right on schedule and approaching on plan. We are going to bring you in to D4. That's docking station four where we have made the adjustments for the X-102." Docking station four was on the opposite side from the *Hope* orbiter, allowing plenty of room to off-load the *Lewis*. "On my count, please give me a two-second burn on your starboard rockets for a twenty-three-degree right turn on your horizontal axis."

Rocket counted down and made the burn, turning the required distance. "Very good. Now give me a stop burn on your port. Perfect. Now, if you will fire reverse rockets, we'll do the rest."

"Roger, we are firing reverse rockets," replied Rocket. Thompson pushed two buttons simultaneously. The nose of the ship eased into a large doughnut ring that closed around it and hugged the TopAir craft tight against the space station. The round door on top of the X-102 matched up with a short tube from the platform. The tube being controlled by Morgan interlocked with the X-102. The hydraulic doors snapped open, revealing electrical, hydraulic, and life-support connections. The five hundred points of contact lined up perfectly. A green light went on in front of Morgan.

"You are clear to board."

Thompson cleared his throat and said, "Thank you."

Rocket secured the systems and shut down the X-102. Space Station Delta now provided basic life support and emergency lighting. Thompson turned to Haistings and said, "We have three hours to deploy the lunar craft. So I would suggest we get started."

Colonel Thompson led the way to the cargo bay. Upon entering, he gasped at the bulky size of the *Lewis*. "Wow, she is a big ship."

Floating in behind Thompson, Bobby replied, "That she is, Colonel. But her maneuverability far surpasses other ships."

"Amazing."

Thompson seemed almost giddy. Bobby hadn't seen Frank as a wide-eyed explorer in years. He had always assumed that ambition had trumped adventure somewhere between the Pentagon and Mission Control.

Thompson maneuvered into a spacewalk suit and clipped his safety line on the twenty-gage zip line running down the right side of the cargo bay.

"Dr. Kubo, where do you want us?" Bobby asked, after securing Thompson's helmet and sliding into his own suit.

"Captain Graham, you take the main doors and keep me clear on the right side. Major, if you could take the front left side, I'd appreciate it. Dr. Street, take the back left. Don't let me hit the landing pods. It will do us no good if you can't land the thing. I'll handle the arm."

Margo and Bobby hooked onto the left side zip line just as Rocket made it into the cargo bay. Rocket latched on to the right side and headed for the control panel. Thompson, already positioned in front of the panel, said, "I can handle the doors." With eagerness, Thompson lifted the six-inch control handle, moving it from locked and closed to unlocked and open. With a whoop and a thump followed by a loud hiss, the doors began to open.

"Whoa! Whoa! Whoa! Not yet, Rocket! Not yet!" Dr. Kubo yelled.

Bobby peeked underneath the *Lewis* just in time to see Rocket body check the colonel, pushing him out of the way. The doors closed and locked. "I beg your pardon, Colonel, but there are shipping braces that need to be removed before we can open the doors."

Bobby winced. *This could be trouble.*

Thompson turned away from Rocket, making a fist with his thickly gloved hand. Bobby thought he heard the colonel's molars milling as he spun back around, going helmet to helmet with the captain. "Don't you ever handle me like that again! Do you understand me, Captain?"

Thompson went off on a tirade about his superior rank and intellect. It was a new song only to Margo. After a string of colorful metaphors, Thompson went on to blame Dr. Kubo for not being more prepared and the rest of the team for being slow.

"I'm sorry, sir. But it's just . . ."

"There is no 'but,' Captain. Be advised, you are on my short list."

"What's the problem, gentlemen?" Bobby was not interested in another verse of the old song.

"We're okay, Bobby. I just got a little anxious."

"Well, simmer down. We need to remove all the restraints, and now we need to inspect for damage. We need to be thorough, but we need to be quick. The clock is ticking."

The restraints were large padded braces held in place by over-center locking latches. The locks were disengaged with the press of a button; the latches were released with a tug and a pull. The colonel floated up and released the two restraints topside, while the rest of the team released and removed the other restraints. Dr. Kubo called, "All clear?"

"We are clear on the top!" informed the colonel. "No damage."

"Clear on the right," Rocket reported.

"Clear on the left," Bobby added.

"We are all clear," Thompson commanded.

"Open the doors," Dr. Kubo instructed.

With a whomp and a thump followed by a loud hiss, the doors began to open again. Pop! "Whoa, whoa, whoa, back her up," Dr. Kubo instructed.

Rocket closed the doors once again. Gazing up, he saw the top restraints still in place. "Hey, Colonel, could you go ahead and remove the restraints?"

"Captain, this is your responsibility. I have more important things to do than just babysit you." The colonel turned away from Rocket to address Bobby. "Major, I'll brief Morgan on our timetable. Please alert me when you have unloaded the *Lewis*." The colonel unhooked himself from the safety line and moved hand over hand toward the bulkhead doorway. The team watched in silence. They waited for him to transfer and the doors to close behind him. Then they all breathed a great sigh of relief.

Rocket shook his head in disbelief. "He's going to get us all killed."

"He'll be okay. He's just anxious," explained Bobby.

"Don't make excuses for him, Bobby."

"I'm not. But it has been a while since he's flown in space."

Margo looked at Rocket and then over to Bobby. "Is there something I need to know?"

"We are flying into deep space," added Kubo. "We need to be able to trust each other. Do we have a trust issue?"

"I've got a trust issue," said Rocket. "Bobby, you are going to have to keep an eye on the colonel."

"Check and double check," said Bobby. "We all need to keep our eyes open."

"Let's get busy." Dr. Kubo's voice echoed in their helmets.

The doors finally opened wide, with Dr. Kubo handling the boom arm that had been attached before liftoff. With a joystick in each hand, Dr. Kubo controlled the speed with his left hand and the direction with his right.

As the *Lewis* cleared the X-102's doors, Margo caught a glimpse of the Earth. "Wow!"

"Congratulations, Dr. Street," Rocket offered.

"Margo, please."

"Congratulations, Miss Margo. Few humans have ever experienced this scene. You are looking at the earth from 240 miles above the Pacific."

"Amazing." Three or four small meteors shot by the space station within one hundred meters and burned up in the Earth's atmosphere.

Bam! A small stone ricocheted off the nose of the *Lewis.*

Margo grabbed her tether line with both hands. She was no longer comfortable floating independent of the ship. Her heart raced, but she managed a smile.

Rocket grinned. "Miss Margo, as soon as the *Lewis* is docked with the station, you can prep your equipment while we disconnect the arm."

"Thank you." Margo moved forward quickly. Unhooking her tether line after moving through the bulkhead doors, she glided to the forward cargo bay and began inspecting the few pieces of geological equipment that were not already on the *Lewis,* including two lunar sensors with optics and a new high-tech core drill. However, it was the two unmarked crates aboard the *Lewis* that she was most anxious to inspect.

CHAPTER THIRTY-SEVEN

Once on Space Station Delta, a research lab orbiting earth, Margo took a quick look around. Feeling inquisitive, she entered the day room. Two magnetic chessboards on game tables and a poker table sat in the middle of the room, arranged in a triangle. To her right was a small kitchenette with a microwave, a refrigerator, and a pressurized coffee pot; a door leading to unknown places; and a large world relief map that covered half the wall. It was nothing special; she had seen thousands before.

On the opposite side of the room sat two exercise bikes and a rowing machine. In the corner, two muscle retention suits hung limp. Muscle atrophy posed a threat to long-term space exploration. Enlisting the help of thousands of rubber bands, the muscle retention suits created just enough tension to mimic earth's gravity. Morgan had his team on a daily routine.

When Margo's eye caught the curtain on the far wall, her curiosity leaped. She pulled back the drape and gasped. Millions of stars with a slice of the Earth in the bottom right corner appeared in the large picture window. She stood there in a daze, appreciating the aesthetic moment.

She nearly jumped out of her skin when she felt someone breathing down her neck. His breath was hot, and his cologne was familiar. What a joy.

"Have you ever made love with a view like that?" Thompson asked, wrapping his arms around her waist. Street was immediately thankful for her one-piece flight suit that zippered to the neck. Street grabbed his little finger and pulled it back to his wrist, providing persuasive motivation.

"I think it's time to leave." Margo headed for the door. Thompson grabbed her arm and swung her around. She faced the window again. Thompson floated behind her, holding each arm at the elbow.

"Come on, sweetheart, we might as well make the most of our opportunities."

"Back off," she barked, loud and angry, but Thompson tightened his grip.

"I don't think you really want me to do that." Thompson pulled her body into his.

"I think she does," Bobby interrupted. His muscular frame filled the door. Arms hanging limp at his side with his shoulders square, he surveyed the room. Just as he had remembered, the room even smelled the same—stale coffee and burnt popcorn.

"Major, the clock is ticking. You have work to do."

"No. We are good until launch." Bobby never took his eyes off Thompson.

"Good, now you're dismissed." His demeaning tone irritated Bobby. Street finally broke free and leaped over next to Bobby. Thompson, in close pursuit, grabbed her by the arm. Bobby gripped Thompson's left arm with his right hand and twisted it clockwise, causing pressure on Thompson's left elbow. Then, with a light shove, he pushed him back. Thompson's face turned beet red. The large artery on the side of his neck ballooned out. He regained his up-and-down perspective and placed himself eyeball to eyeball with Bobby.

Bobby turned and winked at Margo. "If Samson could kill a thousand Philistines with the jawbone of an ass, I can take care of one ass."

"And you wonder why you've never made colonel."

"No, sir, I don't wonder at all."

Morgan's voice on the intercom interrupted the feud. Colonel Thompson was needed in the debriefing room.

Thompson moved toward the door, brushing up against Bobby just enough to knock him back. "The time is coming." He then leaned toward Margo. "The time will come for us as well."

CHAPTER THIRTY-EIGHT

The stars looked bigger and closer than Margo had ever imagined. The earth was sharp and clear. A hurricane blew off the coast of South America, and two more storms were lining up off the west coast of Africa. Margo couldn't deny the magnificence.

"For what it's worth, thanks." Her breathing had slowed with Thompson's exit. She was now alone with Bobby in the day room.

"No worries."

Turning toward the window, Bobby's eyes widened. The sun now rested behind the space station, making the expanse of stars mind-boggling. "You know, Margo, when you see the universe from this perspective, the Earth seems small and insignificant."

They stared out into the universe in quiet awe for a long time. Then Bobby asked, "Have you seen the latest Hubble pictures?"

"Yes, they stretch your comprehension."

"Astronomers tell us that our solar system is one of billions in a crowded universe." With laserlike focus, Bobby stared deep into space.

"That's what they say."

"What are the odds that we are alone?" asked Bobby.

"Small. The odds are favorable that somewhere among all the millions of other solar systems, there is another planet sustaining life." Margo's mind drifted off into a far corner of the universe.

160

"What are the odds of all this happening by chance?"

Margo returned her attention to Bobby. "What's the alternative?"

"Design."

"I don't buy it." She seemed almost perturbed. "As awesome as this is, I still see no need to jump to some kind of religious conclusion. As a geologist, I have studied the Earth for years and I just don't see how intelligent people can take such huge leaps."

Bobby smirked, "After looking deep into space, both Hubble and Einstein, men smarter than me, saw clear evidence of design."

"It just doesn't work for me."

"What doesn't work?"

Margo ignored his question and leaned in toward the window to look back at planet Earth. Her eyes were drawn first to the east coast of Florida. Clouds obstructed any view of the cape. Her eyes moved north to DC and then west. Not yet visible, she imagined what the western states would look like. Then she waved.

"What are you doing?" Bobby wondered out loud.

"Just in case someone is watching."

Bobby's watch beeped, and he smiled, "We are in a sleep period, Margo."

"See you in six hours." Margo exited the room, slipped into her berth, and slid into her bunk as Bobby disappeared into the crew quarters. Only seconds had ticked by before she saw his long nose hair protruding from his nasal cavity. Margo indignantly said, "Good night, Colonel."

Thompson eased down onto the bunk and placed his left hand on her hip. "You still owe me. We made a deal. You're on the mission. I expect the favor to be returned."

Margo sat up, pushing Thompson into an upright position. "Sir, if you grab me one more time, I will slap you into tomorrow."

"Choices, Dr. Street. Let's not forget our choices."

"Leave, Colonel."

Thompson grabbed Street by the back of the neck and began to draw her in for a kiss. Street rammed her right knee into his crotch, slipped her left arm under his right arm, and rolled his shoulder over—his head dove for the floor. In the microsecond that it took for Margo to force Thompson to the floor, she braced her foot against her bunk, retrieved a teardrop-shaped knife from her belt buckle, and put the blade to Thompson's throat, piercing only the first two layers of skin. "Was that good for you?"

Unable to look Margo in the eye, Thompson replied, "We're good, for now."

Street released the colonel and climbed back into her bunk. "Good night, Colonel." Margo rolled away and faced the wall. Thompson left without a word.

As Street dozed off, she felt someone looking at her. She bolted up, ready for another fight.

"Excuse me, Margo." Surprised and embarrassed by Street's reaction, Rocket jerked back. "I didn't mean to startle you."

"What is it, Rocket?" she asked with a perturbed sigh.

"Well, I just wanted to make sure you were okay, this being your first space trip. Can I get you anything? Have you seen the picture window yet? The sun is going to peek around the Earth in five hours. You don't want to miss a once-in-a-lifetime sunrise." Rocket forced a quick pause. "Would you like me to wake you?"

"Do you always talk so fast without giving the other person a chance to speak?" Rocket turned away to hide the blush. Margo smiled. "We have work to do. We need to do it."

"Yes, ma'am. But this won't interfere with our mission. It's just a peek at glory."

"Just a peek, nothing more?"

Rocket smiled big. "Just a peek."

"You're on, but now let me get some sleep."

"I'll be back in five hours."

Margo drifted off to sleep, thinking, "Never get attached to people you may have to kill."

CHAPTER THIRTY-NINE

"Colonel, can we repair this ship?" Mr. Rogers didn't know why he had given up so quickly on the *Santa Maria*.

"You saw the skewered computer as well as I did," Anderson whispered.

"Maybe we are looking at this wrong. Life support is up and running."

Anderson tilted in for more.

"It's quad-redundant," he explained. "We have four different computer systems. If we lose one, we still have three more. Maybe we have enough. Maybe we could free the ship from the rift and head home on our own power. We need to check. We have to try," pleaded Rogers.

Andy Rogers moved into Marty's seat and ran the quad-redundant through a systems check. "Colonel, the triplet is down, but the final quad computer is up and running." He swallowed hard. "It is doing what it was built to do. The quad computer has taken over. That's why life support is up and running."

Anderson's eyes widened in anticipation, "We have hope. I don't know why I didn't think of this earlier. Mr. Rogers, we don't have to wait for a rescue."

Andy Rogers kept typing—no exuberance and no expression. He just kept typing. The colonel zeroed in on Mr. Rogers's face.

She couldn't look at the screen. Her heart sank when she saw perspiration rise on Mr. Rogers's forehead.

"What is it?"

"It's our navigational system. When the number one computer was punctured, it was hit in the navigational hub." All four computers connected at the hub. "All four were shorted out."

"Is it repairable? Can we fix it?"

"It's hardware, Colonel. You saw it yourself." Rogers massaged his neck. His breathing seemed labored. "We can't just wait here to die. I want to fight." He turned to Anderson: "If I have to die, I want to die trying something. I'd rather try to eyeball it home than sit here and wait for death."

Anderson forced a light cough. "The odds of eyeballing it home are zero to none."

"I know, but don't you want to try something?"

"I do. But if rescue is on the way, I don't want to miss them."

"That's a big 'if,' Colonel." Rogers rubbed the side of his ribcage. "Let's keep trying to make contact. But if we find out they are not coming, I say we try something." Rogers winced in pain.

"Are you okay?"

Rogers shook his head and craned his torso. "It's my chest. Breathing hurts."

Stifled, Colonel Anderson leaned over closer to Mr. Rogers and unsnapped his suit down below his sternum. Anderson swayed back. It looked bad. The left side of his chest had a charcoal ring with just a hint of Prussian blue and purple that feathered out into three shades of yellow around the edges. Colonel Anderson felt her legs begin to quiver.

"What happened? When did it happen?"

"When I was jerked out of the rift, I landed hard on a large rock."

"Why didn't you say something?"

"Marty's legs were broken. It was no big deal. I was just happy to be alive."

Colonel Anderson took a big gulp of air and tried to maintain some objectivity. "Well, let's hope it's not a big deal." She gently examined his ribs. "I'm guessing a couple broken ribs, so try to stay still." Any hope of freeing the *Santa Maria* depended on Rogers's health and ability to help. That hope was fading fast. Profound isolation swept over the colonel like a drug-induced rush. Her eyes sunk deep as her fingers combed through the short, gray, permed hair on the sides of her head. Her composure slipped severely. She knew her reason would begin a free fall.

Colonel Anderson forced herself to sit up straight. With both hands now resting palms down on the console, she began a series of controlled breaths.

Rogers sat back up. "Colonel, it's hardware, right?"

"What is?"

"Our problem is hardware. The navigational module in the triplet has been damaged."

"Go on."

"Didn't we disconnect the number two computer's navigational system to silence the alarm?"

"We did."

Rogers squirmed in his seat, trying to find a position of comfort. "Maybe it's not fried. Can't we cannibalize that navigational module and exchange it for the module in the quad computer?" Hope reentered the *Santa Maria*.

CHAPTER FORTY

The air stood still, thin and crisp. Glassy-eyed creatures of the forest lined the mountain road, singing their songs. The deep blue sky contained only the lone early evening star that shone brightly on the black SUV as it approached the Cheyenne Mountain Complex. The ground squirrels chattered as a big buck in velvet, with three does in tow, darted across the road just in front of the transport. From a distance, the mouth looked like no more than a highway tunnel. But this was no tunnel.

"Why did I come?" He was busy. Rescue One orbited the Earth preparing for the Moon. He resented the distraction. He worried about revelation.

"Because four stars beats two, sir." The driver never took his eyes off the road.

The SUV stopped at the mouth, and General Buchholz exited the vehicle and climbed directly into the front right seat of the four-seat golf cart being driven by Sergeant Reed.

"Sir, I'll take you the rest of the way." With hands shaking, Buchholz wiped his head with his handkerchief. Senior Master Sergeant Reed smiled. "It can be a little claustrophobic." Buchholz continued to take in the tunnel. "Sir, have you been to Cheyenne Mountain before?"

The general's eyes darted about; his skin turned clammy, and his breathing turned erratic. "Sir, are you okay?"

General Buchholz pulled his tie loose and unfastened the top button. Exhaling hard, he said, "I'm okay. And yes, I've been here before." He checked his cell phone for messages.

"Sir, cell phones don't work in the mountain."

Cheyenne Mountain housed NORAD deep within granite walls. Divided into the four areas of space control, missile warning, battle management, and the combined intelligence watch centers, NORAD was a sophisticated underground complex linking a worldwide network of US radar and other high-tech electronic sensors capable of detecting, assessing, and implementing a response. General Buchholz had been in contact with the Space Control Centre, which kept a close watch on NASA and other space exploration regardless of origin. NORAD sponsored the lunar outpost with extreme interest.

As they passed the two thirty-ton blast doors, General Buchholz wiped the sweat from the back of his neck. *What did they know? How would they know anything unless someone talked? Thompson's mouth ran a little wild in the presence of women. Maybe he screwed it up. Could he be that stupid? How else would they know? Surveillance. Who's watching? How long have they been watching?*

The general's mind went back to a rainy afternoon in the South Island Inn on Key Largo. They were all careful to use proven evasion tactics.

Colonel Thompson arrived last. The sun had come out and now beamed through the open blinds into a room filled with nervous laughter. He shut the door behind Thompson and then slowly pulled a small black bag from his briefcase and laid it on the table. *I should have shut the blinds . . . Why didn't I shut the blinds?*

The occasion had called for a celebration. Ignoring the ban that outlawed smoking in public buildings and had turned most of his cigars into pacifiers, he had pulled a new *Montecristo* from his travel humidor and then held a flame to the outside edge of the foot and rotated the cigar to evenly toast the edge. It was a ritual he relished. *I could use a cigar right now.* After the outer wrapper and binder turned ashen, he clipped off the end and eased the cigar between his lips, giving it two spins. It was always two spins. Then, using a second match, he held the flame about a half an inch from the cigar and rotated the cigar as he drew in the fire. With a puff and a flame the cigar was lit. He loved a good cigar. *Why didn't I shut the blinds?*

"At a thousand dollars a gram minimum, this one bag is worth over four billion dollars." He opened the bag and poured out the clear crystals onto the table. Looking more like quartz than diamonds, they didn't look valuable.

"While slicing the lunar core samples brought back by Survey I, my nephew Rodney"—Buchholz nodded toward his nephew who sat on the bed—"a NASA lab tech, came upon a large piece of what looked like broken glass but had the molecular structure of gold—clear gold.

"A paper-thin lens placed on a penlight can cut through a ten-centimeter steel plate," Buchholz had explained. "We have only begun to dream about its applications for energy production. The laser weaponry alone could change the world."

What did they know? How much did they know? *I should have closed the curtains.*

CHAPTER FORTY-ONE

General Buchholz continued to sweat. No words were exchanged, but many thoughts were explored as the golf cart made its way down the narrow corridor to the Space Control Centre. The cart stopped with a squeak, and Buchholz unloaded into the firm handshake of four-star General Albert Bermen, a six-foot-five-inch 260-pound monster of a man with a kind, gentle voice.

"Good to see you, Lee."

"Albert."

"Thanks for coming." As if he had a choice.

"What's up?"

"Come into my office and have a seat." The office wasn't actually his; he had taken it over under the circumstances.

The two men strolled across the concrete floor past the windowless concrete walls and through another heavy steel door. The office lay sparsely decorated with a single family photo sitting on the cherrywood credenza next to a crystal candy dish filled with peppermints. The matching desk sat on a twelve-by-twelve foot Persian rug with a busy floral pattern. The opposite wall held an eighty-four-inch flat screen showing the white dome of a computer-controlled fifty-inch Boller & Chivens telescope with high-quality Ritchey optics.

With a kind hand gesture, the general offered, "Have a seat."

Buchholz sat in a burgundy leather wingback chair. General Bermen took his chair behind the desk and said, "What's the status of Rescue One?"

Buchholz stared suspiciously, pulling a cigar from his inside coat pocket. Bermen didn't blink. "You can suck on that, but don't light it." The cigar slid back into the pocket. His misgivings intensified.

"General, we need your help. Rescue One must succeed."

That's odd. "Yes, sir. We plan to do everything possible to recover the crew of the *Santa Maria.*"

"Excellent. But the *Santa Maria* is no longer your primary mission."

General Buchholz stared into the eyes of Bermen, looking for a clue. Eyes thinned; teeth clamped. "What's this all about?"

Bermen grabbed the remote control off his desk, stood to his feet, and gestured with his free hand, "Step over to the flat screen . . . please." The words came out gently, but they were not a request.

Buchholz stood up and did a U-turn around the wingback and found himself standing in front of the flat screen. "This is the Manastash Ridge Observatory in Washington State—one of many at our disposal."

"What does this have to do with Rescue One?"

"That's a fair question. My point is we watch—everything." General Bermen reached over his desk and pressed a red button located just under the lip. The buzzer sounded, opening a portion of the wall adjacent to the flat screen. The wall sunk in and slid into a pocket. Buchholz moved into a small, dimly lit room where the air was stale and a lone technician sat behind a deck of computers. Above the computers flashed another flat screen taking up the entire wall. A magnificent live shot of the lunar surface looking like a bloodshot eye stared back.

"Is that our moon?"

The young technician with pale skin and a full set of luggage under each eye sat transfixed. A trash can full of empty Coke cans explained a lot. His long slender fingers plowed through his black oily hair quickly and then made an attempt to tuck in his shirt.

Stepping out of the dark corner stood a young nondescript man with light brown hair and a clean shave. He had the kind of face that blended into a crowd. Nothing stood out. His charcoal gray suit said "Government." He extended his hand to General Buchholz and said, "Maxwell, NSA."

Buchholz shook his hand, shifting his eyes back and forth between the unmatched trio. "Somebody want to tell me what the hell is going on? Why am I standing in Cheyenne Mountain with the head of the Space Control Centre, an agent of the National Security Agency, and an overworked technician?" The technician smiled in agreement. He finished another Coke and then crushed the can in his hand.

Bermen and Maxwell exchanged several apprehensive glances. Finally Bermen spoke to Maxwell. "Success requires shared information." Maxwell stared hard at Buchholz, sizing him up.

"What information?" Buchholz's voice was loud and agitated.

Maxwell moved up close to Bermen. "Careful."

"General, we are here to explain." He nodded toward the young airman. "Take a look at these pictures," Bermen asked.

The technician moved his curser to Run Slide Show and a beautiful harvest moon appeared on the screen. "That was the Moon one year ago." The next slide showed the same angle but with two faint fault lines running parallel down the center of the moonscape. "That was the Moon three months ago."

The next slide showed the Moon from the same angle but with active volcanic activity. "That was three days ago. More than two hundred peaks have erupted."

"So you think the Moon is breaking up? You think we should scrub the mission?"

"Not at all."

"So what's your point?

"Take a look at this peak on Mare Crisium's rim." Bermen painted the rim with a laser pointer.

The video began to run, showing a new peak, designated mc7, about five kilometers east of the *Santa Maria*. It swelled in seconds. "This is real time." The peak erupted! In the midst of the fire and lava, thousands of sparks took flight. "Keep watching the sparks." Most died out but a large number just kept going. "Within the group, there are forty sparks with a slightly different hue flying directly toward the earth."

A new angle was addressed that recorded the sparks' journey toward earth. "Notice the two on the outside. They actually speed up."

"What is this?"

"They made the trip to Earth in eight minutes."

Buchholz's head spun. "What am I seeing?"

"Now watch as they hit Earth's atmosphere," Bermen instructed. The picture shifted to a ground base shot looking up into the sky. All forty sparks came through and into view and then disappeared.

"They burned up on entry?" Buchholz offered.

"We don't think so. We had them in sight, then nothing."

"Did you track them on radar?"

Bermen's eyes narrowed. "Our radar *never* saw them."

"So what are we talking about here?"

Bermen sat up quickly, rubbed his nose and then his chin. "We aren't ready to say."

"What are you ready to say?"

"We need your team to deploy not only the lunar sensors but three lunar satellites."

"Spy satellites? I think it is a grave mistake to get NASA involved in the spy business."

"You're already involved. You just don't know it," Maxwell said smugly. "Why do you think it was so easy for your man to gain control of the Omega Satellite System?" Maxwell's voice was condescending. "Why did Bonham loan you a five-billion-dollar aircraft, may his soul rest in peace? Bonham was no patriot. He was a money hungry, enterprising vulture who preyed on the egos of the wealthy."

"Bonham's dead?"

Maxwell grimaced with an inadvertent wink and said, "Accident."

"Is that what happened to Miller?"

"Accidents happen."

Buchholz pulled on his loose tie, raised his eyebrows, and said, "We have already launched, but you know that by now. So what's the point of this conversation?"

"We have an agent on board who will deploy our equipment. We need you to make sure they make it into lunar orbit. You can't let them pull out."

"One of my crew members works for NSA?" General Buchholz locked eyes with Maxwell. Buchholz's jaw stiffened, and his lips pinched together. The vein on his forehead pulsed. Maxwell looked calm; his face relaxed; he smiled as if posing for a picture. "Who?" demanded Buchholz.

Maxwell closed his smile and rubbed his top teeth with his tongue. "'Who' is not important. What's important is that they be successful. The security of our nation—the security of our entire planet may be at risk."

"Lee," Bermen interrupted, "we need you to get your team into lunar orbit so they can deploy the equipment. I hope you can get your team back, but we must deploy the satellites and sensors."

"What is this really about?" Buchholz's mind churned. "If it's not about spying, why the secrecy? What do you hope to see?"

"Best case scenario—nothing but an unstable lunar surface. Worst case scenario—a staging ground, a hotbed of extraterrestrial activity. If they are gathering on the Moon, we need to find out why. We need data and we need it fast. Your team must succeed."

Bermen stood with Buchholz. "Lee, I know it's a lot to process. But I need you on this one. Don't let me down." Buchholz turned away. "I need you to keep a lid on this. If word gets out, martial law will not be enough to control the panic."

Maxwell grabbed General Buchholz's right forearm just before he passed through the threshold. Buchholz glared; Maxwell smiled. "We'll be watching."

CHAPTER FORTY-TWO

It was a risk. The higher anxiety that accompanied going out again would expend more oxygen, not to mention the possibility of further injury. Going out onto an unstable lunar surface was not safe.

But any real chance of going home in their own power required going out and cannibalizing the navigational module's motherboard from the number two computer and using it to replace the board in the quad-redundant.

As her foot touched down into lunar dirt, extreme trepidation rippled through Anderson's head and down her spine. Rogers was already kneeling beneath the underbelly of the ship. With tool in hand, he unscrewed the thirty-two fasteners that held the protective cover snug against the ship. "I need some light, Colonel."

Anderson knelt beside Rogers and shot a beam from her flashlight. "Here you go."

Once the panel was removed, the guts of the number two computer were exposed. Rogers studied the unit for a few seconds before it all went dark.

He turned toward the colonel for help. Anderson swept the beam over the lunar landscape in a rapid side-to-side motion. Perplexed, Rogers asked, "What are you looking for?"

Anderson did not respond immediately. She kept the light moving, her breathing accelerated.

"Colonel?"

Still nothing. Then something. She said, "I thought I might have seen something . . . I guess not . . . It was nothing." Her skin had turned ashen, and her eyes looked disturbed.

After another aftershock, Anderson shot the flame of light back onto the inner workings of the number two computer. Careful examination brought Anderson's heart to a near standstill. The navigational motherboard was held in place by six very small Phillip's head screws. Removing and replacing internal computer hardware from outside the command module was not on NASA's to-do list. Disconnecting the electrical connectors was going to be tricky enough. Removing the screws without damaging the board would be a Herculean task given the clumsy gloves in which they had to work. Anderson looked at Rogers. "Any suggestions?"

"Cautious precision."

"I'll pray."

With gentle persuasion, Rogers removed the first two screws before it went dark again. Anderson was searching the crevasse. Rogers lost light two more times before freeing the board.

"I keep seeing something move in my peripheral vision," explained Anderson.

"I'm not seeing anything," Rogers complained, "but I feel something coming." They held on to the ship and waited for the vibrations to stop.

"Let's pick up our pace," encouraged Anderson. "I want to get out of here."

Rogers moved quickly to the quad excess panel. "Keeping that light on me would help."

With his left knee in lunar dust and his right leg extended down into the rift, Rogers removed the panel. He found that the navigational board had a burn mark running through the middle of it. "That won't work at all." He had the board out before it went dark again.

"I'm telling you, something is out here." Kim flashed the light back at the quad. "How can I speed this up?"

Rogers said, "Hold the screws, and keep the light up here."

With the board replaced and the panel reconnected, they headed for the stairs. "We are going home, Mr. Rogers."

"Yes, we are, Colonel Anderson."

Anderson glanced to her right, only to see a kinked oxygen line. It didn't appear to be ruptured—yet. One more, strong aftershock might be their doom. "Let's move."

CHAPTER FORTY-THREE

"Where you headed, Rocket?"

Rocket startled upright, smacking his head on the corner of his bunk. The moonlight illumined Bobby's face; his eyes were still closed as he lay on his pillow. Rocket hesitated. "Rocket, we don't have time for nonsense."

"She's not nonsense."

"I know you, Rocket. I've seen the way you look at her. What I can't figure out is why. She's an astronaut wannabe who seduced Thompson to get on board what might be her only chance of going to space. I'm guessing the woman has issues, Rocket." Bobby sat up straight.

"Who made you judge?" Rocket floated down to eye level.

"Not judge, just observer."

"What do you observe?"

"Rocket, you've always been attracted to strays."

"What are you talking about?"

"College. Every girl you dated was a wounded heart. Most had more baggage than Samsonite."

"Kinda like you."

Bobby stretched out on his bunk. "Yeah, like me."

Rocket paused at the bulkhead door. "I'm not stupid, Bobby."

"I know, Rocket. I'm on edge. Something's not right." Coming up on his elbow again, Bobby added, "I've seen . . . there's . . ."

"What?"

"Bad mojo."

"Mojo?"

Bobby cocked his head. "Bad mojo."

"You haven't used that word since we were kids."

"I know. But I can't think of another word to explain how I feel. It's strange. Strange things, Rocket. At times I feel like I'm being . . . watched."

"Okay, okay. Thanks for the update."

"Film at eleven."

Rocket turned to leave as Bobby's eyes drifted shut again. "These are dangerous times, Rocket, don't let your heart screw with your head."

Rocket glared back at his best friend and said, "Don't let your head forget your heart."

Moving out of the crew compartment alone, Rocket made his way down the corridor, stopping just outside Margo's cubbyhole.

"Rise and shine, Miss Margo."

She really didn't remember sleeping, but Rocket was back at her side shaking her arm.

"Come on, now, or we'll miss it."

Margo forced herself up. They moved across the hall and into the dimly lit room. Only a small under-counter light in the kitchenette shone. Rocket grabbed two bags of coffee from the microwave and clumsily handed Margo one of them. He grinned, she yawned, and they stared out the window.

In the darkness, the Earth began to take on a light ring. Then, ever so slowly, more and more light burst from the right-hand side of the sphere. Splashes of bright white and yellow light erupted in the window. Margo leaned toward Rocket, who reacted in kind. Rocket's heart throbbed against his ribs. His eyes were fixed, not on the window, but on Margo. Her soft auburn hair against her smooth tanned skin struck him dumbfounded. He watched the sunrise in her eyes and wondered what the future might hold.

Curious about everything, Margo asked about stars and constellations; she wondered about planets and galaxies. Rocket relished the ability to answer her questions.

"Wow. Did you see that?" She asked. A huge meteor blazed by in the direction of Earth. Then another and another then hundreds lit up space.

Eyes glued to the window, "I've never seen anything like it, Margo."

Margo's hands began to shake. The shaking moved up her arms and rattled her core. She pushed away from the window, smelling death and feeling sick. Fear squeezed her mind. She wanted to leave. She turned away and pleaded with Rocket to close the curtains. Rocket paused with the curtain in his hand as the meteors stopped. One final light crossed his range of vision, seeming to slow down. Then it was gone. *Bad mojo?*

"Something is out there, Rocket, something wicked. We aren't safe."

"We're safe enough."

"We aren't alone."

"I'm open to that possibility."

Margo squeezed out a hesitant grin. "Extraterrestrial life?"

Rocket squared his body toward Margo; his eyes sparkled. "Listen, since the beginning of time, man has placed his confidence in truth that worked for a while and then crashed and burned. There was a time when we thought the earth was flat, and that belief worked until we expanded our horizons. There was a time when we thought the universe revolved around us, and it worked until we expanded our horizons. There was a time when we thought the atom was the smallest entity. And that worked for us until . . ."

"We expanded our horizons. What's your point?"

"True truth—that which corresponds to reality—will stand forever. I have no interest in placing my confidence or my life in a belief system that changes as more facts become available."

"And you know this system that doesn't change with time?"

"As a matter of fact."

The clarion sounded, and they were jolted back to the reality of a rescue mission that was falling behind. Could they repair the *Lewis* in time?

CHAPTER FORTY-FOUR

Bobby shook his head. "You have got to be kidding." After the sleep period, Bobby found the team in the prep room. They needed to get Dr. Kubo into a space suit for a walk.

"You said 'check and recheck.' I did," explained Dr. Kubo. "One bolt on the topside jet of the *Lewis* was damaged in the off load." No one said it out loud, but everyone knew it was Colonel Thompson's failure to remove the brace that had caused the damage. Now it had to be replaced.

The unscheduled maintenance threatened the timetable and made everyone uneasy. "A little help would be nice." Dr. Kubo couldn't reach his helmet after securing his shoulder clamps.

Thompson entered the transfer station, ricocheting off the wall panels. He surveyed the now silent room. Everyone stared at Thompson as a jury might stare at the accused. Bobby went back to work helping Dr. Kubo secure the suit. Eight hands checked and rechecked all systems.

Thompson gave a half-hearted look at the suit to see that all the hoses and straps were in place. "Just get the jet back in place and bolt it down. Then get back in here . . . We are on a time schedule, and we are starting to fall behind." If everything went according to plan they would only fall behind by about three hours. Their ten-hour window would be cut to seven. Bobby lowered the helmet onto Dr. Kubo's head, turning forty-five degrees to secure it in place. Bobby tapped on his head and asked, "Are you ready?"

"Yes, sir."

"Check communications," came the words from Rocket, who adjusted the keyboard that would keep them in touch.

"Check one, check two, check three." Everyone heard him.

"We gotcha," Rocket confirmed.

"Okay, let's go," Thompson commanded. He moved around in front of Kubo to gain his attention and explained the two-jet system. Coming from each elbow was a fourteen-inch cord. At the end of each cord was a control button that could be held in each hand. The right-hand control button controlled the right side jet, and the left-hand control button controlled the left jet. Pressing them at the same time propelled you forward. Pressing them one at a time turned you. Never press them for more than a three-second blast, and stay close to the ship. Kubo took it all in, staring at the two red plungers in his hands.

"I've tested them before," explained Dr. Kubo.

Thompson smiled, "I understand. This being your first real space walk, I need you to focus. Pay attention to your work, and don't snag your suit."

"I'm good to go, Colonel."

Bobby flipped the toggle switch on the control panel that opened a large hydraulic door. Dr. Kubo stepped into the small room and the doors closed behind him. Morgan then began to take away atmosphere. Bobby watched the dial go to zero.

"Stand clear. The doors are opening," Morgan warned. Bobby then pressed a series of eight buttons, which unlocked and opened the exterior doors. The doctor drifted out.

Using the handheld controls like a seasoned explorer, he glided over to the *Lewis* like a dandelion puff on a gentle breeze. Nothing else seemed to move. Only nervous breathing could be heard.

Back inside Delta, the team watched silently until Dr. Kubo reached the *Lewis*. Margo pushed away from her vantage point on the port-side observation post and whispered, "How long should this take?"

"Hard to say." Bobby glanced at his watch. "From this point, it shouldn't take Dr. Kubo more than another hour."

"We can't afford for it to take more than an hour," added Thompson. "I'm estimating a four-hour loss as it is." Thompson was rounding up, but Dr. Kubo's prep did take longer than anticipated.

Thirty-five minutes later, Thompson asked, "How ya coming out there?"

"Just fine. I've got the jet back in place and flush with the mount, but I'm having trouble with the bolt."

"Just focus, and get it done. We are falling behind," barked Thompson.

Rocket watched Dr. Kubo's vitals spike. "Hey, Doc, try to relax and control your breathing."

"I'm trying."

"You're doing fine," added Bobby.

"Hey, can any of you see the solar panel?"

"Negative." Bobby pressed himself against the view window. "The solar panel is out of our field of vision. Why? Something wrong?"

"No. Not necessarily. There's a strange light next to the panel."

Bobby narrowed his eyes and looked harder. "It's probably just the moonlight reflecting *off* the panel."

"Yeah, maybe."

Rocket leaned toward Bobby and whispered, "Bad mojo?"

"There. The bolt is in place. Now all I need to do is get this nut started." His heavy gloves impaired his movements. After a few anxious moments, the nut bit the threads. *Now, tighten the nut down.* Moving in slow motion, he worked the nut.

With a grunt, Dr. Kubo tightened the nut and then placed the large cotter pin through the core. Then, using needle nose pliers, he bent the two ends back in the opposite direction, securing the jet. "I've got it. Mission complete."

He spun himself around to face Delta once again and fired his hand jet to move him back inside.

As Dr. Kubo hit the transfer door, he grabbed the handrail next to the door and spun around one more time to check his work. "Boy, I do good—"

Blam! A seam in his space suit split, shredding his suit and sending the doctor into a spiral.

"Doc!" Hot plasma exploded in Bobby's brain. "Get him back in here."

Rocket looked up at Dr. Kubo's vitals on the monitoring board. He had flat lined. He had no vitals. "It's too late. He's gone." Rocket rang the alarm, sending the Delta crew to their stations.

Bobby closed his eyes and leaned on the window in disbelief. Looking up, he saw the doctor's body drifting further and further away. The blowout had ripped his suit at the tether ring where his safety line connected. Now, without a line, he would drift in the direction the blowout sent him.

"What happened?" asked Morgan as he entered the room in a hurry.

"Not sure. Either a seam blew or something hit him," offered Rocket as he frantically adjusted knobs and switches, looking for Dr. Kubo's vitals.

"Something?" Bobby begged for an explanation.

"Morgan stared out the view window, examining Dr. Kubo's suit and seeing the rip. "Where did you get that suit?"

Thompson straightened up. "I got the suit."

"I told you the number four had a bad seam." Disgust painted Morgan's face.

"We used number three, not four." All eyes turned to the rack of spacewalk suits. A suit hung in the number four position. "I know how to count," explained Thompson.

Bobby had had enough. "I'll suit up and go and get him."

"That's not a good idea, Bobby. He's already out beyond any tether line," informed Rocket. He watched Bobby remove the number two suit from the rack.

"I'm going."

Like rubberneckers at a traffic accident, the Delta crew stared at the doctor's body, floating further and further away.

Thompson spied Dr. Kubo's body well over one hundred meters from Delta. "He's gone . . . It's too late."

"I'll find him and bring him back." Bobby was determined.

"I can't let you do that."

"You can't stop me." Bobby stood upright and slid his right arm into the jet-pack harness. "I can't leave him."

"Bobby!" Rocket positioned himself directly in front of his friend. "I know what you're thinking. But you're wrong." His voice softened. "You are not responsible."

"I should have checked and double-checked his suit."

"You wouldn't have known. It was no one's fault."

"Accidents happen, Major," interjected Thompson.

Rocket shot an incredulous glare toward Thompson and then returned to Bobby. "It was an accident." Bobby's countenance dropped. "It wasn't your fault."

Thompson instructed, "I want you to take off that jet pack, get your things on board the *Lewis,* and be ready to launch in thirty minutes." Thompson turned toward the others, who stood by gawking. "That goes for all of you. A launch in thirty minutes puts us behind schedule by three hours and twenty minutes. Let's go, people."

"Come on, Bobby." Rocket released the jet strap.

Bobby slipped out of the jet pack and squatted in a heap near the floor next to the transfer chamber. He felt dizzy. "I should have checked it myself."

Rocket released Bobby's shoulder clamps. "Come on, Bobby, other lives are still on the line."

Bobby stared off in disbelief. His facial expression froze. His eyes glassed over.

Margo looked at Rocket. "What do we do?"

"Give me a minute."

Rocket squatted in front of his friend and gently brought his fist down on Bobby's right knee twice. "For such a time as this . . . I don't know why God has us on this mission, but he does. In his sovereign wisdom, he has trained us and given us skills few other people in the world have. And now he has called on us to rescue our fellow astronauts. He has called on us to do our very best in an effort to rescue our friends. Bobby, it's time to step up to the plate. It is time to forget the past. Come on, Bobby. Let's make it happen."

"Rocket, do you think it was an accident?" Bobby whispered.

Rocket leaned in toward Bobby and said, "That or bad mojo."

"If we checked the fourth suit, would we find a bad seam?"

"We don't have time to run a test."

Bobby sighed hard. "Check and double-check everything."

CHAPTER FORTY-FIVE

Rich oxygenated blood electrified the cells in her brain. Her mind worked in overdrive only slightly faster than her hands. Colonel Anderson was almost giddy. The quad's system check revealed all systems were up and running. The navigational system still crunched numbers and launch sequence possibilities. She watched and waited.

Rogers administered more painkillers and encouraged Marty with hope of a launch.

"You cleared the gear, right, Rogers?" Anderson never stopped her preflight.

"Yes, ma'am."

Rogers had gone out alone to inspect the ship's exterior and ensure that all four landing struts were clear. He found two struts jammed up, an oxygen line pinched, and the satellite dish, their communication's lifeline, dangling on a thin wire. He started with the oxygen line that was braced against the front left landing strut.

The three-inch patch, lined with rubber and two over-center clamps, covered the kink. Using limited muscle power, Rogers had straightened the line, being careful not to snap it in two before securing the clamps. It would not win any awards, but the line contained oxygen flow with very little pressure. It would have to work.

He moved on to the front left gear. The same gear that had crushed Marty's legs had been shaken deeper into the rift. Eight inches of lunar rock and dust covered the sixteen-inch circular pad. Using the small spade from the equipment locker, he cleared the debris and then moved to the second strut pad.

Not as deep as the first but wedged in under a large embedded rock, Rogers started pounding. Five minutes of hammering did nothing more than break the D-ring handle of the spade.

Rogers knelt beside the rock and brushed the lunar dust to the side. Finding a small crack, he jammed the shovel blade into the fault. After a brief search, Rogers found a large, loose lunar rock. Rock in hand, he brought it down hard on the broken handle. Two more strikes broke his rock and sunk the blade three additional inches. Rogers pushed, pulled, and twisted on the handle. Sharp pain rippled across his chest. He pushed through the ache. The crack widened, and the blade sunk. Mustering all his remaining strength, he again pushed, pulled, and twisted. The rock split, the gear was freed, and a large shadow moved over the ship.

Rogers moved out from under the ship and investigated the source of the shadow. He found nothing. His breathing picked up its pace. He grabbed the lunar candle and flashed the light down into the rift. He saw nothing that would account for the shadow. He would have preferred to return to the ship, but he had one more task.

The mount had broken at the bolt, along with one wire. When? He did not know. But now the small satellite dish hung down into the rift. Rogers replaced the dish on the servo that turned and adjusted the bowl for maximum reception. Using two plastic ties, he secured the dish in place. Then, using a splicing coupling, he connected the two ends of the broken wire. Now the possibility of communication would be improved. Now they could let the rescue team, if there was one, know that they were coming home.

"We are at two minutes and counting," explained Anderson.

Rogers strapped Marty in on the floor and then took his seat next to the colonel. "This nightmare is almost over."

"Let's pray it is."

Andy Rogers smirked, "We don't need prayer. We need skill. Let's light the fire."

"Main engine start."

Rogers lifted two toggle switches and then pressed a red button marked Main Engine. The ship shook as flames shot down into the rift. Colonel Anderson increased the thrust, and the *Santa Maria* began to lift off only to slam into the side of the rift. The main engine exhaust cowling had been bent and pushed off center in the quake. Rogers had missed that detail.

As the colonel increased the power, the ship began to spin and the struts bashed side to side in the rift. The cowling hit the rift lip hard, turning it almost perpendicular. The thrust now coming out sideways slammed the ship back onto the surface. The front left strut dug itself into the lunar rubble as the colonel shut the main engine down. The ship came to rest with two aft gears jammed eighteen inches below the rift lip.

No words were spoken. Colonel Anderson shut down the launch sequence and restored the ship to emergency power. Rogers sat motionless, staring out at the lunar landscape. After unbuckling Marty to make him more comfortable, Anderson returned to her seat. Still not a word was spoken.

Anderson began to play with the radio. Using a control toggle, she repositioned the small satellite dish. She then cranked up the volume, filling the cabin with static. They listened to the static for a surprisingly long time. Then words came.

Anderson asked, "Was that our one chance?"

CHAPTER FORTY-SIX

Soggy ground, wet grass, and damp sidewalk: the all-night rain had left its mark. The surface winds had diminished. The clouds were thick and still with a strange green tint. No birds flew; no crickets chirped in the air that smelled of stale salt. Dr. Sooner stood quietly, studying the weather just outside of Mission Control. Rebecca, a category four hurricane, was blowing 220 miles off the coast, south by southeast of Houston. The Texas governor had ordered an evacuation of the coast from Port Arthur to Galveston. Interstate 45 North was gridlocked. More than half of Houston had shut down and boarded up. Moving quickly, the National Weather Service didn't expect Rebecca to create more than a two-day disruption. But two days of disruption were too many.

With the *Santa Maria* in trouble and Rescue One running behind schedule, Dr. Sooner would not be leaving. He dismissed all nonessential personnel from the Johnson Space Center but ordered a ride-out crew to stay behind. But for what purpose, he wondered. He did not even know if anyone was still alive on the lunar surface. *Why should I risk more lives? Should I pull the plug? Should Rescue One be abandoned? If Anderson is alive . . . if anyone is still alive, we have to try. Who will be alive when we get there? I've got to find out before they launch from Delta.*

Sooner reentered Mission Control and made his way to the command center, speaking to no one but noticing two unknown faces. He looked for photo badges but saw none. His pass card opened the main doors; his familiar voice gained an immediate audience. "I need confirmation of life on the *Santa Maria*. And I need it now." He turned to see the doors close, excluding the two strange faces. The room came alive as the effort to contact the *Santa Maria* intensified. Sooner moved past his secretary and instructed her to get General Buchholz on the phone. Line one flashed before he got to his desk.

"General, I need confirmation of life before we launch the *Lewis* from Delta. Too much time has passed. We don't know that anyone has survived."

"I trust they are hanging on."

Waves of doubt and suspicion rolled over Chief Sooner. "There is nothing stable about the lunar surface. I need to know they are still alive."

"Chief, I've seen incredible pictures. You're right, the surface is unstable but Mare Crisium is sound. The LZ is holding steady. We will not pull off mission. I'll be in your office in two hours. Until then, I want them on task and on schedule. Is that understood?" Buchholz didn't wait for an answer. He pressed the Off button on his satellite phone and left Sooner wondering.

"Dr. Sooner, we have the *Lewis* on the line."

Running from his desk, Dr. Sooner ignored the piece of paper that his secretary held out for him to take. "It's a message from family services. They need to talk to you . . . It's important," she said.

Sooner quickly entered the control room, placed a headset on and exclaimed, "Lewis, this is Houston."

"Go ahead, Houston."

"Bobby, I'd like to confirm life on the *Santa Maria* before we risk your crew."

"We are ten minutes from launch." Delta was whipping around the earth, preparing to slingshot the *Lewis* toward the Moon. Timing was everything. To delay would mean another orbit. To delay would mean death for those aboard the *Santa Maria*.

"But I have bad news, Chief." Bobby's voice was matter-of-fact.

"I don't need bad news."

"Well, you're going to get it. We've lost Dr. Kubo."

Sooner's vision blurred. "What? What happened?"

"Seam blew out. There was nothing we could do, Chief."

"Do we need to scrub?" This was reason enough to shut the mission down in Sooner's mind.

"Negative," Thompson interrupted. "All systems are *go.* We are at 8:57 to initial burn." Thompson glanced over at the major, who continued prepping for launch.

Sooner ignored Thompson. "Major, have you had any contact with Anderson or anyone from the crew of the *Santa Maria?*"

Bobby spoke into the mouthpiece. "No, sir. We have tried."

"We may have lost the *Santa Maria,*" informed Sooner. "We have detected major volcanic activity on Mare Crisium's outer rim. Without confirmation of life, I don't want to risk your life."

Colonel Thompson interrupted again, stopping his preflight. "We can't leave them to die."

"They may already be dead," Sooner insisted.

"Jack, a delay would seal their doom. Let's launch." Bobby said.

"I don't like it."

"I don't like it, either," Bobby said. "I'd rather be home kissing my bride and playing with my little girl. But if there is a chance that Kim or any of her team is still alive, we need to try. Let's keep the possibility open. If we do not hear from anyone on the *Santa Maria,* we'll do a fly-by orbit and head for home."

Jack Sooner looked up at the number one screen showing a real-time picture of Delta. "Okay. Go ahead and launch. We'll keep trying to connect with the *Santa Maria* on our end. You keep trying to connect on your end. But if we don't hear from Anderson before lunar orbit, I want you to loop the Moon and head for home. Do not land. Do you understand me, Major?" Do not land."

"That's a roger, Houston," Thompson chimed. "Let's prepare for burn," Thompson instructed as he terminated the transmission.

CHAPTER FORTY-SEVEN

"Survey III, do you copy?" Terror filled the cabin. "Survey III, do you copy?" More dread. "Colonel Anderson, this is the USS *Lewis*, are you there? Kim, are you there? Come on Kim, answer the radio."

Anderson heard the radio, but she dared not move. With heart racing, the colonel tried to open one eye very slowly and only slightly. It moved across the cabin slowly, smelling like decaying fish on a stagnant pond—a presence that Anderson had not yet seen but had felt for the last hour.

Finally, the eyelid cracked and Anderson could see Martinez propped up against the opposite wall. She hadn't heard Martinez moan in a couple of hours. The mission commander stared hard, looking for chest movement. She couldn't be positive. A shadow crept over her head; Anderson let the one eye gently close. Whatever it was, her opossum strategy seemed to be working—no physical contact had yet been made. She wondered if the presence was the being she saw earlier. Not likely. This creature seemed darker, bolder, and more curious. It moved down in front of Anderson—nose to nose, only inches away. It now smelled of maggoty decomposition. The colonel shuddered, feeling its hot breath on her cheek. *Oh God! This is no dream.* She tightened her gut to suppress the gag reflex but feared the creature that straddled her legs may have observed the body movement. Staying calm and still, she swallowed the breath in her mouth. Suddenly the rancid visitor made a loud gurgling/sucking sound that vibrated the entire ship.

"Survey III, do you copy?" The transmission was clear. The colonel's hope sunk. "Survey III, this is Major Robert Haistings aboard the USS *Lewis* en route. Do you copy? Is anyone there?"

Oh, God, they are coming. But they are going to think we're all dead. They are going to call off the rescue. I've got to answer. I've got to get to the radio. I can't move. She could feel the creature's legs press against her knees. Bobby called for two more minutes before the radio fell silent.

Bobby, please don't give up.

Her one eyelid slid open again. The creature now squatted in front of Martinez. Head tilting back and forth in an awkward rhythm, two arms and two legs made it humanoid, but the skin was thick, slimy, and rubbery with a flat gray-brown tint. It had four fingers and a thick thumb on each hand, but its feet were two-toed like the Vadoma tribe of the extreme west part of Zimbabwe. Each toe was long, with a heavy crescent nail looking more like an eagle's talon than a human toe. They were dirty, broken, and chipped. With a quick snap of his head, the creature stared directly at the colonel. She recoiled, pressing her head against the bulkhead. *Don't move.*

The hairless face with bug eyes looked angry. Small flat nostrils flared as the chin elongated, opening its mucus-laden mouth with no apparent teeth. A loud, hideous noise shook the craft again. Fire red eyes stared in her direction but no longer directly at the colonel. The creature's attention seemed focused above Anderson. Then another hideous noise came from overhead as a chilling frost settled on the nape of her neck. The bug-eyed creature moved quickly out of Anderson's field of vision. The smell of rotting flesh dissipated quickly, but Anderson held her position. She let her eyelid fall and tried to relax before the next close encounter.

CHAPTER FORTY-EIGHT

As the *Lewis* burned toward the lunar surface, Bobby sat alone, detached, bewildered, and despondent. The command center seemed cramped and stuffy to Bobby, with the command seat fitting more snuggly and less comfortably than he remembered. Wearing a NASA-issued jumpsuit similar to the flight suits worn by fighter pilots, only white in color, with sealed zippers and a biotransmitter used by Houston to monitor vitals, Bobby stared out the front window. Houston lost reception of the biotransmitters three minutes after the *Lewis* launched from Delta, but he didn't care. His life had just fallen off a precipice.

Buchholz could have held the information about Bobby's wife from Thompson. But he did not. Thompson could have held the information about Bobby's wife until they returned but chose not to do that. If Thompson wrestled with telling Bobby the news, it was only for a moment. His demeanor was cold and uncaring.

"There has been a terrible accident." Bobby's face went flat. "Involving your wife." His heart hammered his chest. "They couldn't save her." The flame snuffed out; Bobby's eyes retracted deep into his skull. "She was pronounced dead at the scene." His whole being went numb. All muscle strength vanished. Major Robert Haistings shut down.

Bobby had two twelve-inch computer monitors to his left, each with its own keyboard. The joystick was thick and mushroomed out into a half-moon with communication controls built in. To his right lay two throttle controls, one for each of the two main engines. Just below the throttles sprawled a bank of red safety toggle switches used to manually fire the twenty-one reaction control system rockets used for steering during the trans-space glide. Below the front glass sat radar, altitude, and speed screens. Gauges, lights, and switches of all sorts filled every other inch overhead and to the right.

Further to the right, Rocket sat grieving his own loss and being deeply concerned about his friend. Rocket fidgeted as he ran both a voice and telemetry systems check in the right-hand seat that mirrored Bobby's. He watched as Bobby's right leg began to shake. Bobby's body turned and twisted; he looked as though he were in serious pain. Rocket ran a check on the oxygen purge system without ever taking his eye off his friend. Bobby unfastened the top neck snap and stretched his neck. *Hang in there, Bobby.*

Directly behind each of the two front seats and one step up were large swivel chairs that only locked into place facing forward. Rocket glanced back at Margo, who sat directly behind Bobby in her unlocked chair, facing her own computer monitor but gazing out the view window just above it.

Sitting back to back with Margo, Colonel Thompson continued to monitor the life support system. Bobby's vitals were on screen. His blood pressure pulsed up, along with his heart rate. Thompson said, "You okay, Major?"

Bobby didn't answer. He didn't move; he just stared hard at his now-blank monitor. He sat perfectly still for the first time in over an hour.

"Bobby." Rocket tried again. Bobby didn't flinch.

"Keep trying, Captain," said Thompson.

Rocket leaned toward Bobby and eyed sweat seeping from every pore. Like an out-of-shape horse, Bobby was lathered up. His breathing seemed labored, and his skin looked tacky. Rocket reached over and grabbed Bobby's arm. "Bobby, you okay?"

Bobby snapped upright and blinked several times, wiped his head with his hand and said, "It's hot in here."

Margo handed Bobby a cool dry handkerchief. "Here you go, Major."

"Thank you . . . Margo."

"You're welcome, Bobby."

Rocket glanced around the command center.

"What do you want to do, Bobby?"

His chin fell to his chest. "I want to go home . . . scoop my little girl up in my arms, hold her tight, feel her chubby arms around my neck, smell her breath, kiss her cheeks, and let her know her daddy loves her very, very much and that we will be okay." He lifted his head up and said, "Rocket, I've got to get back to my little girl."

"I know you do." Rocket looked back at Margo, who offered an understanding countenance. "As fast as possible."

"Are we there yet?" Margo's question allowed everyone to exhale a smile.

"No, we're not there yet. If all goes well, we will touch down or be headed for home in forty-two hours, two minutes and eleven seconds," Rocket announced.

The atmosphere conditioning unit offered a faint hiss. "Wake me in twenty," asked the colonel as he pushed deep into his seat. Eyes closed, his mind surely drifted. Who knows what a man like Thompson dreamed? Bobby didn't care; he didn't want to know.

Margo sat motionless, directing her attention to her window and the great expanse. "The stars are right there, floating in a sea of darkness, hanging on nothing. I feel like I could reach out and grab one or blow them all away with a whisper." Her eyes sparkled with fantasy.

Margo removed her heavy gray harness, allowing her to lean further toward the window. Looking back, she could just see the faint shimmer of the water planet in the background. "Absolutely amazing," she marveled. Collapsing once again in her chair, she turned her head toward Bobby, and their eyes met for a brief moment before Bobby's fell to his lap, where he cradled in his hands a picture of Carol—caressing, worshipping, and dreaming of earlier days. With the Sierra Nevada Mountains behind her, Carol stood holding a pair of skis, wearing a teak green ski overall with a lily white cashmere sweater underneath. Her pearl white sunglasses provided a beautiful contrast against her sun-darkened skin. It was a Christmas vacation he would never forget. Bobby's mind gently floated off. He could see her wiggle in her cute, tight-fitting ski suit. He remembered how, after he put snow down her back in the chairlift line, she knocked him back with a swift elbow to the rib cage, causing a domino effect; about fifteen other skiers went down. They began to wrestle in the snow and were asked to leave the lift area when the wrestling turned to hugs and kisses.

Thoughts of being run out of the supermarket later that same day bounced through. In the produce department, with a half-filled basket of food, they armed themselves with the water hoses and had a battle. They took out one orange display, two signs, and three bystanders. They were escorted out of the store without making a purchase. Come to think of it, they had been kicked out of a lot of places—they were all great memories.

Tears began to roll down his face. Embarrassed, Bobby quietly removed his harness and stole away into the cargo compartment. Getting comfortable in the boom chair, Bobby strapped in and looked back at planet Earth. Hot, thick tears now saturated his face. Carol's picture still covered his palm.

"How is any of this good?" His nose smoldered, and his hands shook.

"Stacy will never again sit on her mother's lap or hear her sing a lullaby or feel her sweet lips on a scraped knee. Who will teach her to dance and play? Who will teach her to move with grace and strength? Who will teach her to be a woman? How is this good for Stacy? It's not good. It's never good. I don't understand."

Bobby's questions generated a tinge of guilt. But he pressed, "My heart burns like fire. Oh God, it makes no sense. Lord, flood my ignorance with knowledge, help me understand."

After popping every knuckle on both hands, Bobby stared toward Earth. He then lowered his head into his left palm. "Oh, God, why did Carol have to die?" His head throbbed; his voice slowed and dropped an octave. The question dripped from his lips in pain as he realized for the first time that he was talking out loud.

"Why didn't you take me?" His head fell, and his face burrowed into his arms against the control board. Wet eyes opened for only a moment before closing tightly as great anguish thrashed in his chest and a cry of sorrow bucked from his mouth. "Oh God, Stacy. Don't let her be scared. Please, God, take care of my little girl."

Bobby sat up. "I've got to get home. I have got to get back to my little girl." Bobby's mind rifled through possibilities, surveying every scenario. He couldn't just turn around. He couldn't just desert his friend on the lunar surface. Or could he? Bobby felt nauseous, his vision went fuzzy, and anxiety clamped down on his soul. He'd been here before. "God, I'm not going to make it."

Chapter Forty-Nine

Consciousness returned with pressure on Anderson's left side. Something moved up against her, sending cold needles down her spine. "Colonel, you awake?"

"Mr. Rogers, where have you been?"

"What do you mean 'where have I been'? I've been sleeping right beside you for the last couple of hours. You should have heard my snoring. My wife says I can wake the dead. I can't believe you didn't hear me." His voice was soft and strained.

"Did you see anything . . . anything strange?"

"Like what?"

"Did you hear the radio?"

"Colonel, I've been fading in and out, but I didn't hear anything and I didn't see anything other than Martinez slipping closer and closer to death." Rogers's eyes moistened for the first time. "Why? What did you see?"

The colonel sighed hard and then looked around the cabin for a long minute. "Nothing, nothing. I didn't see anything. I just had the strangest dream."

Mr. Rogers crawled over to Martinez and felt his carotid artery for a pulse. It was faint but present. As he eased back over next to the colonel, two sets of desperate eyes locked onto each other. "Will this be our coffin?" Rogers asked.

The colonel ignored the question and moved to the radio to call for help. Maybe it wasn't all a dream. Maybe Bobby did call and rescue is on the way. She tried for forty-five minutes to make contact but received no response. She adjusted the radio between emergency channels, hoping someone was monitoring. For another ten minutes, the colonel cried out for help, receiving only dead air. She let the mike float free and settle on the station counter. Anderson moved back down next to Rogers.

Exhaling hard, the colonel rubbed her worried face and said, "So do foxholes have atheists?"

No words were offered, but his eyes told a story of perplexity. Staring nowhere and everywhere, Mr. Rogers seemed to take the question deep into his soul. Finally, "Do you think I need there to be a god right now? Death is banging on our door. He's screaming to get in. Is believing in a god going to change that?"

The colonel's head drifted side to side. Mr. Rogers continued. "You believe in a god and death is coming for you, the same as me. How would taking a leap into religion change my present circumstance?" The question ushered in a deafening silence—long and uncomfortable. Like some guilt-induced avoidance technique, the two astronauts avoided eye contact. After about ten painful minutes, they both rested their gaze on Martinez.

Colonel Anderson finally spoke. "I'm not saying it would."

"So what's the point?"

"What if there is more to life than our present circumstance? What if there is life after death?"

What looked like a meteor caught Rogers's attention, and he was lost in wonder. Another meteor screamed past, then another and another. Each seemed to have a color of its own. The colonel leaned forward and looked back to see what had caught Rogers's attention. Half a dozen meteors burned through the thin lunar atmosphere and on toward earth.

"And you believe that all this happened by chance?"

"Actually, I think what we are witnessing is evidence of what I call modified evolution. Before our eyes, we are watching our moon morph, which will affect our planet and maybe our solar system. We are seeing natural causes produce significant change. Now I'll admit the Earth is being acted upon by an outside source.

And maybe the whole evolutionary process had help from an outside source. But it doesn't have to be a supernatural god. Could it possibly be that the Earth had two moons at one time and the other moon disintegrated, and its actions upon the earth started the evolutionary process? Is it possible that alien life from another solar system started the whole process? For all I know, we are a giant ant farm—someone's lab experiment. Maybe they are watching the whole process unfold. Can you prove I'm wrong?"

The colonel sat dumbfounded as Rogers continued. "You can't answer because there is no answer. We are mere specks in the universe who are subject to the events that completely happen at random. Consider this: if you are walking along a sidewalk and there are ants crawling about on it, does god control which ants die when you step on them? We are just like that too. As far as the forces of nature and the universe are concerned, we are just like ants—only bigger. Thousands can be killed at a stroke. No one weeps, and no one cares. Your belief in god is for your own comfort because you don't want to face up to the brutalities of life."

"No disrespect intended, Colonel, but we are probably going to die in this titanium can. I can't help that. We can't start whining about it. Let's face our own mortality like grown-ups and let it happen."

"But what if . . ."

"Colonel, you're a good person. What kind of god would leave you up here to die? I could understand leaving me up here. I've never given your god the time of day. I don't even believe he exists. But why would he leave *you* up here, or Martinez? The man was an altar boy—he gives money to his church. He has his boy in a Christian school, and he is dying on the lunar surface. Your god is either unable to help, which would make him a rather small god, or he doesn't care, which makes him unloving. Either way, he's not a god I'd want."

"I can't say that I haven't had similar thoughts lately," Anderson remarked. "I only have one request. Get me home. Is that too much to ask?"

"I'm with you."

Martinez let out a horrific cry of anguish, squirmed a bit, and then fell back into unconsciousness. His eyes never opened, so neither the colonel nor Rogers moved toward him. They let him settle into unconsciousness without assistance.

"If God doesn't get me home, I'm going to be . . . disappointed. But I still believe in him."

"If that helps you, Colonel, more power to you. It doesn't help me. It just ticks me off. Think about it, Colonel. Why did the Moon have to split under us? Why would your god let Lathem and Davenport die? Why did he have to cripple the *Santa Maria*? If there is a god, I have a thousand questions for him. It just doesn't make any sense to me. Why would a supposedly loving god leave you up here to rot?"

"Oh, we won't rot, much. The rotting process depends on oxygen-breathing creatures. We'll be preserved up here for all time and eternity."

Rogers shook his head in disgust. "Shut up . . . ma'am."

The colonel stared out the window for a moment. "Call me, Kim." She stuck out her hand as if they were meeting for the first time.

Their hands embraced as Rogers said, "Call me Andy."

"Andy, I'd like to do a little experiment with you. I want you to stare at Marty but be conscious of your peripheral vision."

"What's this about?"

"Just trust me."

"Okay."

"What do you see in your peripheral vision on your left side?"

"I see a bit of the desk and radio."

"Can you see the walleyed window?"

"Not quite."

"You can't see the viewing port?"

"No," Rogers insisted.

"When was the last time you had your vision checked?"

"Colonel, what's your point?"

"Okay. Do you see the oxygen gage just to the left and above Marty's head?"

"I see it."

"Focus on that and tell me what you see in your peripheral."

"Whoa!" Andy Rogers leaped over the colonel, holding on to a support handle just above Kim's head, and then pushed his feet to the floor. "What was that?" His terrified eyes were now focused on the walleyed view window that revealed nothing but lunar dust. "What was that?"

"Tell me what you saw?"

"A face, a white face with no hair. No eyebrows, no eyelids, just smooth skin. But it had long, white hair that seemed to waft in a breeze. And it was leering. Did you see it?"

Seeming distant and confused, Kim said, "I've been seeing it for two days."

"I think we may be in trouble."

"You think?"

CHAPTER FIFTY

"You okay?"

Surprised and irritated, Bobby jerked upright. "Do you need something, Doctor ... Margo?"

"No, just checking on you."

"I'm fine." Bobby wiped his face on his sleeve and returned his gaze to the window.

Remaining quiet and feigning inspection of her lunar drills, Margo loitered. Bobby knew she wanted to help. Must be that mothering instinct that pushes women to reach out and try to help the wounded. She adjusted her suit for the fifth time, pulled on her right ear nervously, and finally said sheepishly, "I don't understand. I don't know that anyone truly understands."

Bobby acknowledged her comment but didn't pursue it. Margo moved his way.

"Life is the pits and then you die. My goal is to enjoy the pit the best I can."

Bobby smiled politely. "I'm sorry. I'm not the best company right now. I'm angry. I'm tense. And my only hope is glory."

"If we make it home, there'll be enough glory to go around."

"That's not the type of glory I'm talking about."

"What are you talking about?"

Bobby wiped his chin and then stretched both arms over his head as he turned toward Margo, who was now sitting next to him. "If this world is all there is, then God is a villain." The words came out mean. Bobby gulped down a breath to try to take the edge off. "Margo, we live in a fallen world where evil seems to have the upper hand. Life in this world is neither fair nor just. Wicked people prosper, and good people suffer. But this world is not all there is to life. There is a whole other world that we know little about—another life in which God will make it right. Justice is coming. There are no side doors and no under-the-table deals. No one escapes. Why Carol had to die? I don't know." Bobby stopped speaking abruptly and withdrew into himself. The minutes ticked away as Margo waited quietly. Five, ten, fifteen minutes ticked by. Finally, wiping his face with her handkerchief, Bobby sat up straight.

"I don't pretend to understand the mind of God. However, just because my finite mind cannot understand or even begin to comprehend the infinite wisdom of God is no reason to reject Him. It's frustrating—I'll grant you that."

"To say the least." Margo's eyes showed confusion.

"Margo, what do you want?"

"What do you mean 'what do I want'?"

"In your heart of hearts, what is it that you really want?"

"Get out of debt—I owe a train load of cash." They shared a light smile.

"That's not what I mean."

"I'm not following."

"It's not about this world. It's about the hope of a better world."

"And you feel you have that hope?"

Bobby's heart sank. *I want to say yes, Lord.* The silence screamed for an answer. Margo waited. With pleading eyes, Bobby finally said, "I have that hope."

"Where did you find that hope?"

"I first saw it in Rocket." Bobby peered into Margo's eyes. "You've seen it too, haven't you?"

"What is it about Rocket that makes you want to be near him?" she asked.

"He's a Christ follower who actually follows Christ with more than just words." Bobby noticed a tinge of pink in Margo's complexion. "It may be a little bit more than that for you, but that's what it is for me."

Dink, dink, plink. "What was that?" Margo's attention diverted to the view window. Bobby swung around as he replied, "Small meteorites striking the ship."

"What is that?" Margo focused on the window.

Bobby leaned in and stared at what looked like a thousand tiny stars clustered between the *Lewis* and the Moon.

"Let's move up front." Bobby didn't wait for affirmation. He pulled himself along, hand over hand, through the cargo compartment to the command center hatch. With a ninety-degree spin of the handle and a metallic thunk, the door opened. He squeezed through with Margo on his heels. Bypassing the sleeping colonel, he floated up and then down into his command seat.

Dink. Bonk. Bang. "Wow." Margo scrambled up between Bobby and Rocket.

"Meteors," Rocket replied. "They've been pinging the ship for the last hour. The last three were bigger than the rest, and they all struck the windshield."

Then the light show began. Thousands upon thousands of white lights exploded from the lunar surface and sped through space toward the USS *Lewis*.

"Everyone, buckle in. We are in for a ride," said Bobby.

Margo slunk back into her seat and pulled the heavy two-shoulder harness on over her head. Reaching between her legs, she grabbed the heavy nylon strap with buckle and connected the harness. The now fully awake colonel didn't need any encouragement. He harnessed into his seat before Dr. Street tightened her straps.

The lights were on top of them in less than a minute. They streamed past the *Lewis* at speeds that boggled the mind but caused no disruption. Scattered throughout the white lights were occasional groupings of reddish orange lights. At first Bobby thought it was one large off-colored light. However, as they approached and past, the individuals within the group stood out.

One particular large group of reddish lights on the port side caught the attention of the entire crew. All eyes were fixed on the red lights, which began to slow down. Both Margo and the colonel removed their harnesses and moved up close to Bobby and Rocket. "What is that?" asked Bobby.

Bam! A meteor slammed into the front glass, filling the cabin with blinding red light. Margo's forehead bumped hard against the back of Bobby's head and both of her arms struck the back of his seat. The colonel turned slightly and took the impact of Rocket's seat in his shoulder.

The lights went out like someone had hit a switch. All the meteor lights dispersed. The cabin lights no longer illumined the command center.

"Major, the instruments."

Nothing registered. The emergency system came on, revealing all gages pegged at zero.

Margo pleaded, "What's happening?" The panic in her voice only added to the tension in Bobby's gut.

"Sit back and strap in." The words came out of Bobby's mouth like machine gun fire. His mind swirled as his hands moved quickly about the gages. Both Bobby and Rocket set and reset everything.

"Colonel, what's the status of quad-redundant?" asked Bobby.

Colonel Thompson reached to his right and pressed a large, two-fingered button marked QR. The power came back on; lights lit and spirits soared. Before Bobby could say the words, Colonel Thompson had quad-redundant run a complete systems check.

"What's quad-redundant?" Margo asked.

"Quad-redundant," Rocket explained, "is our backup computer system. We have three computer systems that run simultaneously. If one system disagrees with the others, then the one in disagreement does an independent check and then reevaluates the issue in question."

Rocket's hands never stopped moving as he checked every gage within his reach. "If the check comes back still in disagreement, all three computers do a systems check and reevaluate the issue in question. If the three systems remain incongruent, all three are disengaged and the fourth takes over. The trio continues to work at resolution. If they don't come to agreement, they never come back online."

A loud and annoying buzzer sounded. Warning lights flashed across all three computer screens. The command station blinked and flashed like a disco ball. Bobby, Rocket, and Thompson quickly worked on resetting the computers. "Run CBX on all systems," Thompson ordered. Compliance was immediate. The Computer Bug Extermination system went to work in the trio.

"There." Thompson declared. "We have a bug. It has been quarantined in the backup computer system."

"A bug?" Margo asked.

Thompson said, "When the programs were originally written, there must have been a defect, an error." He glared at Bobby. "That little error can cause life-threatening consequences for us." All eyes shifted about the cabin. "Care to explain why there is a bug on your ship, Major."

"I don't get it." Bobby kept working his fingers. "How can we suddenly get a bug?"

"Maybe it was dormant," Margo offered.

"Maybe, but we did a sweep prior to launch. We ran the systems through every possible scenario. Geeks far more computer savvy than I never found an error. A dormant bug is unlikely."

"Wait, wait, wait! It's moving," the colonel informed. "It's a worm. It is moving into life support!" Worms have the ability to reproduce and run themselves. The panic intensified.

"I thought it was quarantined." Margo's heart vaulted.

"It was. I swear it was. The quarantine didn't hold." The colonel postured the CBX to control the number one computer system. He set a trap and captured the bug just before it moved into flight controls. The screen showed an orange dot flashing just behind the life-support symbol on the computer schismatic. Four bars came down, surrounding the orange dot. "I've captured the bug."

"You said that before," Margo taunted.

"I said I've got it." All watched as the four bars disintegrated and the orange dot split into two, then four, then eight orange dots.

"Shut it down, shut it down!" Bobby stared at Rocket for two bloated seconds. Then Rocket grabbed a small screwdriver from a tool kit hanging on the side of the number one computer cabinet. Opening an access panel on the number two computer and locating the primary cable, he unscrewed the two matching thumbscrews and unplugged the number two computer from the number three computer. The trio was now one. Margo and Bobby looked on as the colonel continued to work CBX.

"Did we stop it?" Bobby asked Colonel Thompson, who shut down both the number one and the number two. Now the number three functioned independently.

Thompson replied, "I think so."

"You think so? I need more than an 'I think so.' I need a yes, a confident I-know-what-I'm-talking-about yes!" Margo begged, with an attitude.

Colonel Thompson paid little attention. His fingers were typing fast and furiously. "I said, I think so." His words were slow and measured. He was insulted by her demand.

"What happens now?" Margo asked.

Bobby took a deep breath and then moved back into the command seat. "The number three should run fine." Punching a series of keys on his left side keyboard, he ran both navigations and life support through a systems check. "I think we're okay." His eyes never left the screen, where a rectangular box appeared with a green gyrating barber pole indicating one minute forty-nine seconds until completion of the systems check. "Colonel, what do you have?"

The colonel's fingers flew across his keyboard. Rocket continued to pull panels revealing the inner workings of the number three computer and the quad-redundant.

"I take no comfort in CBX. If it let one bug by, why not others?" Rocket suggested.

"Captain, I think we are safe," Colonel Thompson instructed.

"Run the tests and show me a clean system, and I'll put it back together."

Colonel Thompson pulled up the computer system schematic showing all systems and their relative relationship as rectangular boxes with a three-letter designator. As the CBX checked each system, the box and its three letters turned green. Beginning at the top, the boxes started turning green. One after another, the green boxes soon outnumbered the red boxes. The crew stared, mesmerized, at the color transformation. Margo and Rocket watched Thompson's screen; Bobby watched his own monitor. Smiles were shared as the final two boxes turned green.

"All right. We are still in business." Margo exclaimed. "We are still lunar bound."

Bobby turned toward his crew only to find perplexity in Rocket's face. "Are we?"

"Sure, why not? You said the number three would be fine," Margo insisted.

"We can't turn about, captain," the colonel explained as he began to run life support through a routine test. "We'll have to loop the Moon to return home anyway. I'm not ready to abort the mission yet."

Margo looked toward Bobby again. "I agree with Colonel Thompson. We press on toward the Moon."

Bobby then craned his neck around to look at Margo, who had moved in directly behind him. "Dr. Street, we are hours away from orbit. Regardless of the status, we will be moving fast. If you want to run any tests at all, I would suggest you prep them now."

"I'm way ahead of you." She had already started a computer check. Three minutes later, she moved. "I'm headed to the cargo bay." She disappeared into her instruments as Rocket replaced the final screw on the panel.

"Not too fast, Rocket." Bobby's eyes were fixed on his screen. A small backup communications system returned red. Bobby felt the colonel peering over his shoulder. The box returned to green again. Bobby wasn't smiling. He didn't move. He had seen this before. The box turned red again and then began to flash. "Colonel?"

"I see it."

Fingers moving at ninety words a minute, the colonel cried, "Hold on, Captain. It may be just a glitch." Rocket had already removed a screw.

Bobby's eyes narrowed, watching the one box blink back and forth between red and green. Then a steady orange light beamed.

"Crap!" Bobby grabbed a screwdriver.

"Capture it! Kill it before it kills us all!" Bobby yelled.

Colonel Thompson continued working the keyboard as Bobby and Rocket removed the last two screws from the number three computer cabinet. "Hold on, Major. Hold on, hold on!" The colonel screamed. Bobby didn't know Thompson's voice got that loud, but he wasn't slowing down.

"Not yet! Not yet!" Colonel Thompson pleaded with Bobby to wait for him.

"We can't risk infection." Bobby removed the two thumbscrews, and in a blink of an eye the number three computer was disconnected.

The crew compartment went dark, save a full moon shining through the front shield. Every computer screen went blank. No overhead light illuminated. The panel lights behind the gages did not shine. On Bobby's command console, a small red light blinked, indicating the emergency system had engaged. The three men went statue still.

Dr. Street eased the door from the cargo bay open and asked, "What happened?"

"I told you to wait, Major." His tone of contempt was unmistakable. "Major Haistings may have just killed us all."

"Or saved our lives," Rocket offered.

"Major, I said wait."

Bobby turned away from the colonel, who had returned to his seat. Dr. Street moved up into her seat and fiddled with gages and lights, looking for some evidence of power.

"There is no power," informed Thompson. "The major disconnected the number three before it was safe. He blew the main circuit breaker."

"I thought the system was created to take over for the number three."

"Not like this," Bobby explained. "The quad-redundant system is set up to take over for the trio. The systems are handed off. We didn't hand if off. We literally, physically disconnected the computers from each other. I didn't expect to blow the circuit breaker on quad-redundant."

"We have emergency life support that will last approximately forty-eight hours. We are on course and on schedule." Rocket glanced at his watch. "The problem is that in seven hours, we'll either crash on the Moon's surface or ricochet off the lunar atmosphere into outer space without the computers. We must get the quad back up and running."

"I told you to wait."

"I heard you, Colonel. I wasn't willing to take the chance. If the quad was alerted, it would have pulled data from the trio. It would have pulled the bug."

"You don't know that, Major. He doesn't know that. You are just trying to cover your ass." The colonel's hands shook as his fingers rubbed his now greasy face.

"Colonel." Rocket stood up and placed his hand on the colonel's shoulder. "Colonel Thompson, sir." Thompson shook his shoulder loose. "I think Bobby made the right call. We had an infectious bug that spread from the number one through two and into the number three. We captured and quarantined the bug and it got away from us. The CBX could find it and trace it, but it could not contain it. If Bobby had waited, the door would have been opened. If the bug infected the quad, we would all be dead." Rocket looked toward Bobby then back toward the colonel. "Bobby made the right call."

"It was my call," the colonel demanded.

"No. It was my call, my ship." He looked at Rocket and offered apologetically, "I couldn't wait." Bobby turned around, only to meet Thompson's fist in his nose. His head snapped backward, striking the corner of the air exchanger. The dime-size gash spewed blood immediately. Bobby regained his balance and got his feet back under him, only to be knocked back verbally.

"You self-righteous, bombastic idiot."

Rocket stepped in between. "That's enough." He pushed Bobby back against Margo's seat.

Margo pushed Thompson back. "You want to dance with me again."

"I said that's enough." Rocket hooked his right foot under Margo's chair and stood erect.

"Why didn't you wait?" The words exploded from the colonel's mouth.

"We didn't have the luxury of waiting."

"That was my decision."

Bobby turned away. "As commander of the *Lewis*, it was mine." Every muscle flexed, every joint stiffened, every fiber of his being ached. *Oh God, I've screwed up.*

"We live and die with our choices, Major."

Bobby stared off. "I know."

"Bobby, do you know how to get the quad back on line?" Rocket pressed forward.

Bobby looked at the colonel and then at Rocket and then back at the colonel. Shaking his head, he said, "No, but it is in the manual."

"The computer manuals?" Rocket asked.

"There are hard copies in the back."

The colonel bellowed, "What are you waiting for?"

CHAPTER FIFTY-ONE

The lunar shadows grew longer. The stars were still bright, and Orion still hovered over the crippled ship. Time ticked by very slowly—in the great expanse of space, little changed, until now.

Anderson watched as the lunar crust erupted, twisting and heaving. The left side of the main rift pushed up over the right side and then closed against the heave, creating a wall two meters high and its own dust cloud. At the far end of the crevasse, the rift splintered away from the craft. Colonel Anderson realized that any chance of recovering the body of Sam Lathem had just vanished. The consequence of earlier decisions manifested. "Rest in peace." A single tear pooled in her right eye. She captured it with a handkerchief.

The ship began to buck violently. Rogers fell against Marty's leg, inadvertently releasing the tourniquet. A deep guttural groan came from Marty, as the quake forced him to roll right. Rogers pushed himself off Marty and grabbed the emergency release handle overhead.

The *Santa Maria* seemed suspended over the gorge. She had broken free. For a moment Anderson felt relieved. Then, as if some mysterious hand had grabbed the strut and slammed it back into the rift, the ship sat deeper in the rift than before and tilted another ten degrees.

Anderson's eyes focused first on the moonscape. Was the bucking over? Then her eyes shifted back inside the lunar craft, where Marty slumped against the aft bulkhead. Sitting opposite Marty, Kim stared at his chest in the dim emergency lighting. She wanted to believe that Marty had returned to quiet rest. Kim thought she saw the rising and falling of his chest.

Kim wanted to believe that Marty would be okay, but the pool of blood beside his body told a different story. How much blood can a person lose and still be alive? She could hope. Kim gestured to Rogers to check on Marty. Not wanting to face the inevitable, he shook his head no.

Kim knelt beside Marty. Two fingers to the carotid artery on the left side of his neck confirmed Kim's fears. With her thumb and forefinger, she opened Marty's left eye and turned his head toward the light, looking for pupil movement. Nothing.

Kim pulled the blanket over Martinez's head. "He's gone." She wiped away another tear and then offered the handkerchief to Andy. He declined and then punched the bulkhead.

Collapsing next to Andy Rogers, Kim looked up at the oxygen counter, which read twenty-nine hours thirty-seven minutes.

Andy asked, "Do you think that line ruptured?" The words came out slow and labored.

"Let's hope not. Either way I need to refigure our oxygen intake based on two people instead of five." Kim punched into the computer the correct data. "We'll need to keep a close eye on it." The numbers on the counter started to spin and came to a stop at forty-four hours three minutes twelve seconds and counting down. "Our margin of error has improved a bit."

"Where's all our help?" Rogers asked with sarcastic disgust.

"They're on the way."

"Yeah, right. I'll believe it when I see them. I think we've been left!" Rogers leaned back against his workstation and stared into the woman's heart. "Let's be brave, Kim."

Chapter Fifty-Two

"What am I looking for?" Margo flipped through a black one-inch binder. Each crew member had at least one binder in hand and another close by.

"It should be in LC-7," Bobby declared after finding "Quad Start-up" in the index manual. "Who has LC-7?"

Rocket found LC-7 in his bundle, flipped to the table of contents, and located "Quad Start-Up" on page Q-3. "This doesn't look good. To restore power and reboot the quad after an unsafe shut down and power loss requires a manual reset. The system thinks we are in the docks."

Bobby's chin fell to his chest. Rocket continued reading quickly but quietly. His lips moved but only produced a mumble. Bobby rubbed his hands together as Rocket looked up. "It's going to require more than pushing a button, Bobby."

"I was afraid of that." Bobby shrugged.

Rocket tilted his head to the side and said, "We've got to reset it from the outside."

"Major Haistings got us into this mess. He can get us out," jabbed Thompson.

Bobby felt sick but believed the colonel to be correct. "I'll go." He sighed hard. "I know the system better than anyone else."

Ping, ping, bang! Another volley of meteors blew through. Bobby looked toward the colonel. Thompson wagged his head in disgust. "If we do nothing, we all die. You put us in this predicament. So you'll go and reset the quad."

"I said I'd go."

"If you're fast enough, you might make it before the next round of meteors."

"It's my ship. I said I'd go . . . I'll go. Rocket, if you and Margo would prep a spacewalk suit for me, I'd like a little time reviewing the procedure."

"Move, Captain. Let's get the suit ready for a walk," insisted Thompson.

Colonel Thompson shot through the bulkhead door in front of the others with flashlight in hand. In the transfer room five suits hung in five cubicles. Each crewmember had been previously fitted. Bobby's suit hung in the number three cubicle. Rocket and Margo set up three large, battery-powered lights to illumine the work area. Using tie straps, they secured the lights strategically. One light was fastened to tubing just above the bulkhead door, shining on the exit door. The other two were placed above Bobby's and Margo's cubicles, which sat juxtaposed to center.

With lights in place, they pulled the suit out on its stand while the colonel prepared the helmet. Rocket first attached an oxygen supply and then a small bi-jet pack.

"Let's go, Major Haistings. Time is precious." The colonel's voice reverberated through the ship's hollow corridors.

There was no reply. "Where is he?" All eyes turned toward the bulkhead door. "Dr. Street, would you please go get Major Haistings."

Margo torpedoes through the passageway, finding Bobby with the manual in front of him, but he wasn't reading it. Bobby's mind traveled back to his final words to Stacy. "I'll be back, I promise." *Lord, my little girl is counting on me. I've got to make it back. Please protect me! Please give me the skill to reset the quad. Please don't let me screw this up.*

Margo placed her hand gently on Bobby's shoulder. "You okay?"

Bobby looked up slowly, his face pale with anxiety. His bloodshot eyes pleaded for help. "No."

"You scared?"

"A long time ago, my daddy taught me that courage is not the absence of fear but the overcoming of fear. I've got to find it in myself or we're all dead."

"You're wrong, Bobby." Rocket entered the room. He lowered himself down until he was eye level with his friend. Margo situated herself close by, with her hand still perched on Bobby's shoulder. "Real courage, supernatural courage, is not found in overcoming fear with a great human grunt. Real courage flows out of the knowledge that you are dead already."

Bobby looked up into the eyes of his closest friend and saw rock-solid courage. His eyes fell to the floor. "I don't know, Rocket. I don't have that kind of courage."

"I do. Bobby, I'll go."

"No!" Margo's response was fast and directive.

"Thanks, Rocket, but I can't let you do that."

"No, he can't."

"Bobby, let me do this for you . . . You've got to get back to your little girl, remember." Their eyes locked. Bobby looked for some hint of fear or hesitation but found none. Rocket was running into the burning house, toward the overturned tanker, into the face of death. Rocket smiled. "Help me suit up."

Margo grabbed Rocket by the forearm. "You can't go, Rocket. The suit is prepped for Bobby."

"No worries. Our body type is so similar we have interchangeable parts."

"Please, don't go. Please."

"There is no greater love than this, Margo, that a man lay down his life for his friends."

"No, Rocket."

Rocket slowly slid his right hand gently onto her neck and caressed her cheek with his thumb. "You . . . are my friend."

She leaped into his arms and kissed him hard. "I love you, too. I can't lose you, Rocket. I need you. I need you to live."

"I'm not gone yet."

Bobby stood to his feet. "Thanks, my friend." They shook hands and then embraced.

"Can we roll the ship, Bobby? It will keep me out of the meteor rain."

Bobby's mind searched for answers. "I think I can do an atmosphere purge on the right by manually opening the valve for a couple seconds." The carbon monoxide produced by breathing was collected by exhaust fans, filtered out, and stored in a collection reservoir. On long missions, the tank would require purging. On this trip, purging was optional. "The purge should roll us. I could stop the roll with a purge on the left. Yeah, I should be able to do it. I'll roll it. You change."

Rocket changed quickly into the orange pumpkin suit that had the proper connectors for the spacewalk suit. As he porpoised through the prep-room door with a small flashlight in his mouth, Thompson let out a train whistle: "Roo-roo!"

Rocket paused just above the open shoulders of the space suit, removed the flashlight from his mouth and said, "Nonsense."

Bobby erupted through the door having successfully rolled the ship. "I said I'd go."

"Coward."

"Don't be ridiculous." Rocket shimmied down into the suit, filling every canal with the proper appendage. "I volunteered."

"Feet?" Bobby asked as Margo checked the suit and jet pack for irregularities.

"They're good."

"Fingers?"

Rocket started wiggling his fingers. He touched each finger to its thumb and then made two loose fists. "I have all ten." Margo nervously attached the jet control module to Rocket's left arm. He would have to control his motion with his left hand but could release the module without fear of losing it.

Bobby reached into the chest cavity and pulled out a four-wire connector. "What's the point?" Rocket asked. "The transponder will send the info, but you won't be able to read it."

Bobby retrieved the male end of the four-wire connector from the orange pumpkin suit and made the connection. "We will, after you reset and reboot."

"Let's go, gentlemen," Thompson ordered, standing behind Bobby with helmet in hand. Bobby pulled the inner liner up over Rocket's shoulders and zipped it closed on the right shoulder. He pulled a flap of stretch material over the zipper and sealed it in place.

"My grandmother is slow, but she's dead," the colonel complained as he bounced around the transfer room.

Bobby pulled the exterior suit closed and fastened it at the shoulders. The clamps fit together, sealing the suit at two points. Margo handed Bobby a helmet seal that he lowered over Rocket's head and secured it in place on the collar.

"Let's go. Let's go. Let's go," the colonel urged as he literally bounced from one side to the other.

Thompson turned around at the bulkhead door as far away as he possibly could have been—then Bobby declared, "Waiting on you, Colonel."

"I don't think so." The colonel pushed off the door and collided with Margo, who stopped his motion. "A fortuitous bump." Margo's left eyebrow went up in disdain. She grabbed the helmet and handed it to Bobby.

"Ready?" Bobby asked. Rocket nodded.

"No, wait." Margo said. She leaned over and slowly, gently kissed Rocket. "You come back, okay."

He turned a tinge pink. "That's my plan."

"Are we done?" asked Thompson with irritation.

"Review the jet control system for me one more time. I've never used one of these new-fangled things." Rocket addressed Bobby but never took his eyes off Margo.

After a heavy sigh, Thompson stepped in and reviewed the two-jet system. Bobby moved around in front of Rocket and said, "Never press them for more than a three-second blast and stay close to the ship." Rocket took it all in, staring at the two red plungers in his hands with one eye and Margo with the other.

"Okay, I've got it."

"Ready?"

"I'm ready."

"Margo, you want to open the oxygen valve on the back as I set the helmet in place—it's just a button?" Margo moved around behind Rocket as the colonel moved toward the exit door control panel.

"There's no power to the door system," Thompson declared.

Bobby hesitated just before setting the helmet on the seal. He lifted the helmet up about an inch and a half. "Rocket, you do understand that after we leave and secure the bulkhead door, you will have to open the exit door manually. We can't shut it, so just leave it open."

"I understand."

"Your flashlight and tools are attached to your belt on retractable tether lines. They will go where you go."

"That much I know."

"Reset the main circuit breaker, then reboot."

"Bobby, I read it. I know what I'm doing."

"Let's go, Major."

Bobby secured the helmet as Margo opened the oxygen valve and said, "You are good to go, Rocket."

Rocket nodded and gave a stiff thumbs up before positioning himself in front of the exit door. He grabbed the release handle and then turned toward the others as if to say, "Get out of here."

Colonel Thompson exited before Rocket grabbed the door. Margo eased through the bulkhead door in front of Bobby, who attached Rocket's tether line to an inside D ring and then paused at the bulkhead door, looking back at Rocket he prayed, "Lord, have mercy on my friend."

CHAPTER FIFTY-THREE

The world stood still. The bright blue sky smelled fresh and clean. The cirrus clouds spotted the blue canvas. He stared up at the clouds for what seemed like hours. In the lower left-hand corner, a white VW bug crawled by. It must have been a ragtop; he watched the top slowly blow off. Within minutes the VW crashed into a fire hydrant, which changed into an elephant with a giraffe's neck. Center left, a cat with a rat's tail and a bird's beak ran from the VW. The rat's tail broke off and morphed into a saucepan. Ever so slowly, the world drifted along.

He tried to make something of the other cotton blobs, but they were too random. Then a small barn swallow flew into his field of vision without making a sound and danced in the wind. Turning right, diving left, darting back and forth, the barn swallow quick stepped it across the sky. It was surreal; it was unfamiliar. No, wait. The sweet smell of fresh-cut alfalfa, mixed with the strong scent of horse, wafted in the air. He was back on his uncle's farm.

The gentle exhale of his favorite gelding let him know he was close. Tilting his head back, he could see Popper, a twelve-year-old chestnut quarter horse, which grazed three meters away. The chomping was peaceful, calm, and almost hypnotic. A honeybee hopped from one flower to another, but he couldn't hear the bee, just horse molars grinding clover.

Beside him lay a green halter and a red lead rope. He would take Ole Popper for a ride. Rolling over on top of the halter and lead rope, he stood to his feet slowly, shielding the tack from the horse.

"Whoa," came the command, said as deeply as his ten-year-old voice could go. Popper stepped away but was drawn back by a handful of fresh alfalfa. The lead rope slinked around his neck in a flash—Popper was captured. The horse went back to grazing. He slipped the halter on and then clicked on the lead rope—not on the chin ring but on the intersection of the nose and chin strap of the left side of the halter. The little boy led Popper over to a stump, where after throwing the lead rope over the horse's back—being careful not to let go of the halter—he tied the lead rope to the other side of the halter. Now he had reins.

In a very fluid motion, he slid under Popper's neck and up onto the stump, and then with a hand full of mane, he leaped onto Popper's back. He had ridden bareback before but never without his dad close by.

Things went rather well until Popper turned his attention toward the barn. Popper's walk turned into a trot, which turned into a canter, which turned into a fast canter. Popper wasn't paying any attention to the little rider, who had dropped the lead rope and was now latched onto his mane with both hands, screaming something unrecognizable.

They came down from the upper pasture, splashed across a small creek, and lunged up the steep bank. The rider didn't make it up the steep bank. The rider rolled off his backside, landing on his back—head down and feet up the bank.

Popper continued home. His rider struggled to breathe. He had gotten the wind knocked out of him. He laid there, upside down on the bank, waiting to catch his breath. Staring up at the light blue sky, the barn swallow was back, dancing in the wind. How long he watched that bird waltz in the wind, he could not be certain, but the light was diminishing. His head started to pound. Night showed up. He figured he had been upside down for a long time. He still couldn't move.

In the fog of bare consciousness, the very much alive Major Sam Lathem searched for clues. Then he heard a high-pitched squeal. Another squeal with a different tone joined in. The individual squeals turned into a high-pitched hum just over his head, or was it just below his head? In the black of darkness he still couldn't orient himself. Was he upside down or right side up? *Upside down—certainly,* he assured himself.

"Where am I?"

His world began to shake violently and it all came back. He felt pressure on his left shoulder then on his right. The pressure released, and his feet felt heavy as the sensation of falling overtook him. The lunar quake shook him deeper and deeper into the lunar crust. The high-pitched hum got louder and louder. Then his descent stopped, and so did the squeals.

His shoulders were too broad to fit through the opening. Half of his helmet peeked through the roof of what looked like a lunar cavern. A light source of unknown origin cast enough light to reveal a cave or some sort of lunar tunnel leading into darkness. With only an inch of his visor through the opening, his peek was very narrow.

High-pitched squeals returned from behind. Their volume increased quickly to the point of pain. He would have covered his ears if it were possible. Then colored lights exploded in the tunnel, forcing him to close his eyes. Traveling at incredible speeds, the multicolored lights flew through the passageway. The squeals and the lights stopped in unison.

Lathem still couldn't move. He was still confused.

CHAPTER FIFTY-FOUR

The bulkhead door locked and sealed. The exit door opened, and Rocket floated outside the ship only to find a strange light sitting on the right-hand solar panel. "Bad mojo?" Flipping himself around, Rocket positioned his body in the desired direction, released the door jamb, fired both jets, and then headed for the access panel located just below the right side landing pod doors.

Unable to see or communicate with Rocket, Bobby and the rest of the crew found their respective seats in the command center and watched blank computer screens and various other instruments for any sign of power. No one uttered a single word for the first thirty minutes. They did, however, take turns peering out the colonel's view window in hopes of seeing some action. No one ever did. Empty space, a million stars, and the leading edge cowling of the starboard side rocket filled the view window. Bobby looked for the fourth time.

Finally the silence broke. "If the power is not restored, how long will we last?" Margo asked, never turning her head toward the front. It was her turn at the window.

Both Bobby and Thompson checked their watches. "The emergency lights run off the solar panels. They'll run forever. Life support is another story. Realistically, we have forty hours, maybe a little more if we are lucky." Bobby replied.

"That's about right," added Thompson.

"Will we stay on course?"

"We should." Bobby leaned to the right and looked back at Margo, who swiveled her chair around front.

"Will the ship reach lunar orbit?"

"It should. We are on the right glide path. Actually, with no power the Moon's gravitational pull will draw us in. Depending on our angle, we may orbit the Moon a couple of times, but eventually the *Lewis* will be drawn to the surface."

"How long until orbit?"

"About six hours." Bobby replied.

Margo said, "Could we still launch the probes?"

"Not without power. There would be no way to open the doors. Without power, we are dead in the water," Bobby explained.

"Could we launch them manually?"

Bobby smirked. "We need Rocket to get us back online."

"How's he doing?" she asked.

Bobby turned toward Margo again. "Rocket is probably still working on the access panel. The panel is secured with twelve fastened screws—four across the top and bottom and two on either side. They'll take some time."

Rocket inserted the torque screwdriver attached to his belt into another screw head. His hands seemed thick, and his gloves were unusually clumsy. Rocket had done this type of work many times before, but this time felt different. He felt rushed—anxious. Not only was he on the clock; the clock ticked loudly in his head. He looked around the outside of the ship before depressing the next screw head about a quarter of an inch and then turning it counterclockwise 180 degrees. The screw head popped out about a quarter of an inch from the surface, releasing its hold. Rocket painstakingly repeated the process two more times before the panel floated loose. Attached to its own six-inch nylon tether, it would not float far.

As he reached up for the reset handle, Rocket shuddered in his suit. A shadow moved over him. His eyes shifted from right to left before he slowly turned around. A grayish green mass twice his size began to rotate about twenty feet off the ship's starboard side. The rotation accelerated, elongating the mass into a fifty-foot cyclone.

Your battle is not against flesh and blood, but against powers and spiritual forces of darkness. The words were profound in his mind.

Inside the *Lewis*, Bobby looked at his watch and then grabbed LC-7 and opened it up. His eyes moved quickly across the pages. "After the panel is gone, Rocket should see a large black plastic D ring lying flush against the craft. He'll grab the handle, pulling it away from the craft and then down until it is flush again. A small light should then come on next to the handle." Just as the words spilled out, the cabin lights came on with a flicker.

Smiles ruled the moment. All lights flashed brightly. All flight controls registered functional. Major Bobby Haistings and Colonel Frank Thompson busied themselves resetting blinking lights and adjusting gages. "We are back in business," Margo declared.

"Not quite. Everything is up and running, but we need the Quad to navigate this ship. Rocket still has to reboot the Quad," Bobby explained as he opened communications.

"Rocket, how are you doing out there?"

"Okay, Bobby."

"Just okay?"

"I'm doing well." A collective sigh inside the *Lewis* revealed that hope had returned. "I've replaced the first panel, and I'm now moving toward the Quad control access panel."

Rocket stopped. The cyclone positioned itself between him and the Quad panel. Looking back at the exit door, he considered returning to the ship. But without the Quad, they were still dead in space. He steadied himself against the fuselage of the *Lewis*, set his jaw, and moved toward the spinning mass.

The cyclone tightened its spin, shortened its tail, and tipped its top, revealing a red cloud slowly rotating in the opposite direction. The mass then moved quickly toward Rocket, stopping within arm's reach. Rocket lifted his hand, pushing his palm toward the spinning vortex. Unsure what would happen when contact was made, he whispered a prayer.

A vile reptilian mouth from a long snout, with razor teeth and dripping thick slime, launched itself toward Rocket. He closed his eyes quickly and shot another prayer. He opened his eyes to quiet space.

Margo pushed out of her seat to Rocket's view window. "I can see him." Both Bobby and the colonel joined her at the window. Rocket turned the third of twelve screws 180 degrees. Bobby smiled to himself as Margo tried to help Rocket turn each remaining screw with the tilt of her head. "Why is it taking so long?" Margo asked.

After turning the final screw and removing the access panel, a large keyboard and small monitor stared Rocket in the face. "This isn't easy. NASA engineers never intended us to have to reboot the computer in space."

His gloved hands made it impossible to type. So placing two screwdrivers on either side of the middle finger of his left hand and the index finger of his right, he pressed Control+Alt+Delete. The screen came on. "Okay. We are looking good." Shouts of cheer erupted in the command center. Everyone's screens came on. "My computer's up," Margo reported.

"Hold on."

Everyone stared at the same screen—blue background with a black box in the middle asking for "User name" and "Password." Bobby cried out, "The user name is 'NASA.'"

Margo typed NASA but nothing happened. She tried moving her mouse; still nothing. "Something's not right."

"This is just the start-up menu. Our keyboards are locked out. Rocket has to unlock them from the outside."

"Rocket hit the final Shift+A and the word "NASA" stood in the box. "You do know the password, don't you?" Rocket asked hopefully.

"I wouldn't have let you go out there if I didn't. Type lewisandclark underscore 1804, all in lowercase." Bobby turned toward Margo. "That's the year *Lewis* and Clark set out on their great adventure."

"Do you know that to be correct?" Margo asked.

"Eighteen-o-four? Yes, that's the right year."

"No. Do you know that to be the correct password?"

"Yes. It would not have been changed without us being notified."

"I hope you're right, Major." The colonel's voice was grave. "With communications down, there is no way to confirm."

Bobby shrugged it off and avoided looking at the colonel.

After typing in the password, Rocket pressed the return button. Every screen went blank again. They stayed blank for a long three seconds. Then they flashed blue with a new box displayed. This box contained five smaller boxes in a column, each designating one of the ship's computers, with the bottom box being an All button.

"Rocket arrowed down to the Quad and hit return." Bobby still had the manual in front of him. Once again the screen blinked on and off, causing great anxiety. Then across the top came the words "WAIT! THE QUAD-REDUNDANT IS RESTARTING."

"Now," Colonel Thompson declared, "we are back in business."

"Don't get 'froggy' and leap too quickly. It will take about four minutes to boot up. In the meantime, Rocket, you need to come on in." Bobby's stress factors would drop a hundred points after Rocket was safely inside.

Rocket had already replaced the access panel and three screws. "I am on my way, with nine screws to go. I'll be at the door by the time the Quad is up and running."

"I've got his vitals," Margo announced. "Blood pressure is good, external body temperature is up, and so is his heart rate." The words came out slow and with concern.

"Of course they are! I'm working out here! I've been sweating like a dog for the last hour."

"Dogs don't sweat. They pant," Bobby corrected.

"Thanks for the update," Rocket said.

"Film at eleven."

"Whoa!" Margo spun around to face Bobby. "What's happening?"

Bobby looked out the view window toward the Moon. "We're rolling." He stared back at the colonel.

"The autopilot is righting the ship."

"Wait until he's back inside," Margo begged.

Thompson urged, "Tell your buddy to move faster."

"I am moving faster. I've got one more to go." Rocket let out a battle cry of victory and then gave a great sigh. "I'm coming in." He dropped his tools, which zipped back to his belt, and grabbed the two jet control devices. Glancing one last time at the moon to his right, he pushed off the *Lewis*, turning back toward the exit door that was now moving away from him. His tether line kept him close and connected. With one leg against the fuselage, he lined himself up and then depressed both buttons for a three-second blast. "I'm on my way."

Bobby moved away from the window. "Margo, you want to keep an eye on Rocket's vitals until he is in and the doors are locked and sealed?"

"I'm watching."

"Colonel, let's run every system through CBX. I don't want to take any chances." Bobby's concern had diminished only slightly.

"I'm way ahead of you, Major."

Eyes sharp, hands busy, a sense of excitement and anticipation filled the command center. Bobby called out, "Rocket, where are you?"

"I'm two meters from the door."

"Don't look now, but we have trouble," Margo cried. With her eyes fixed on the right side-view window, she froze in her seat. Bobby's chest tightened as the colonel moved up, adding another set of eyes staring down another round of white lights. But these lights were not coming from the lunar surface. They were coming from deep space. The lights formed at some point thousands of miles out and began rushing toward the Moon.

"Rocket, you may want to pick up your pace a bit," Bobby urged.

As the first of the white lights streamed by, Margo hoped, "Surely he's inside by now." The last words stumbled out of her mouth as she moved back to check his vitals.

"Rocket . . . Rocket, are you there?"

Bobby quickly swung his head around toward Margo, who cried out, "Where'd you go, Rocket?" she begged.

"Where is he?" Bobby leaned toward Margo.

"I think we lost him. Oh God, I think we lost him."

"What do you mean 'we lost him'?"

"It's like he unplugged. I have no reading. Rocket, are you there!"

Bobby squirted out of his seat and began hitting the Reset button repeatedly. "Could he be inside already?" Margo asked.

"I hope so."

Colonel Thompson moved behind Bobby and Margo, mumbling something about finding out. He passed through the bulkhead door and down the narrow passageway, with Bobby and Margo in his wake. He stopped at the door leading into the transfer room and peered through the small six-by-six-inch observation window.

"What do you see, Colonel?" Bobby asked.

"I see an opened door, an empty room, and about seven feet of tether line." The colonel opened the control panel located on the right-hand side of the door. A lit panel of buttons waited to be pushed. Colonel Thompson closed the exit door and then restored atmosphere to the room. By the time he opened the bulkhead door, Bobby and Margo crowded at the hatch.

"I can't believe this is happening." Bobby entered the room first. All three astronauts gathered near the exit door and stared at the charred end of the tether. Grabbing the tether line, Bobby slid his hand down it, stopping about a foot from the end and about two inches from the black melted residue. Flinching and ducking at the sounds of small meteors striking the ship, he turned the end over and over.

"It's burnt," he explained.

Margo slouched down and stared off blankly. "Rocket, no."

Thompson said, "Like a semi hitting an armadillo on a West Texas highway, quick and painless."

Margo slapped the foul, insensitive comment deep into the colonel's cranium. Thompson took the blow without retaliation. The air grew heavy as the tension mounted. Like a poorly tied bow, ribbons of "AB negative" drifted about the chamber. "Striking me won't bring him back, and it won't change the fact that he was out there because of Major Haistings's screwup."

Thompson headed for the hatch. "No time to hunt for or recover the body. Let's secure the area and get back to work."

CHAPTER FIFTY-FIVE

No word. No contact. The *Lewis* was on course to collide with a shattering moon. Orbit could mean death; landing would be impossible, save for the grace of God. Jack Sooner sat perfectly still at his desk, staring at his "Fifty Years of Space Travel" coffee cup. Mercury, Apollo, and two generations of space shuttles adorned the large blue mug. The chief drained the coffee and then wiped the mug clean with a tissue before placing it in the box beside his desk.

His eyes then went once around the haunting office, pausing at pictures of him with each of his crews, which decorated his walls. The most recent pictured the crew of the *Santa Maria*: Kim, Sam, Marty, Andy, and Ed—he knew them by their first names. Having memorized each of their jackets and spent personal time in their homes, the chief bonded with his crews. Extreme disappointment flooded his lower lids.

Moving on around the room, he stopped at the first of two CASE awards. He read the words slowly: "For Courage in Advanced Space Exploration." He read them again and again, pausing at the word "courage," then mumbled, "If I were all that courageous, I would have stood up to Buchholz from the beginning . . . Kim, I am so sorry." The two plaques found themselves in the trash.

"Chief, I've got another idea. I know how we can get through." Meekerson's shaky voice betrayed his desired confident persona.

The communications specialist did burst through the doors without knocking. NASA's Chief Jack Sooner barely managed a grunt. He placed a couple more personal desk items in the packing box and then looked at the young engineer, whose small rectangular glasses had slipped down his nose.

"What do you suggest?"

Meekerson nervously shuffled toward the visitor's chair but stopped short of sitting down. "The *Lewis* is scheduled to touch down on the lunar surface in just under six hours. While we have made contact with Delta, they have yet to make contact with the *Lewis*." His eyes never left the floor.

"I know. They may be risking their lives for nothing."

"Yes, sir. But Delta's orbit is going to place her on the far side of Earth. The Earth is going to eclipse Delta and the *Lewis*. They will no longer be able to contact the *Lewis*."

Jack rubbed his temples then raised his right hand, gesturing to Meekerson to wait one minute. Opening the middle drawer on the right-hand side of his desk, he retrieved a prescription bottle of painkillers. After taking two pills without the aid of a lubricant, he motioned to Meekerson to continue.

His hands slid into his front pockets. "We can contact the *Lewis* ourselves."

"Haven't we been trying, without success?"

"Yes, we have been trying to make radio contact. But there is another way."

"I'm listening."

"Do you know anyone at NSA?"

"Tell me more, Meekerson."

"NSA controls the Omega Satellite System, whose web extends out beyond Delta's orbit. That system cannot only receive and transmit up and down the frequency dial, but it can also transmit and receive using microwaves, hi-def, and infrared simultaneously. We put our abort text message through the Omega System, blanket the frequency spectrum, and we'll get through to the *Lewis*."

"Maybe." Jack's defeated demeanor said a lot more than words. He placed a couple more items in his box before staring off blankly and adding, "We may be able to contact the *Santa Maria*—see if anyone is still alive."

"We could try. So do you know anyone at NSA?"

Jack tapped his left forefinger on his desk seven or eight times before looking up at Meekerson. "As a matter of fact, I do." He shooed Meekerson out of his office, picked up his phone and called Washington. After five computer menus and two live voices, he was talking to General Buchholz.

"General, I've only got a second. The press are breathing down my neck. They want a statement." The office was empty. The press had been locked out.

"What can I do for you, Jack?"

"Any word on Miller?"

"Accident. A run-of-the-mill hit-and-run by a drunk."

"Yeah, right."

"I'm serious."

"I need the Omega Satellite System."

"What for?"

"It's the only way to abort the *Lewis*."

"Why would we want to do that, Jack?"

"Have you seen the Moon lately? I don't want them to land." Jack's stomach twisted as his hand squeezed the black out of the telephone receiver. "We haven't heard from them in days. They're lost, General. I see no reason to risk more lives."

"Okay, Jack. But listen: they must deploy the probes."

"General, that's all I've wanted. I mean that is *all* I've wanted. They have to loop the Moon to slingshot home anyway. We'll send a message to abort the landing, deploy the probes, and head for home."

"All right, Jack. You can have the system. Give me an hour, and the system will be yours."

"I'll need codes, General."

"I'll open the channel and send the encryption codes. The only password you'll need is 'WETHEPEOPLE.' That will get you in."

"Thank you, General. It's the right thing to do."

"We are in this together, Jack."

"Yeah, sure."

CHAPTER FIFTY-SIX

"I apologize for my earlier insensitive comments." The colonel's conciliatory tone caught Margo off balance. She took a quick peek at the colonel through the corner of her eyes.

"Apology accepted."

"I think I can make it up to you."

"How's that?"

"With a little help, I'll do more than make it up to you."

She smiled and quipped back playfully. "I thought you were helping me."

The colonel had followed Margo to the cargo bay to help her prep the probes for deployment—at least that's what he said. Bobby stayed in the command center to finish running the Quad through CBX and then do a navigational systems check.

"Maybe we can help each other," he offered with a wink as he opened a deployment canister.

"What did you have in mind, Colonel?"

"I haven't told you everything." He spoke with coy mischief.

Margo continued to load the probes into the deployment canisters. A smile widened, "I haven't told you everything either."

The colonel stopped, his brow furrowed to corduroy. His glare intensified. "Nothing happens on this mission without my approval."

Margo never paused, but her smile hardened into resolve. "We can squabble, or we can cooperate. What's it going to be?" She opened another canister and loaded probes. "Let's help each other, Colonel."

Colonel Thompson turned away and stared out at a bright full moon in the view window. "Come on, Colonel." He turned back toward Margo, and after two false starts, the words finally fell out.

"How can I help you, Doctor?"

"I have probes and three satellites."

"Satellites?"

"I need you to slow down the ship, allowing me to deploy three satellites, spread evenly around the moon. I have the coordinates."

"You'll need the major's help."

"You could convince him."

"I'll help you convince the major to slow down the ship, if you help me convince him to land this thing."

"Land?"

"On the lunar surface . . . I have the coordinates."

Margo twisted her mouth. "Go on."

"If we don't hear from Colonel Anderson, there will be no apparent reason to land."

"But you still want to land."

"Yes."

"This trip was never about rescue, was it?"

Thompson moved over close to Margo. "Well, let me tell you a story."

Margo slowed her work without stopping. "I'm listening."

"One rainy afternoon I pulled in to the South Island Inn on Key Largo. The note read 'room 207 at 1500 hours.' I tapped lightly twice before General Buchholz opened the door. Four people sat around the table, and four sat on the queen-size bed. Buchholz shut the door behind me and then slowly pulled a black bag from his briefcase. It was about the size of a small loaf of bread—noticeably heavy. He said it was serious money."

"What was it?"

"Buchholz opened the bag and poured clear crystals onto the table. Looking more like quartz than diamonds—he asked Rodney to explain."

"Who's Rodney?" Margo motioned to the colonel to help her move a bulky trunk, loaded with more probes, over to the deck of deployment tubes.

"Rodney is the general's nephew. Buchholz had never thought much of Rodney or the other lab rats until that late-night phone call. Rodney had been slicing the core samples pretty thin when he came upon a large piece of what looked like broken glass. Broken glass didn't make sense. Two more hours of focused examination, with cutting-edge technology provided by NASA, revealed it had the molecular structure of gold—crystallized gold."

"Never heard of it."

"Crystallized gold didn't add up to me either. Rodney wasn't sure of its application, but he thought it could be worth a lot of money, so he took some. He had never stolen anything in his life, but he didn't think this was stealing. No one owns the Moon."

"NASA's mission, NASA's lab—he stole some."

"For further examination. In fact, he collected all the gold from all the samples for safekeeping."

"That was big of him."

"Fortunate for us."

"Funny how creative a greedy mind can be."

"The story is not over. The next night he was back, and the next and the next. He couldn't shake his curiosity. With long tweezers, he picked up a small cube of clear gold and held it over his Bunsen burner. Looking through a large magnifying glass, he observed the gold clear up. It became smooth with no fault lines. Wanting more light, he grabbed his penlight from his belt and shot the beam of light through the now crystal clear gold. The gold refracted the light and, with a pop, burned a hole through the metal countertop in less than a second. Margo, we are talking laser technology. At that point he called his uncle, General Buchholz."

Margo had stopped prepping. Thompson had her undivided attention.

"The crystals liquefy at eighteen hundred degrees centigrade and can be molded into any form. We can press it out to one-tenth the thickness of twenty pound paper."

"What's the point?"

"Regardless of its form, it has the ability to magnify light millions of times. We are talking incredible lasers. A paper-thin lens placed on a penlight can cut through a ten-centimeter steel plate. We have only begun to dream about its application." Thompson's perverted imagination took him for a short stroll down despot lane. "The laser weaponry alone could change the world." A hawk took flight. World conquest marched in his eyes. Margo recoiled.

"Clear gold?"

"Crystallized gold. We estimate its worth at about a thousand dollars a gram, minimum. That one forty-kilogram bag of lunar crystals is worth over four billion dollars. I can't explain it. We don't have to explain it. We just want to profit from it."

"We?"

"Margo, Sam Lathem was a part of the original ten. Even if the space station was a bust, with another forty kilograms of crystals we would all be rich."

"You're already rich."

"Up and back and grab another forty kilograms. Sammy pulled the first cores. He knew exactly where to pull the next. The *Santa Maria* took off quickly. We wanted another chance to gather cores."

"Sam was to pull the cores with crystals and then replace them with the two retrieved on the first trip, minus the crystals of course. We would be the richer, and no one would be the wiser, and no one would get hurt. Who knew a moonquake would cripple the ship? A million square miles, and it cracks under our ship. What are the odds of that?"

"So what do you want from me?"

"Sam's dead. There are at least two cores with crystals sitting in the *Santa Maria*. Help me get them, and we'll give you Sam's cut. It's got to be worth a half billion dollars. That's billion with a 'b.'"

"Can this ship make it?"

"Down and back and we head for home. We can do that."

"Why can't we cut Bobby in?"

"He's a boy scout. He won't bite. He'll want to turn the crystals over to the authorities."

"We are talking billions of dollars."

"Trust me, we tell Major Haistings and the NSA will be all over it. Can't take that risk."

"Why did you take the risk with me?"

"Had to choose one of you. I thought paying off debt would appeal to you. Besides, handling cores is what you do."

Margo placed her hands in the small of her back and stretched. "You'll make sure the cores don't fall into the wrong hands?"

"Of course. I'm still a patriot."

"Colonel," her delightful smile returned, "I think you have yourself a deal. Rescue if we can, probes and satellites before gold. Deal?"

"Probes and satellites before gold, Dr. Street."

CHAPTER FIFTY-SEVEN

With faces glued to the front view window, Bobby and the crew of the USS *Lewis* cringed at the incredible volcanic activity visible as they entered lunar orbit. Looking like the Mississippi delta with fire red tributaries, the ominous moon bulged and contracted. "It looks more like an egg than a ball," Margo noted.

"There!" Bobby pointed at the apex of a giant heave just as a peak exploded, leaving a formation with sharp edges and smooth sides. "Is that . . . thing growing?"

"It's almost as if something . . . inside . . . is trying to get out." Fear and wonderment collided in her speech.

Bobby studied the moon as it retched, pitched, and rumbled. The surface looked alive as molten lava flowed across the moonscape. "This makes no sense." Burning lava on the lunar surface defied the laws of combustion. Normality had fled. Face-to-face with an encounter, Bobby begged, *Oh God, what am I looking at?*

Bobby looked over at Colonel Thompson, who tried to sit up straight and hide his fright. He was chewing gum at ninety miles per hour. Bobby hadn't seen him blink in over five minutes. He knew the colonel was scared speechless, but there were no words to relieve the fear. Besides, Bobby preferred the colonel quiet.

Margo set her jaw, puckered her lips, pushed out three fast pants, and then whispered, "I can do this." Bobby figured it was good self-talk.

"Let's slow down the ship to launch the probes and release the satellites," Dr. Street announced.

"Satellites?" Bobby turned toward Margo. "No one has said anything to me about satellites." The probes could be deployed at any speed. Satellites, however, could not. Slowing down the ship placed them in greater danger from flying debris and would delay their ETA back on Earth—the only place Bobby wanted to go.

"Just three small ones," Margo explained, "out far enough to keep an eye on this beast. I have the coordinates."

"That will take time that we don't have." The colonel had come alive again. "Major, loop the Moon. We are heading for home." Balls of light flew past the ship like tracers. "We will not be landing on the surface." Pulling back from his view window, the terrified colonel proclaimed in a wobbly voice, "Forget the satellites. There will be no slowing down. We need to get the hell out of here!"

Bobby's eyes danced quickly between Margo and Colonel Thompson. "For once, I'm with you, Colonel."

"Colonel!" Dr. Margo Street yelled, with iron in her voice as she moved toward the bulkhead door. "I came to launch probes and satellites, and that's what I intend to do. If you have changed your mind about going down, that's fine by me. But we will be launching the probes and satellites."

Thompson parried with his own steel. "I'm still the commander. If I say there will be no slowing down, there'll be no slowing down."

The ship rocked violently, interrupting the duel. Margo slammed hard against Dr. Kubo's station. The ship returned to calm immediately, but Margo moved forward quickly and both she and the colonel stared down at the Moon. "What was that?" she asked.

"Like I said, we need to get out of here, now," Bobby said. The cabin temperature dropped more than ten degrees. Bobby was sure everyone felt it, but no one mentioned it. Six eyes darted about, as every light in the cabin dimmed by ten lumens.

"Colonel, I'll forget your *research* on the surface," razor-sharp determination blocked and countered, "but not the probes and satellites."

"Maybe I didn't make myself clear." The colonel positioned himself squarely in the number two seat and then fired the main rockets, speeding up the craft. "There will be no slowing down."

He came across smug, reminding Bobby he was still Frank Thompson. Even when he was right, Thompson came across like a jerk. Rocket used to say that some people had a jerk gene. Thompson must have been the host.

With eyes forward, Bobby heard a metallic click and then turned to see a round cylinder at the colonel's head. "Slow it down," she said.

Thompson turned to look down the barrel of a .45. He froze. It was a deer in the headlights. "Who are you?"

Bobby moved toward Margo, meeting her left outstretched hand. "Stay there, Bobby. I work for NSA. On order of the President of the United States of America, it is critical, gentlemen, that we launch the probes and satellites. I respectfully ask for your help. If you cannot give me your help, then I will insist that you stay out of my way. I am prepared to do whatever it takes to make this happen." It was a speech that she had rehearsed numerous times. Strong and confident, she delivered the words without a hiccup.

"What's going on?" Bobby's head spun. *Think, Bobby, think.* The synapses fired only blanks. He would never have guessed this scenario in a thousand years. *Where the heck did she get a gun? Had she been carrying it the whole time? How did she get it on board? How did an NSA agent become a part of NASA and then maneuver into this particular mission?* The explanation ought to be really good.

With the gun still pointing at the colonel's head, Margo explained her mission. Her meeting with the colonel was no coincidence. NSA had a thick file on Colonel Thompson—they were well aware of his womanizing and used it to get her on board. The colonel relaxed with the realization that his life had been captured. Any mystery dissolved in the moment.

Colonel Thompson slumped over in his seat. "So what are we doing here?"

"This was a rescue mission, remember," Bobby insisted. "There are real people stranded on the lunar surface . . . or were . . . There were people stranded."

Margo ignored Bobby's answer. "We have clear and undeniable evidence of extraterrestrial life. We believe our moon has become a staging ground of sorts, a gathering place for these creatures. Their comings and goings have been observed over the past ten years. However, in the last two years, the traffic has picked up considerably."

"How so?" Bobby asked.

"In the last thirty days, we have concluded that they are colonizing the Moon. We need to find out why. Why our moon? Can we coexist with our new neighbors? What are they building there? For all we know, they may have been building something inside the Moon for the last thousand years. Is it a peaceful colony or a military outpost? The survival of humankind may depend upon the information that the probes and satellites supply."

Bobby looked over at the colonel, who sat terrorized at the sight of the unstable moon. "Colonel." There was no response. "Colonel, did you hear what she said?" Bobby looked at Margo. "This is the real thing?"

Margo nodded at Bobby as her coy smile returned. "There is no more time. Whatever is happening on the Moon is happening now. Help me deploy the probes and launch the satellites. That's all I'm asking. Let's give the people on earth a fighting chance." With her one hand open and a face that begged to be listened to, she pleaded. "We are the only hope they have. Help me. Time is running out."

With a sad affect, the colonel just stared off at nothing. Bobby wondered if he had heard anything.

"Colonel, the only story I'm telling is the story of your heroics." Margo moved in close to the colonel. "Help me, Colonel, and we'll all go back as heroes. You'll go back as the man who saved the world. Did you hear what I said? We are talking ticker-tape parade in Time Square. You, Colonel Frank Thompson, saved the world from an alien invasion. That alone will be worth millions! Save the world, and you'll never have to work again."

She was laying it on thick, but the colonel seemed to be responding. His eyes began to sparkle, and the right side of his mouth cracked into a hint of a smile. "Unbelievable."

"What do you think, Major?"

"Let's make it quick. I want to get home to my little girl."

"Let's do it. Let's do it and then burn for home," Thompson said.

Colonel Thompson fired the reverse rockets for a three-second blast, slowing down the *Lewis* to deployment speed. Then the three-person crew of the *Lewis* scrambled for the bulkhead door, heading for the cargo bay. Pulling up the rear, Bobby paused at the door, hearing the buzzer. A message was coming in.

"Go, go, go! I'll catch up." It had been two days since they had received any kind of message, so Bobby couldn't let it go.

The text message from Chief Sooner read:

> "The Santa Maria is Lost
> Deploy the probes and come home"

Bobby sent a return message.

> "Rescue aborted
> Deploying probes and satellites
> Heading home"

Bobby looked up just in time to see a hundred lights descend on the lunar surface. Margo and Thompson had deployed the first of nine rounds of probes.

By the time Bobby made his way to the cargo bay, the doors were opening. The three crew members gathered in a small control room off the cargo bay. They watched through a glass window and TV monitors as the second round of probes deployed. Thompson controlled the doors and positioning jets of the *Lewis*. Margo controlled the satellite, and Bobby grabbed the boom controls. The claw had a secure hold on the first satellite as Bobby maneuvered it out of the bay. Stretching the arm to its full extension, Bobby released the small satellite into orbit.

Margo deployed its solar shields and then engaged the computer navigation system, which fired the appropriate subrockets, placing it in the correct orbit for maximum effectiveness. "Now she'll keep an eye on this sector. Let's move along."

Colonel Thompson closed the doors and then returned to the command center to fire the main rockets. Bobby kept working. It would be thirty minutes before they deployed the next set of probes and an hour before they launched the next satellite, but Bobby didn't want to waste any time. Maintaining control of the boom arm, he worked at positioning the claw to capture the next satellite. He would be ready for a quick deployment once the doors could be opened.

The lunar surface continued to heave and contract on the far side. Explosions were frequent. The *Lewis* pitched and rolled as meteors pelted the ship, sounding like a bad hailstorm.

"Are you scared?" Her words were measured, revealing veracity, not mockery.

"Not as much as I thought I would be. You?"

"More than I thought I'd be." Margo wiped perspiration from around her eyes. "Are you still skeptical?"

"About what?"

"Extraterrestrial life. I mean, just look at the Moon. That ought to convince anybody."

"Do I believe that intelligent beings exist outside of earth? Yes." Bobby paused for a moment, looking back at planet Earth. "I believe in God. He's an intelligent being."

"I'm not talking about religion. I'm talking about real life."

"So am I."

"I don't get it. If there is a God, why didn't he protect Rocket?"

"Are you sure he didn't?"

"What's your point?" Margo fiddled with her probes and rearmed the deployment canisters.

"Glory." The word poured from his mouth with great affection.

"Now you sound like Rocket."

"I'm still learning from him. Margo, it's the hope of seeing Carol and Rocket in glory that prevents a free fall into utter despair. It's glory . . . the hope of glory. I still have that."

"I'm intrigued but not convinced."

Bobby rotated away from his view window and smiled at Margo. His gaze returned to the expanse of space, and he replied, "I am."

"Bobby, how can you look at clear scientific evidence and then dismiss it?"

"I don't think I am."

"Look out there, Bobby." Margo moved to Bobby's side. "What do you see?"

Bobby looked out of his view window and saw a hotbed of molten rock. "You're not going to find that in your Bible."

Then four strange lights appeared just off the *Lewis*'s port side. They paced with the ship. "What do you suppose those are?" Margo asked, pulling back from the window a bit.

"I don't know."

"Bobby, you see with your eyes and yet refuse to believe."

"No, I see with my soul and believe deeply. I just don't always understand what I see."

"But the data. What do you do with the data? You can't just ignore it."

"I'm not ignoring the data. I'm interpreting it differently."

One of the four lights turned red and rushed the ship. Margo recoiled from the window as Bobby stood up straight. With his hands over his head, he grabbed a conduit line just above the window and pushed his feet to the floor. Bobby's body shielded the window from Margo, who now peeked up.

The hot scarlet light rushed the ship, colliding with a white light just as it entered, knocking Bobby back with a force he had never felt before. The lights were bright and painful; his skin burned as the luminaries bounced around in a strobe like manner. They circled faster and faster, creating a vortex that picked up everything not secured, including Bobby and Margo, who tumbled as they spun. Margo's mouth opened, and her neck tightened, suggesting a scream, but Bobby couldn't hear anything over the howl. As they spun faster and faster, Bobby could feel the skin on his face pull and his head snap back. He closed his eyes and felt a cool breeze wash over him. Taking in a deep breath that smelled like the early morning in the Colorado Rockies after the Aspen have already turned, Bobby's whole body relaxed. He could feel the tension drain from the crown of his head out the soles of his feet.

A smile blossomed as Bobby remembered his girls. The sheer joy on Stacy's face as she leaped from the diving board settled deep in Bobby's memory. He couldn't have been more proud.

The recollection of Carol's slipless silhouette stirred a hunger in him. Her feisty attitude and playful demeanor fanned his love for her into a blaze. How would he ever live without her?

"For such a time as this."

"Who said that?" Bobby looked right and then left but could see no one through the rain. He peered hard as the curtain finally parted just enough to see his backyard visitor. Bobby yelled, "What do you want?"

"For such a time as this."

The curtain of rain closed before Bobby could respond. The drops were big and came down hard. Bobby could feel the waves crash against his shins as he heard himself yell, "Lance!" He dove into the surf with arms whipping, reaching, stretching, and groping. He felt his left triceps pull hard and every knuckle in his left hand crack in rapid succession. A small hand held tightly to his. As he strained to see, every vein in his eyes surfaced and splintered, only to reveal a blue sleeve and a woman's face. Margo held tightly as she mouthed the words, "Help me."

A blinding white light washed everything away and Bobby found himself standing in front of the view window. The red light that rushed the ship stopped just outside the window and then darted away. Bobby rotated back toward Margo, who with wide eyes and windblown hair, asked, "What just happened?"

"I'm not sure." For a reason that defied explanation, he knew that Margo's experience was different from his own.

Thompson interrupted. "We have another satellite to launch."

Having already slowed the *Lewis* to deployment speed, Colonel Thompson opened the doors, and the satellite was released into orbit. Spying a flashing orange light on the satellite, Margo exclaimed with great satisfaction, "Our satellites are transmitting!"

"How do you know?" Bobby asked.

"The orange light tells me the two satellites are talking to each other. Now, whether or not Cheyenne Mountain is picking up the transmission through the Omega Satellite System is another story."

Bobby closed the doors just as Margo deployed two more sets of probes. "Let's move quickly, people. Colonel, would you please fire the rockets?" Colonel Thompson returned to the command center, leaving Bobby and Margo alone just outside the cargo bay.

Margo watched as Bobby captured the last satellite and prepared the boom arm for extension. His steady hands on the boom control joystick surprised even him. Bobby hurried but had a peace that he couldn't explain. Time ticked on.

"I still want to understand." Her curiosity had dissolved into a fear that needed answers.

"I want to know the truth. I'm listening, Bobby. Help me understand the truth."

"What truth?"

"Real truth. Rocket spoke of a truth that would stand the test of time."

"How do you verify real truth?" asked Bobby.

"That's truth." Margo pointed her finger out the window toward the Moon. "Verifiable facts. I see it, I believe it. After everything that we have seen—verifiable facts that contradict your book and you still hold on to it. I just don't get it."

"What contradictions?"

"The Moon breaking up, the extraterrestrial life. We have hard data."

"So where is the contradiction? None of this actually contradicts the Bible. It is just not mentioned."

"I don't get it." Margo looked more interested than confused.

"Listen, we can discover truth through the hard sciences using our five senses. I am completely on board. However, I also believe that there is another reliable source of truth."

"Which is what?"

"Revelation. Supernatural revelation. God has revealed truth to us. There is no natural explanation, ergo supernatural. Now when our discovered truth contradicts his revealed truth, I go with revelation."

"You want to put a sock in it, Major." The intercom was on. Bobby made a mental note to turn it off once back in the command center. "You need to deploy the last three sets of probes. Reverse rockets will fire in five minutes for satellite launch."

Margo moved over to her seat and loaded the probe deployment cylinder with Bobby's help. Priming the charge, she then fired and hundreds of probes spread across the Moon's northern hemisphere. They loaded the cylinder again, primed the charge and fired into the southern hemisphere. Loading once again, they fired the last set of probes across the Moon's equator. "All probes are deployed."

"One more satellite and then we burn for home"—there was pain in Bobby's voice—"without Kim or her team."

"Let's go! Let's go!" Thompson surged through the bulkhead door and took his position. He was opening the cargo doors before he was sitting. The doors opened, and the satellite launched without mishap. Margo spread the sail, and the orange light blinked.

"Let's close her up and go home," snapped Bobby as he quickly retracted the boom.

Thompson closed the doors just behind the boom arm and Margo headed for the command center ahead of the two men.

The ship was whipping around the Moon as Bobby and Thompson made it into the command center. "Take your seats and buckle in tight, boys and girls. We are headed for home." Bobby gave orders that no one resented obeying. "Run all systems through CBX, Colonel. We are three minutes to primary burn."

"Mayday . . ." A faint but hoarse voice was heard over the intercom.

"Did you hear that?" Margo asked.

"I didn't hear anything," Colonel Thompson insisted. "You want to turn that intercom off, Major."

Bobby reached over to the intercom, but instead of turning it off, he turned it up. Static filled the cabin. "I said, turn it off, not up."

"May . . . mayday . . . San . . . Maria," pleaded a familiar feminine voice through garbled static.

Bobby recognized the voice, and his heart skipped a beat. "There it is again."

Bobby placed his headsets on and cued his mike. "This is Major Robert Haistings aboard the USS Lewis. Come in."

"Thank God. Don't leave . . . to die. Bobby, help me, please."

The colonel threw his headset at the front view window. "I told you to turn it off!" Colonel Thompson reached over the middle console and switched off the radio. Bobby turned his head slowly, with eyes wide open. "Don't even think about it, Major. There is no way we are landing this craft."

Bobby's heart raced; his mind swirled. *Lord, what do I do? What do I do?* His nostrils flared with the memory of salt air. Bobby was back on the beach, stomping up and down while his brother drowned. He could see his brother's bloody face and hear his cries for help. "And you did nothing," graveled a mean, angry voice in his head.

Shut up! he cried. *What about Stacy?*

"Do something before it's too late, Bobby."

"You're my hero, Daddy."

"Coward."

"Bobby, help me."

Both hands scratched the back of his head, as his forearms squeezed his face. *What do I do, Lord?*

"Coward."

"I'll be back, I promise."

"Bobby, help me."

"Your hesitation cost your brother his life. Don't let it happen again."

"I said, shut up."

"Don't tell me to shut up, Major," corrected Thompson.

"Wasn't talking to you."

"It's all about you, isn't it, Major?—you and your messiah complex. You just have to be the hero. You don't care about anyone else, including your own daughter."

"Shut up."

"You gonna leave her an orphan?"

"I said, shut up, Colonel." Rage boiled in his blood as he grabbed the colonel by the collar. "Don't even speak of her." Bobby pushed the colonel back into his seat. "And for the record, I've never rescued anyone in my entire life. I told you that before we left the cape. This rescue mission was your idea."

For such a time as this. Rocket's words came out of nowhere and echoed in his head. *Crucified with Christ, we're dead already.*

Disturbed and confused, Bobby looked back at Margo, who sat without expression. She turned away, not allowing him to see the fear in her face.

Margo had accomplished her mission. Now what? The momentary exhilaration of a mission well done quickly gave way to confusion. Margo abhorred helplessness. She needed control. The serpent of vulnerability choked her spine, leaving her mind momentarily paralyzed. Teeth clenched, hands clasped together, she rubbed the silver scar on her left wrist with her thumb. She needed control. She still had the gun.

"We can't go down there, Major." Thompson demanded.

Margo's eyes fell shut, her lips quivered, tears welled up. *Give me eyes to see.*

The view window lit up as a white ball of fire squared off in front. Margo took a breath, filling every lobe of her lungs with fresh oxygen, as the light exposed every pore of her skin.

"Major, we are not landing this ship." Thompson pounded his fist on the console.

The colonel looked over to Margo, who appeared to be in some euphoric state of mind, smiling gently at the lights that were two-stepping across the galaxy.

"'Don't leave me here to die.' Those were Kim's words, Colonel. She's alive." Bobby scrutinized the lunar surface. "I can't leave her."

"If we go down there, we may never come back." The colonel began to eye Margo's right ankle, looking for the gun.

"We have to go down. We don't have to come back." Bobby couldn't believe those words came out of his mouth. *For such a time as this, Bobby Haistings.*

"I liked you better as a coward." The colonel watched as Margo slowly reached for her gun. "You may not have to come back, but we do. We can't let you take this craft down to the lunar surface, Major. Why risk three more lives to *possibly* save one?" Thompson's mouth blossomed into a smile.

Bobby turned to see Margo holding her gun. It was pointed at him. Their eyes met. Bobby's stare plumbed the depth of her soul. "We have to try."

"No, we don't." Thompson started setting a course for home.

Margo moved toward Bobby with the gun outstretched. "You're wrong, Bobby . . . you rescued me."

Bobby reached up and took the gun that was offered. "It is your call, Bobby."

For such a time as this.

"Are you insane? He'll kill us all!"

Ignoring the colonel's hysteria, Margo whispered, "Rocket said that there was no greater love than this . . ."

"That we lay down our lives for our friend."

"It's the right thing to do," Margo said.

Thompson could not believe what he was hearing. "You both have lost your minds."

Bobby turned on the transmitter and keyed his mike. "We're coming, Kim. Hang in there, we're coming."

Chapter Fifty-Eight

"Nancy, I'm going to call it a day." Eight o'clock in the morning ended a long, wakeful stretch for Chief Sooner. With a team on a mission, he usually slept in his glass office until touchdown but not this time. Chest fallen, lips dragged down, and a hollow stare focused on the carpet told a different story.

"Okay, Chief." With glassy eyes, his secretary of twelve years forced a nervous smile as Jack walked out the door with a half-filled box under his arm. He never looked back after his hand hit the knob. Two engineers who talked quietly in the dreary control room caught his attention. Their somber voices froze as they spied Chief Sooner shuffling across the back of the room toward the exit. Jack nodded to the only two men still trying to contact the *Lewis*. "Chief, our world just got more complicated." Jack paused as Meekerson took two steps toward him. "A meteor the size of a Winnebago just took out the Dome of the Rock in Jerusalem. The Jews are calling it a sign from God. The Islamic world has threatened Israel with a nuclear stick. All hell is about to break loose."

"Best of luck to you, gentlemen."

As the heavy security door shut behind him, the halls appeared eerily vacant. The lights flickered, and the thunder grumbled, but Jack kept moving. The two shadows that he had picked up—sent by General Buchholz, no doubt—were gone. "It must all be over now."

Jack Sooner trudged out to his car in a light sprinkle. He placed the box in his trunk, next to two other boxes, and closed the lid. He then collapsed behind the wheel and began to shudder. No tears rolled, as deep anguish plowed ruts across his forehead. He pounded on the steering wheel with his fists and then embraced it with his arms. Torso sagging and head tilting, his eyes saw a blurry world. "I am so sorry."

He had already lost two teams. He didn't want to lose a third. But all hope dissipated with the latest pictures from the lunar surface, revealing a gauntlet of meteors and dust. The pitching and heaving of the surface made the Moon a certain death trap. Even looping the Moon would be a gamble that not even a Las Vegas bookie would take.

Staring out of the front windshield, Jack watched a ring-necked pigeon land on his hood. He started to honk, the palm of his hand hovering over the plunger, but he refrained. "The pigeon has landed." Maybe it was an omen?

The chief started to feel sick. Dinner or breakfast, or whatever you call a meal at four o'clock in the morning, wasn't going to stay down. He opened his door and leaned way out over the parking lot. Nothing. He began to sit back up, when the eruption in his stomach forced him out again. Three spasmodic heaves emptied his belly. His head swirled, and his skin felt tacky. After rubbing his teeth with his tongue, he spit twice before wiping his chin with a used napkin he found on the floorboard. He sat up just in time to see a large owl swoop down, grab the pigeon, and fly off.

With a disgruntled huff, Jack reached into his unused ashtray for a stash of spearmint gum. He removed the foil wrapping quickly and began chewing the gum with a vengeance, anxious for the warm, sour aroma of vomit that saturated his nose, mouth, and throat to give way to the fresh taste of spearmint and liberate his senses. "Thank God for spearmint gum."

He fastened his seat belt and adjusted his mirrors. There, in his rearview mirror was Meekerson. He started to approach Jack on the driver's side but hesitated after seeing Jack's deposit and approached on the passenger's side. The window lowered with the push of a button, and the young engineer leaned through. "Chief, I've got messages."

"Let me have them."

"Space Station Delta has been evacuated. Morgan has loaded his crew on the *Hope*, and they are headed home. ETA is tomorrow morning at 0950 EDS." The chief allowed a smile. "Good . . . and?"

"We've received a text message from the *Lewis*."

"Please tell me that the *Lewis* has looped the Moon and is headed for home."

"Well . . . not exactly."

Jack's head pounded as his body sunk deeper into his seat.

"They have established communication with the *Santa Maria*."

Jack turned pale; his eyes darkened but never blinked. "What exactly did it say?" His lips barely moved as he slowly spun away from Meekerson and stared at the hood of his car. The pigeon had left a present.

"Anderson's alive. Snatch and run."

Jack turned his car on. "Chief, what do we do?"

Jack placed the transmission in reverse and eased on the gas, with Meekerson still peering through the window. "Chief, what do you want us to do?" Meekerson sidestepped to stay with the car. "Chief, where are you going?"

Jack placed the transmission in drive. "To pray, Meekerson. To pray for their souls." Jack drove off, leaving Meekerson standing in the parking lot. It began to rain hard.

CHAPTER FIFTY-NINE

With the computer navigation system engaged and the location of the *Santa Maria* preset in the LPU, Bobby spread the wings and engaged the 360-degree flight control jets positioned on the wings' trailing edge and far tip, which allowed the *Lewis* to maneuver in the limited atmosphere of the Moon. Thompson buckled in tight but hadn't stopped swearing at Bobby since he'd said they were going down. Bobby tuned him out. The colonel may have tried something more drastic, but two with a gun against one without kept him in his seat with his mouth running.

Margo sat in Dr. Kubo's chair, monitoring the locator readout. "There she is." The computer image showed the *Santa Maria* twenty kilometers from Bobby's left sleeve.

"Whoa!" Bobby rolled hard right, avoiding a flaming meteor about the size of a Hummer. He rolled left and pitched up, hopping over the next deadly impediment. Pint-sized meteors beat the drum on the *Lewis*'s underbelly. There was nothing Bobby could do about the small ones; it was all he could do to dodge the big ones.

Two more hard banks produced a string of expletives from Colonel Thompson. He hadn't changed his vote. "Do you have any idea where you are?" Thompson questioned.

The game of dodge had moved the *Lewis* off course. No visible distinctive formations identified their whereabouts. If Bobby had memorized the topography of the entire lunar surface, it would not have helped. The extreme volcanic activity had changed everything.

"Margo, I need a little help," Bobby begged.

Margo struggled to read the lunar positioning unit. If the *Lewis* wasn't rolling or pitching, she was vibrating. The coordinates shook with the screen. Margo strained her eyes with a squint as she tried desperately to read the data. Finally, she placed both hands around the monitor to steady the screen and remove the finer vibrations. "We're off."

"I could have told him that."

"We need to turn about. The *Santa Maria* is twelve kilometers 176 degrees from our present setting."

"We're further away now than we were before," the colonel informed them.

"I'm doing the best I can, Colonel."

"Your best is going to get us all killed. You are an idiot, an absolute idiot. Who do you think you are, playing god with my life?"

"You're not helping," explained Margo.

"Hold on." The last meteor strike pitched the nose toward the lunar surface at a steep angle. Margo spun forward and locked her seat into position. Colonel Thompson latched onto the steering column in front of him and pulled hard. Not that pulling hard helped; they weren't trying to overcome aerodynamics, but earthbound habits were hard to break.

They knifed through the thin atmosphere and slid over the surface at just over one kilometer. Visibility was minimal. Rocks jutted; mountains exploded and dust flew. The *Lewis* continued to take fire as she avoided the larger debris. "Can the ship handle this abuse?" Margo asked.

"Who knows?" Bobby never took his eyes off the front window.

At 2400 Zulu, the USS *Lewis* passed over what used to be the northern ridge of Mare Crisium as a lava tube exploded, sending molten lunar rock toward her underside. Bobby fired the rockets to escape the plume. The ship bucked and went into a yaw spin.

Bobby didn't want to even think about the damage they had sustained. But the rocket blast pulled them out of the spin and shot them past the *Santa Maria*.

"There she is," Colonel Thompson pointed out, "and there she goes. You really aren't very good with this ship, are you, Major?"

Bobby smirked, "It has all been theory until now." Bobby banked to his left, allowing him to keep an eye on the *Santa Maria* and look for a place to set down. The dark craft sat contorted in the rift with no sign of life.

"I hope you haven't risked our lives for nothing."

"We're about to find out, Colonel. I'm bringing her down. Prepare to land."

Inside the Mare, the atmosphere was clear and free from debris. The rifts and cracks looked like a river delta, with the main artery being fed by hundreds of little tributaries. After spotting a clear piece of real estate two hundred meters from the *Santa Maria*, Bobby turned the *Lewis* over to the autopilot, allowing the ship's computer to bring them down.

A squishy thud rattled the ship and shook their skeleton axis. A strange reptilian creature leaped onto the forward view window. Thin skin revealed a massive ribcage that heaved as the creature drew in a great breath. From its mouth of jagged teeth came a gruesome cry that delivered waves of pain through Bobby's frontal lobe. He wanted to cover his ears, but his hands clung to the console. A white light exploded into the side of the creature, sending hot sparks across the *Lewis*. Another white light filled the cabin. Brighter and brighter the light grew, washing everything out.

Bobby closed his eyes and threw his head back. "Sweet Jesus, deliver my soul."

CHAPTER SIXTY

Bobby drew in a breath, slowly filling and expanding his lungs. His chest retched. His eyes wouldn't open. For reasons unknown, his eyelids hung together. Elongating his face, he tried to force his eyes open. Nothing. He took inventory, beginning with his toes. They wiggled freely as did his ankles, but there was no sensation of any kind. No shoe, no boot, and no sock rubbed his skin. Was the wiggle in his mind or in reality? He cocked his head and listened for some sound, anything that would give him a hint to where he was or what was happening. Silence.

One eye finally broke loose and opened slightly. He saw what looked like soft blue sky. He contorted his face again, breaking the other eye loose. His arms still didn't want to move. His eyes felt full of sleep—that quasi-hard, sticky crud that collects in the corner of your eye. His blurry vision made it difficult to get a fix on his location.

The blue looked too close to be sky but lacked the appearance of a solid mass like a ceiling. More similar to a soft liquid with the viscosity of molasses, whatever it was, he was in it. "I think I'm breathing it." As he drew in a deep breath, he could feel the cool goo penetrate his windpipe and ease into his lungs. There was no pain involved, only the strange sensation of breathing thick humid air.

He stretched his head back and took in another gulp. His head pushed into something spongy as his mouth widened into a giant yawn. His eyes closed lazily, and his body relaxed softly as his mind drifted into deep sleep, at least what felt like sleep.

Bobby sensed the cool water on his shins. The bubbles danced all the way to his knees. As the surf went back out to sea, the sand slipped from around and under his feet. The rain was cold; his tears were hot. All of a sudden the horror of his brother disappearing in the waves overwhelmed his psyche. A blood-curdling scream erupted from his mouth. "Lance!" Bobby splashed up and down the beach, "What do I do? What do I do?"

"Bobby." The voice was calm but firm.

Bobby jerked around, only to see the soft blue molasses. His heart slowed down, and he took a deep swallow of thick air. "Am I dreaming?" As his eyes closed slowly, he drifted off into a subconscious world, feeling the cool rain on his face again. The waves continued to surge and crash. Bobby sobbed for hours.

"Bobby." The warm, familiar voice spoke again. This time Bobby didn't turn to see where the voice originated. His eyes diverted to a dark piece of driftwood that looked like an overripe banana. "Bobby," the voice called out in a gracious tone, "it wasn't your fault."

"I was scared," Bobby pleaded, still fixed on the driftwood.

"I know. But it wasn't your fault."

"Don't you remember I told you not to go out?" Bobby tried to turn his head to see the face he longed to see, but his neck stiffened.

"You did warn me. It wasn't your fault, Bobby."

"I should have dove in. I should have swam further and faster. I should have tried to save you. I should have tried harder. I was so scared." He could taste his hot tears as they followed the face crease into the corner of his mouth.

"Bobby, you did everything you could. I wasn't listening. I was twelve years old with one thing on my mind. I just had to be a man. You were eleven years old, and gale force winds stirred the surf. We shouldn't have been on the beach. But Bobby, there was so much more going on that neither of us understood at the time."

Hunched over, Bobby fell to his knees and grabbed two fistfuls of wet sand. "I don't understand." The banana driftwood agitated between his knees. He closed his eyes out of sheer exhaustion. "Lance, I'm sorry."

"Bobby." He recognized his brother's love. The gentle breeze kissed his cheeks. One deep breath and Bobby's heart slowed and the crying stopped. Now, conscious of his shaking, Bobby tried to relax.

"Bobby, open your eyes."

He cracked his eyes open, with his head turned down in anticipation of seeing something that might scare him. While he saw nothing at first, the fine hair on the back of his neck stood tall. A chill ran down his back, and the small blond hairs on his arms rose up. He felt a presence he couldn't explain. As he lifted his head up, there was an explosion of lights flashing and dashing about. Like lightning bugs on drugs, they jolted about—slowly stopping, turning, and then darting away. Faces of light moved effortlessly through the sky. Then they stopped in a line along the beach. Armored legs, arms, and wings seemed to drop out of the balls of light. Their feet extended into the sand but made no impression.

With his heart in his throat, Bobby tried to speak. He swallowed hard again and rose to his feet. "Who are you?" His body shuddered. There was a presence behind him that carried the stench of death. With fight in his eyes, the creature standing in front of him raised his sword up over his head—the sword itself was now parallel with the beach. The putrid aroma intensified. Bobby's eyes burned and watered.

The creature opposite Bobby opened his mouth and released a deafening shrill and then swung his weapon. Bobby dropped to his knees and covered his head as he shrunk down into the sand. Bobby felt the aching of a fractured heart.

"Bobby." The calm voice of his brother spoke again. The beach was quiet and deserted, smelling of fresh salt air. "It wasn't your fault. They came to escort me and protect you."

"Lance, I'm sorry." A small twelve-year-old hand squeezed his right shoulder. Bobby's shaking stopped with the rain, and the clouds opened up. The bright sun beamed hot against his face.

The surf felt warm and inviting. Seagulls flew overhead, squawking with delight as Bobby took in the cool salt air.

"Bobby, just so that you know, I'm okay. I've always been okay."

Bobby's eyes rolled back as he fell into the surf. Once again, he sucked in a big gulp of thick air. Turning his head to the side, he took stock in his surroundings. Dressed only in his flight suit—no helmet, no boots, and no oxygen—he found himself alone in a small antiseptic room with pearl white tile on the floor and walls and an airy blue ceiling. He was lying on what appeared to be a leather mat, blue in color and elevated on a white porcelain pedestal. He saw no door or window and no visible form of egress. "How do I get out of here?"

"I wondered the same thing."

All of a sudden, there she was. Bobby almost fell off his pedestal when he heard her voice. He would have sworn he was alone. But there she lay on her side, head propped up and her right hand on an identical porcelain pedestal. "Margo, were did you come from?"

"Where'd I come from? Where'd you come from? I thought I was alone in this marshmallow room. I have no idea how I got here or where 'here' is, but I thought I was alone. Then I heard you ask, 'How do I get out of here?' and there you were."

"This is so strange. I have the same story. I was alone, then you spoke, and bam!—there you were."

"Are we dead?" Bam. There sat Thompson on his own pedestal between Margo and Bobby.

The three pedestals lay in the shape of a triangle with two meters of empty space between the head of one pedestal and the foot of another, leaving a large opening in the middle.

"Are we alone now, Bobby?"

Bobby raised his eyebrows and then took a slow look around the room.

"I think so. This is so strange. I just don't understand what's happening. It's nothing I would have expected. I mean, it is just way out of the bounds of my understanding. I don't have a category to put this in . . . I remember . . ."

"What? What do you remember?" Margo asked.

"No, no, no. It's not a memory. It was a dream."

"What kind of dream?"

"An explanation."

"What are you talking about, Bobby?"

"It was my choice to try. But it wasn't my choice to succeed."

"What do you mean?"

Bobby explained, "There are other players in the universe."

"Yes, there are." Margo seemed almost excited.

"I opened my eyes to see some sort of light creatures flying around me—balls of light with faces. Then they came to rest between me and the surf. Bodies dropped out of the balls."

"Bodies?" Engrossed in the story, Margo swung her legs into the center. "Light creatures with bodies."

"Humanoid. They had some sort of form-fitting body armor on them. If it was their skin, it looked hard and leathery. They definitely wore a breastplate—a piece of armor—I could see the straps."

"Extraterrestrial storm troopers."

"They had wings. They had large wings, eggshell in color, which seemed soft but rugged. Like four-foot corn on a windy day, they wafted in the wind, but I never saw them flap.

"Were the wings feathered or skinned like a bat?" the colonel asked.

"The underside looked more like skin. But the topside was soft like fine fur. And in their hands they carried . . ."

"A weapon." Margo finished his sentence, with excitement in her voice.

Bobby nodded, and the room fell silent. His eyes continued to scan the room, probing an explanation.

Then Margo asked, "Where does the light come from?" While the room was bright and fresh, there was no light fixture. "Where are we?"

Bobby took a long breath and then offered, "I have no idea."

"We're dead. And you killed us." Thompson bolted off his mat and lunged at Bobby. "If we aren't now, you are going to be."

His body was intercepted in midair by a small figure of a man in a USAF flight suit identical to theirs. "It is too late," instructed the small man who then carried Thompson back to his mat.

"Who are you?" Bobby asked as he stared at the white-haired, dark-eyed visitor.

"'Who are you?' I think the first question is 'What are you?'" Thompson corrected.

"My name is Caleb. I'm your host." Margo moved closer as Thompson moved to the far side of his mat. "I am a malach, a watcher."

"An alien?" Margo asked quizzically.

"Explain 'alien.'"

"Different from us. Non-human. Not of our world," Margo explained.

"You don't belong in our world," Thompson added.

"Yes, by definition. I am not human. I am not of your world. But"—Caleb leaned toward Thompson—"we were here first. So maybe *you* are the alien."

"No, you are definitely the alien," Thompson insisted.

"Regardless, you are all my responsibility for the time being." Caleb's smooth and pleasant voice calmed the nerves but lacked authority. There was something familiar about him that Bobby couldn't place. "So please, I'm asking you to stay here until I get back. If you run into trouble, blow this horn." He removed a thirty-centimeter ram's horn from a small pouch on his side.

"Trouble? What kind of trouble?" Margo's smile straightened into concern.

Handing the horn to Bobby, he added, "Don't lose the horn, Bobby."

"How do you know my name?"

"What kind of trouble?" Margo's head spun.

"When do we go home?" Bobby asked.

"When?" Caleb smiled.

"Yeah, when do we go home?" Margo chimed.

"Soon."

"Soon. What do you mean 'soon'? I'm not staying here. I deserve better than this. I demand to speak to your superior."

Caleb turned away from Thompson and addressed Bobby. "The arrogant one is difficult. They always are." He placed his hand on Bobby's shoulder. "Just stay here until I return for you. I'll explain everything later."

Before their eyes, Caleb transformed into a light creature, still having the basic form of a human except that his substance was pure light. He floated over the floor with no visible means of propulsion. He waved his hand, which left a twenty-seven centimeter light trail before their eyes, and then turned into the wall to leave. However, he was knocked back onto the cold floor. Changing back into human form again, he shook himself off and declared, "I still have trouble with white walls. Don't ask me why. I just do."

The stunned team watched him walk slowly through the wall. On the other side of the now translucent partition, he transformed into the light creature again and then streaked down the corridor of a long damp cave.

Bobby watched as the wall returned opaque. "What do we do now?"

CHAPTER SIXTY-ONE

The Moon shook at full quake. The rocks shattered around his head. His arms vibrated loose. The lunar vise, which had held Major Sam Lathem pinned in a rock tube, released its grip. Sam fell to the floor of a long cave splashing into two inches of water. "Where did the water come from?"

Off his right shoulder, he found the lunar lamp. Sam smirked, snatched up the light, and switched it on. No light beamed. He rattled the light in his hand before giving two firm raps on the bottom of it with the heel of his hand. It worked. "What do you know?"

First to the right then to the left, he directed the light down the corridor. Cylinder shaped, with a five-foot ceiling, the cave ran about thirty meters to the right before bending and about ten meters to the left. Periodic stalactites created a dangerous maze. The floor appeared rocky but there were no sharp edges. Erosion worked to his advantage. But which way should he go?

He wanted out. He needed to get back to his ship. Which way was out? He looked right, then left, then right again. He stared down hard into the water. Squatting with the lamp, he watched. He then stood up into the tube from which he had fallen and grabbed a handful of dry lunar dust. The fact that the tube was now closed did not escape his notice. Squatting back down, he sprinkled the dust into the water and watched as it drifted to his right. He continued to sprinkle and watch until the first drop test disappeared around the bend. Looking left, Sam sighed and pushed off, hoping he was heading up and out.

The going was slow. He couldn't risk a tear on the sharp rock edges. Moving through the maze of stalactites, hunched over, made his back ache. "I hate spelunking." He paused to rest on a ledge and pondered time. He had no sense of it. How long ago was the quake that sent him down the shaft? It couldn't have been too long ago. He was still breathing oxygen. Sam checked his timepiece. It indicated that only minutes had elapsed. But surely, it was more than minutes? His thoughts, sleep, and dreams would have consumed more time than minutes. It didn't make sense.

The second turn opened up into a large room. Sam stayed close to the wall and used the large boulders for cover as he shot the lunar candle around the room. It was empty except for three large pillars—stalactites and stalagmites had come together.

The creek had narrowed to about two feet wide. Winding its way through the pillars, it cut through the great room. Sam wanted to move across the one-hundred-foot span quickly but thought it wise not to give up his cover.

Halfway through the great room, he heard movement. Squeals and splashes were moving toward him at a rapid rate. Sam pushed himself into a depression in the wall, extinguished the light, and wished that NASA had chosen a darker color for their space suits.

Three creatures jumped into the room. One paced as it searched the room. The other pair seemed to be in conversation with clicks, ticks, and some bizarre language. Two arms, two legs, a head, and a torso made them familiar, but the torsos were no thicker than the arms and the legs. Their feet were two-toed, but their hands had four fingers and a thumb. Their skin seemed thick and tight, with a small patch of course hair across the shoulder blades. Sam made mental notes but had no interest in verifying what he saw.

They stopped on all fours in the water. One raised its head as if to sniff the air. The two holes below the two large bug eyes appeared to be nostrils. A long tongue came from their mouths as they lapped up the water like dogs.

Then the more nervous one stood upright like a man and peered directly at Sam. Its nose elongated into the snout of a pit bull. Teeth flashed, and saliva dripped. A piercing shrill shook the room. Sam pushed harder against the wall. Lights flashed and what looked like a lightning bolt struck the snarly creature in the chest, knocking him into the water. The creatures scrambled upright and darted back up the corridor in the direction from which they had come.

Just as Sam leaned out of his hiding place, he heard voices. He pushed back into the shadow. Two men entered the great room fast, stopping atop one large boulder. Dressed in body-length coats with no sleeves, they each held two eighteen-inch blades, one in each hand. Massive arms, ripped in muscles, flexed as the blades cut the thin air in front of them. Their eyes, clear and sharp, scanned the room. The slightly larger warrior spoke first: "Scouts, no doubt." He replaced his blades in a sheath that strapped to the middle of his back.

"I'm surprised by their bravery."

"It's not bravery—it's audacity," said the smaller one. "What do we do?"

"We drive them back. It is not yet their time."

The two warriors ran through the room in pursuit of the creatures.

Sam Lathem stepped out of hiding just in time to see an orange ball of light streak across the room, disappearing in a crevasse. *No time to figure out what that was.* Sam took off across the room. When he hit the water, he stayed in it. The corridor that exited the great room was larger and void of stalactites, allowing Sam to pick up his pace.

Two turns later, the water vanished into a thin lip, and the corridor opened up into stars. Sam's heart exploded. Ten more meters and Sam was out. He bounced back out onto the lunar surface, becoming an astronaut again, a lost astronaut but an astronaut nonetheless. The sky was filled with smoke or dirt or dust. He wasn't sure. Distant peaks glowed red. Nothing looked familiar. The corridor had opened at the foot of a two-hundred-foot hill. Sam decided to climb. Maybe from a higher vantage point, he could get his bearing.

The slope was jagged but gentle. A hop, a skip, and a jump placed him halfway there. Thirty feet from the top, the lunar surface began to rumble. But this time, it was different. It shook with a beat—in a march.

Sam eased himself between two rocks and peered over the summit. Thousands upon thousands of bug-eyed creatures in full battle array marched. Spread across the valley, their number stretched to the edge of sight. Where were they going?

Sam looked down the ridgeline to his left and found his two warriors watching the bug-eyed parade. They spoke softly to each other. Sam couldn't make out what they were saying, but they appeared concerned. Then, in a blink, they transformed into creatures of light and flew back down the corridor. As they vanished into the cave, the orange ball of light flew over Sam's head and bounced down the ridgeline. He watched it bounce from one boulder to another, finally coming to rest on a large flat rock in the rough shape of a turtle. Then it disappeared in a cloud of moondust.

When the dust settled behind the turtle rock, Sam Lathem could see the *Santa Maria*. "My ship!"

Sam quickly dropped down about thirty feet from the summit and made his way toward the ship. From three hundred fifty meters away, he could see the disabled *Santa Maria*—she sat catawampus in the rift. His hope began to fritter away; his joy sank deep into his boots. "There must be a way." He trudged on, one heavy step after the other, hoping to find some company. Together they could free the ship.

One hundred meters from the *Santa Maria*, the Moon split in front of him, creating a blanket of dust and a chasm too wide to jump. To the right were the bug-eyed soldiers, so he would go left in search of a place to cross.

As the dust settled and the chasm narrowed, he saw another craft—the USS *Lewis*. Sam Lathem smiled to himself. He was going home. But first, he needed to collect his valuables.

CHAPTER SIXTY-TWO

Mare Tranquillitatis. In the stillness of limited atmosphere, the turbulent moon pondered her intimate doom in the dust, dust that blew hard against the alien invaders, the brave, the frightened, the battle scared, and the sentries stationed on the rim to warn of danger. And the dust, stirred by the moonquakes, heaved against the troops. Wave after wave of bug-eyed soldiers pushed back and poured out of the lunar core, hungry for human blood.

Yet to the designated east, in Mare Crisium, the remaining crew of the *Santa Maria* quickly boarded the *Lewis* as malach marched in formation. The Moon shook as each foot pounded the fracturing crust in unison. Outlined against the rising sun, myriads of white-crowned creatures stood shoulder-to-shoulder and armor-to-armor around the rim. Flashing swords and burning eyes covered the mare's floor as a trumpet blew, bringing the army to a halt.

In the distance, at the head, a lone warrior sat tall upon his armored stallion. Muscles throbbing with anticipation, eyes piercing the darkness, he scanned for Earth's approach. A single white-headed creature then circled the lunar craft and came to rest on the forward hatch. Solicitous astronauts inside grunted and groaned through their preflight. As the snow-headed creature took flight, weapons readied for battle, he glanced down into the window of the crew module and saw two very familiar, very fragile eyes staring back at him.

*　　*　　*

Armpits soaked and sweat pouring off his face, Thompson sprung to his feet once again. "I don't know about you, but I say we get out of here."

Bobby helped Margo down from her mat and handed her the horn. "Hold this."

"He said to stay put." Margo hesitated; fear radiated from her eyes.

"I've got to get back to my little girl." Bobby moved toward Thompson, who was patting down the walls. "We find our suits, then our ship."

"Then we warn Earth." Thompson worked high on the far side.

No openings, no seams, no indentations, and no cracks. They began systematically pushing on every inch of the wall. Bobby worked his way over to where he thought Caleb exited and gave a push. His hand went right through the wall. He jerked it back quickly. "Here it is."

"What is it, Bobby?

"Watch." Bobby pushed his hand through the wall again and then brought it back. "We go through the wall."

"We don't know what's on the other side," Margo resisted.

"Move," Thompson declared as he puckered his lips and began to pant, gearing up for a run at the wall.

Bobby grabbed Margo's hand, and the two of them simply walked through the wall. They found themselves in a three-meter-wide corridor of the dark cave. The ceiling was barely two meters, causing six-foot-one-inch Bobby to hunch over.

Ankle-deep water on the ground flowed slowly to their left and water dripped quickly from the ceiling. He could see reasonably well but didn't understand why.

Thompson burst through the wall, falling facedown into the water. Turning himself over, he scrambled to his feet. "I wanted to make sure I made it."

"Well, you made it. I don't know where you made it to, but you made it." Bobby peered down both directions.

Margo examined the striations on the cave wall. "We aren't safe."

Thompson assessed the situation in the cave quickly and ordered, "Let's move upstream. Up and out."

Bobby shrugged in agreement. "Why not?"

They followed the cave for two turns and then heard the strange sound of rushing wind. Getting closer and louder by the second, Bobby realized the need to move. The cylindrical shape of the cave afforded no hiding place; running was the only option available.

"Run!"

They scrambled for their lives. The thunderous freight train roared closer and closer. They made a hard ninety-degree turn, and the cave opened up a little, with boulders and numerous notches in the walls.

"Hide!" Bobby yelled. With Margo in tow, they passed Thompson. They dove behind the rocks just as thousands of multicolored lights flew by them and then disappeared down the corridor.

After several minutes of calm, Thompson followed Bobby back out into the corridor that split into a "Y."

"It's clear. Any ideas what that was?"

"I think I know," Margo offered, stepping out from behind the rocks. "Aliens, just like Caleb."

Bobby smiled, "Thanks for the update."

"Film at eleven," Margo smirked playfully.

"The question is are they friendly or hostile?" With eyes like saucers, Thompson backed up against the wall as a dark shadow moved behind Bobby.

Unaware, Bobby stretched his vision down the dimly lit corridor. "Any suggestions as to which way?"

"Follow the alien trail," Margo whispered.

Thompson pressed hard into a concave. "Are we following them, or are they following us?"

"We can't stay here." Bobby motioned to Margo to follow. "Let's go, Colonel."

After stomping another five hundred meters and veering right at two more intersections, they entered a large open chamber.

Bobby estimated the room at just over two thousand square feet with a ceiling reaching one hundred feet off the floor. Murky orange light from an unknown source emanated from the upper left-hand corner. Three pillars stood in the center where stalactites had reached down to hold hands with stalagmites. The walls appeared wet with a sticky sheen. Boulders of various sizes littered the floor, with a large grouping to his right. Bobby moved into the room slowly, using the rocks next to the walls as cover. After an investigative trip around the chamber, Bobby came back around to Margo and Thompson, who had waited by the passageway. "There is no exit. It's a dead end."

"What's that mean, Bobby?"

"It means you're stuck with me." The voice came from behind Thompson. A shadow rose from the misty floor and then scampered up on a rock. With glowing red eyes, it spoke again. "Welcome. I've been waiting for you." Thompson stepped back, Margo moved over behind a stalagmite, and Bobby squared his shoulders.

The creature paid no attention to Bobby and ambled over to Thompson, who backed up all the way to the wall.

"What do you want?" Bobby demanded.

The creature turned his shadowy head three hundred and ten degrees, stopping at Bobby. "You, I want all of you." A frosty mist flowed from his mouth. The humans were suddenly cold.

"You can't have us. We aren't yours." The words spilled from Bobby's mouth with a courage he had always wanted to have.

"Do you really think you can stand up to me?" His words thundered, shaking the corridor. "You fool."

Bobby stepped up quickly. The creature leered at him and then released a deep guttural growl. "You are nothing. You are a gnat in my eye, a mosquito around my ear. Bother me no more." His angry eyes doubled in size.

"Well, I would hate to be a *bother*, but we need to be leaving." Bobby began to back in the direction of the corridor.

"Enough of this chitchat." The creature pointed his spiny finger at Bobby and lightning flashed toward his heart.

Inches from his chest, the lightning was cut in half by the fiery sword of Caleb. "I told you to stay put." Caleb's sword was cut in two pieces, causing the momentary joy of the team to turn to bewilderment.

"Great," Bobby moaned.

The creature gave a sinister chuckle and cried, "Caleb, Caleb. Don't make me laugh. You are no match for me. Go home. I don't want to hurt you. I just want these humans."

"That's a lie. You've wanted to hurt me ever since Budapest."

"That may be true."

"They are my responsibility. They are not yours for the taking. I have stood my ground before. I will stand again."

The creature barely managed a nod in Caleb's direction as he replied, "But you had help. You're all alone now." With one eye still on Caleb, the creature moved his attention to Margo, who had backed away against a large rock. "I'm going to have fun with you." A long tongue emerged from his mouth, which reached down to his belt and then back up, wiping his face.

Caleb turned to Bobby and whispered, "Try to get his attention away from me."

Bobby ran from the creature and dove behind two large boulders. Seeing Bobby run, the creature snapped around and shot a lightning bolt from his long crooked fingers into the rocks. Caleb then shot his own bolt from his broken sword, striking the creature in the chest and knocking him up against the chamber's roof. Sparks flew as the shadow disintegrated. A small, monkey-looking lizard with a short fat tail leaped up on a rock. His red eyes glowing, he spit out his long red tongue, dripping of mucus, and wrapped it around Margo. Repulsed, she tried to loose herself, but the slime did not allow a handle. The foul stink made her breathing difficult. She gagged.

Caleb sailed over to Margo and struck the rancorous tongue with a mighty blow from his half sword. Wincing in pain, the creature retracted his tongue as he leaped onto Caleb's back and gave a hair-raising screech. Some kind of putrid fluid smelling of death oozed from his nostrils. Margo ran to the other side of the cave next to Bobby, trying to put distance between herself and the creature. Thompson had huddled down behind a large rock.

Opening his mouth wide, the creature revealed massive canine teeth, which he then sunk deep into Caleb's shoulder. Caleb faltered for a moment, falling to one knee. Sucking in a deep chest full of air, Caleb reached back, grabbing the creature by the loose skin above his lip and throwing him over his shoulder into the lunar water. Struggling quickly to his feet, Caleb staggered toward Bobby and mouthed the words, "Blow the horn."

Bobby turned to Margo and, speaking softly, asked, "Where's the horn?"

Margo motioned gently with her head and whispered, "Over there in the rocks. I dropped it when he grabbed me."

Bobby spied the horn just as Margo saw the top half of Caleb's broken sword glowing in the water. After a moment of hesitation, Bobby vaulted for the horn. The creature sprung to his feet and tackled Bobby in midair, wrestling him to the wet floor. Caleb then struck the creature on the back of his neck, piercing his skin. Steam vented through the wound, and the creature flew off, bouncing against the walls like an excited monkey in a cage.

Like a trained assassin, Margo dove for and snatched up the broken blade, burning her hand. In one fluid motion, she rolled to her feet and threw it at the creature, which had perched itself high on the wall. The blade impaled the creature's chest, and Caleb yelled, "The horn! Blow the horn!"

Fire burned from the creature's eyes. "No!" He poured out his rage in a deafening screech. Bobby brought the horn to his lips and blew with all his strength. Before the blast from the horn finished echoing off the walls, the room was filled with a bright blue light. The light retracted itself into the form of a large man standing over three meters tall, holding a flaming sword. Dressed in a sleeveless coat, the bronze giant stood with shod feet shoulder-width apart. His long coal black hair matched his eyes.

"Azariah! What is your business with these humans?" The creature's voice was brave, but his backward motion revealed his fear.

Azariah stepped toward the creature. "They do not concern you."

"Not all, but one."

Azariah motioned toward Bobby and Margo. "Step here."

"Why trust him?" the creature gargled "His hands are stained with the blood of ten million humans."

Bobby looked to Caleb for confirmation. Caleb nodded. "Some assignments are difficult." Bobby and Margo stepped toward Caleb.

"Do not be afraid of me, for I am a simple servant of the king." Azariah bowed his head to the humans and then swatted the creature away. Like a fly, it buzzed down the dark corridor.

"An alien king?" Thompson queried.

A strange calm fell on the cave. Bobby moved slowly toward Azariah, who did little more than shake his head at Caleb. Questions filled Bobby's mind, but he knew somehow they would all be answered in due time.

Caleb scratched his head and prepared himself for the rebuke he knew would come. "Caleb, why are they out here?" Caleb looked sheepish and offered no explanation.

Azariah noticed that Caleb was hiding his sword behind his back. "You broke your sword again, didn't you?" Caleb nodded. "It doesn't matter. You are getting faster and stronger." Caleb straightened up. Azariah put his hand on Caleb's back; the wound had already healed. "It is time for the arrogant one to go."

All eyes turned toward Thompson, whose face began to go dark as he retreated into the corner, pressing his back against the sopping wall. "I'm not going anywhere until I find out what is going on."

"You'll find out." Azariah raised his hand toward Thompson.

"Wait!" Thompson yelled. "Help me, Bobby."

"It's not up to Bobby," Azariah interrupted. "The choice was yours and yours alone. It has always been about choices. Make the right one and there is glory. Make the wrong choice and there are consequences. They are consequences with which you must live for eternity."

"What choice? I never made a choice."

"Oh, but you did. Every day of your life." With those final words, Azariah waved his hand in front of Thompson, who rose up off the wet floor and then blew down the dark corridor. He disappeared in the blink of an eye.

Margo turned to Bobby. "Isn't there anything we can do?"

Caleb leaned in and grabbed Margo's burnt hand and began to rub it softly. "I understand how you feel. That creature we fought was once my friend. We had spent much time together in close friendship, and then he turned." Caleb let her healed hand fall to her side.

Azariah nodded in agreement, and then with just a hint of a smile, he said, "It is time. We must move quickly."

Bobby backed away a couple of steps. "What about my little girl? What about Stacy? I can't leave her alone."

Bobby looked up as Azariah placed his large hand on his shoulder. "You have trusted the king with your life. Now it is time to trust him with her life." Azariah then vanished.

Margo withdrew behind a boulder as fear distorted her face. "Where are we going?" She directed her question to Bobby. Her eyes begged for understanding.

"Follow me." Caleb whistled as he took the lead down the corridor.

Bobby followed with feet as heavy as his thoughts. "Bobby, she'll be fine," explained Caleb. "He is the father to the fatherless." Caleb never slowed his pace.

Bobby stared blankly, withdrawing into brokenness.

"I don't understand at all," Margo complained in frustration.

Caleb smiled understandingly. "You . . ." The sound of the malach drowned him out, and in fear, Margo bolted into the crack in the wall, leaving Bobby and Caleb standing in the middle of the corridor.

"Would you like to see?"

Bobby's eyes widened. Caleb eased over to the wall and rubbed his hands against the rough surface. Rubbing in a circular motion, his hands went faster and faster until he dissolved a hole in the wall. The sound of the malach shook their very bones, but curiosity drove them to the opening. Margo squeezed in next to Bobby, and they stuck their heads through. It felt like a wind tunnel. What they saw were thousands upon thousands of multicolored light trails coming from deep down in the lunar core and going out into space toward earth. Thousands more were coming back. They were stunned by the beauty of the colors. Yelling over the noise, Bobby questioned, "What is it?"

"We call it the pipeline. It is our main thoroughfare to and from earth."

Kaboom! Bobby and Margo were thrown to the floor by a quake. They hadn't felt a quake or even a tremor since they arrived. The shake brought back the memory of the whole trip, and how they had got there. All of a sudden they were back on the lunar surface, wanting to go home.

"We must go quickly." Caleb took off down the corridor, expecting them to follow along. They didn't.

Bobby and Margo froze, staring out at two familiar orange lights. They were the two primary rockets of the USS *Lewis* burning for home. Caleb laid his hand on Bobby's shoulder and said, "For such a time as this, Bobby."

"What are you talking about?"

"It was never about getting you home." Caleb then nodded toward the *Lewis*. "It was about getting them home."

"What about Stacy?" Bobby's eyes danced between Caleb and Margo. "What about my little girl?"

"As soon as I get you inside, she'll be my assignment."

"But . . ."

"I'll take good care of her, Bobby. Trust me. You have my word. More importantly, you have the word of the king."

Bobby exhaled with effort. Caleb took off again down the corridor. "We must go now." His pace was fast, causing Bobby and Margo to break into a jog.

No words were spoken, but Bobby's thoughts ran rampant as they passed the white room. *I guess we went the wrong way.*

They had run another four hundred meters, weaving their way through the corridors, when they reached a large domed room with two thirty-meter-high brass doors. Another large twelve-foot malach stood beside the doors and smiled as he saw the team approach. "You are running out of time, Caleb." His voice was deep. His muscular build was massive.

"I know, I know. Just open the door."

They came to a halt, mystified by what lay behind the doors. Another violent shake broke their trance.

"The husk is breaking up," Caleb instructed. "You must go in now."

The large door opened out with flashes of lightning and cracks of thunder. A strong wind and brilliant white light struck them in the face, pushing them back. Standing behind them, Caleb pushed them forward into the light and through the doors. They heard the loud sounds of rushing water.

Bobby's knees buckled, sending him to the ground. Caleb helped Bobby stand up slowly. Bobby raised his head to see a pure white hooded silk robe with two beautiful blue eyes smiling at him. "Carol?"

"Bobby."

Shedding all apprehension, Bobby ran to Carol. They leaped into each other's arms. Bobby swung her around as all the memories of their glorious life together returned. Their lips touched, and Bobby knew he was in heaven.

Margo looked at Caleb in puzzlement. Caleb gave a little smile and explained, "You are home."

"I knew you would come." Margo began to weep as Rocket moved closer and smothered her in his arms. She clung to him, never wanting to let go. "I hope this isn't a dream."

"It's no dream, but it's beyond imagination."

The lunar husk continued to break up as bloodred lava filled the lunar atmosphere. Beneath the red canopy, a massive structure measuring over two million square miles moved toward earth.

"The sun will become dark,
the moon red as blood,
before the overwhelming and terrible day of the Lord comes."
Joel 2:31 (NCV)

Made in the USA
Lexington, KY
15 November 2010